Deadly Dealings

A Detective Liv DeMarco Thriller

G.K. Parks

Copyright © 2020 G.K. Parks

A Modus Operandi imprint

ISBN:
ISBN-13: 978-1-942710-21-9

For the best mom in the world, I love you

ONE

He slipped the ornate headdress out of the velvet bag, examining the shimmering diamonds and glistening emeralds under the light. This was it. The final piece of the puzzle. He'd spent nearly a year planning. Every step precisely executed. No mess ups. No getting caught. He had everything he needed – the skills, the resources, the power. Every tiny piece fit perfectly into his carefully crafted masterplan. Now, with the jeweled tiara in his possession, he could make contact and finally set everything in motion. The cogs would turn and the wheels would spin. There was no turning back now. In a matter of days, he'd taste victory and laugh at his vanquished foe.

* * *

Detective Brad Fennel rocked back on his heels. He swallowed uncomfortably, a thin sheen of sweat coating his skin. I glanced up, watching him gulp down some air, his pallor a sickly yellow-green.

"Are you regretting transferring to homicide?" I asked.

He dragged his gaze away from the body and did his best to play it off, adopting a lopsided grin. "Why? Aren't we having fun?" But I knew my partner better than that.

"Try not to have too much fun or you might vomit on our vic, and the rest of the department will never let you live it down."

"Fine." He glanced around. "You got this, Liv?" I nodded, and he straightened to his full height and sucked in a few shallow breaths. "I'll check the roof."

Waving Brad off, I turned my attention back to the body. With gloved hands, I checked the security guard's ID. Ezra Sambari. His prints matched the photo ID. The Beretta he carried remained holstered. He didn't clear leather. From the looks of it, he didn't even try. Either Sambari had been caught off guard, or he trusted his attacker.

Gently, I turned his head. The bullet entered roughly three inches behind Sambari's right ear. He never saw it coming. From what little remained of his face, I couldn't make out much, except a strong, clean-shaven jawline and a buzz cut. Sambari looked capable of taking down any opponent, which is why the killer didn't give him a chance to fight back.

A pool of blood haloed around Sambari's head. "He died before he hit the ground," the medical examiner said.

Saying a silent prayer, I stepped away from the body. Ezra Sambari was our fifth victim in the last four weeks. "Any idea what kind of gun the killer used?"

"Looks like a nine mill."

My gaze went to the broken window. CSU had already photographed everything before dusting for prints and collecting evidence. "So Sambari wasn't killed by a sniper?"

"No, DeMarco." The ME gestured to a few techs who zipped our vic into a body bag and placed him on a gurney. "Once I complete the autopsy, I'll let you know what else I find, but I don't expect any surprises."

I watched the body get carted off before examining the hole in the wall left by the bullet. The bright red spatter turned my stomach, but I forced myself to focus.

A crime scene tech had already removed the bullet lodged in the wall, and another one directed a laser pointer, indicating the likely trajectory from which it traveled. But since the bullet went through Sambari's skull before it impacted with the wall, it may not have traveled in a straight line. Crime scene markers and glass shards covered the floor and rug. The thief tracked broken glass through the apartment, which meant he used the window to enter.

From what we gathered, the killer fired twice in rapid succession. The first bullet shattered the window, and the second shot, which he fired almost immediately afterward, went into our victim's skull. That's why the guard didn't have time to turn around or reach for his gun, unless the killer shot out the window, waited for Sambari to check it out, turn around, and then entered and popped him. Without surveillance footage, I had to go with my gut. But my gut said it didn't matter. The results were the same, and given Sambari's holstered weapon and no attempts to call for help, our killer most likely fired twice in rapid succession.

"He's a professional," I muttered.

"Thief? I'd say so," one of the techs replied. "Who else can crack a safe like that, exit out the front, and get away undetected?"

"Not undetected," I retorted. "We know he's out there. We're gonna find him, eventually."

"Hopefully before more bodies drop." The tech went back to cataloging the bagged evidence as he placed it inside a box for transport.

Following the trail of glass shards, I retraced the killer's steps. After entering through the window, he went past the body and straight to the safe hidden behind a false back in the linen closet. Our killer knew exactly where to look. He emptied the safe and went out the front door. He didn't falter or misstep. He kept a singular focus based on the trail of broken glass and footprints. Several expensive items remained on shelves and in glass display cases, but the killer didn't waste his time. He wanted whatever was inside the safe and nothing more, just like our four previous crime scenes.

"Does anyone have any idea what was inside the safe?" I asked.

A few people shook their heads or shrugged. I keyed my

radio and asked for an update. Dispatch sent officers to locate the apartment owner, but, as of yet, I didn't know if they found him.

"We just picked him up, Detective," came the response.

"Bring him to me." Normally, patrol would have taken Leopold Zedula, the apartment owner, to the precinct, but I wanted to see how he'd react to the break-in. The shock factor might work in my favor. Though, I secretly hoped the news wouldn't shock Zedula.

"Yes, ma'am."

Since this was a penthouse apartment with no fire escape, we assumed the killer rappelled down from the roof. At least, that's what my partner thought and what the evidence indicated. Plus, I didn't have a better theory. The window broke inward, not outward, but I wasn't ready to rule out the possibility this was an inside job. A copycat could have heard about the string of deadly home invasions and decided to recreate it to get away with murder or insurance fraud.

I stared into the hidden wall safe. Inside sat a tray draped in black velvet. It, like the rest of the safe, was empty. Something shiny caught my eye, and I crouched down to examine a smooth, clear stone. "Hey, take a look at this."

The nearest tech moved closer, taking the pebble from my gloved hand. "Is that glass?"

"You tell me. I want it bagged and tagged."

He pinched it between a pair of tweezers and held it up to the light. "It could be a diamond."

"Put a rush on it." This wasn't good. If that was a diamond, this would be the fifth deadly home invasion with a high-ticket item stolen. Our thief had to be choosing these targets specifically. I just didn't know how. None of the previous four victims connected. Only half of them had been the actual home owners, the other two were staff, just like Ezra Sambari. "Who hires a security guard to protect his vacant apartment?" I wondered.

Before anyone could offer an answer, someone called my name from the hallway. "Detective DeMarco?" An officer lingered just outside the front door. "Mr. Zedula's here. You wanted to speak to him."

"Yes." I peeled off the latex gloves and left the apartment. Two officers stood in the hallway beside a man with molten chocolate eyes, wearing a Rolex and exquisitely tailored suit. Leopold Zedula could have been a movie star or a diamond smuggler. "Check the roof and see if you can find Fennel, Officer Richards."

"Yes, ma'am."

Thanking him, I strode down the hall and dismissed the unis waiting beside Mr. Zedula with a single look. "I'm Detective Liv DeMarco. I have some bad news. Please," I gestured to a bench near the elevator, "have a seat. First, would you mind telling me where you were tonight, Mr. Zedula?"

"At a charity auction," he said, his accent a mix of the Queen's English and something exotic. For a moment, I wondered if he might be royalty. "My home security firm contacted me several hours ago and said my alarm was triggered, but I couldn't get away. I trust my security guard handled the situation. Did Mr. Sambari call you? Is that why you're here? Have you spoken to him? He should be able to answer your questions more easily than I can."

"That's not an option."

Zedula narrowed his eyes. "Why not?"

From here, it was impossible to see the bloodstain on the floor. "Do you know anyone who might want to harm you, Mr. Zedula?"

"I don't know. I could probably come up with a few names, but I thought this was a break-in. My security system reported unauthorized activity inside my apartment." He sat up straighter as if wanting to bolt off the bench and race down the hall. "Where is Mr. Sambari? I want to speak to him now."

"I'm sorry." I watched him closely. I might be new to homicide, but I spent years undercover. I knew how to read people. "I regret to inform you Mr. Sambari was killed."

"How?" Zedula didn't appear upset, just shocked.

"I'm sorry for your loss."

"Yes, of course," Zedula shook his head like a horse annoyed by a fly, "but how?"

"He was shot." I studied the man. "Do you own a gun?"

"I own many guns. They are collector's items." He glared at me. "You think I killed my own security guard? Don't be ridiculous." Suddenly, Zedula was hit with dread. Panic overtook his features. "What happened? Was anything damaged or stolen?" He stood, but I grabbed his elbow, already on my feet and blocking his path. "I have to check my apartment. I have to see if it's gone."

"If what's gone?"

He blinked, fighting with himself on whether he should answer the question.

"Mr. Zedula, please."

"Right." He swallowed, dropping back onto the bench. "You're right. Of course, I'll help in any way I can. I just need to know what happened."

"We'll get to that, but first, I have some questions. Not many people have security guards stationed inside their empty apartments. What did you hire Mr. Sambari to protect?"

Zedula reached into his pocket, and I tensed, my hand coming to rest on my gun. A moment later, he produced a phone and tapped on the screen. "According to this, someone opened my front door but failed to disengage the security system upon entering. That's what triggered the alarm." Zedula searched the hallway, finding a security camera positioned behind him. "You must have caught the intruder on camera."

"It's not that simple." When the killer left, he strode out the front door, which triggered the security system. As soon as we were notified, units rolled in to investigate. When the responding officers found the body, homicide got involved. But that was hours ago. The killer was long gone, and he'd been covered head to toe, making an identification damn near impossible.

"Make it that simple."

"Sir," I did my best to maintain a professional tone, "do you know who would want to hurt you?"

"Hurt me or rob me?"

"What was Sambari protecting?"

"A trinket. Valuable trinkets." He dialed a number,

speaking to me while he waited for someone on the other end to answer. "I'm an antiquities broker, Detective DeMarco. I routinely have millions stored inside my apartment awaiting delivery or authentication. Anyone looking to score would want to rob me. That's why I hired Mr. Sambari. As far as hurt me, I'll get you some names, but first, I need to find out what was taken. This is bad. Very bad."

Before I could ask a follow-up question, whoever Zedula phoned answered. He turned his back to me while he spoke. The door labeled *roof access* opened, and Brad stepped into the hallway. He jerked his head to the side. I pointed at the two nearby uniforms to keep an eye on Mr. Zedula before tucking myself into the corner beside Brad.

"The killer definitely used the roof to gain access to the apartment. I found nylon fibers hanging from an anchor near the edge. It looks like we're dealing with a homicidal cat burglar or possibly a team. Similar skills would have been needed to gain access to this building, just like the other four home invasion sites. I checked with building security, but they don't have cameras on the roof. And you've already seen the footage taken from this hallway." Brad pointed up at the camera. "Our killer kept completely covered. No prints. No hairs. And no fibers, except the nylon cord."

"Did you find anything else on the roof? After he left Zedula's apartment, he went back up. How did he escape?"

"Maybe he jumped. Cats land on their feet, right?"

"Not from fifty stories up. Since when do cat burglars kill armed security guards?"

"I don't know, but Sambari wasn't just a guard. He was former Mossad."

"Shit." I turned back to the apartment owner, wondering if he might be a person of interest, and resisted the urge to snatch the phone away from him. "Why do you have former Israeli intelligence on your payroll, Mr. Zedula? What could you have possibly needed to protect that badly?" Maybe I'd watched one too many spy flicks, but thoughts of WMDs ran through my mind. And given Zedula's vague answers to my question about the content of the safe, I couldn't help but think Sambari might have been guarding a dirty bomb or sarin gas.

"Sambari possessed the appropriate skill set to work as both bodyguard and security guard. That was all I cared about. Obviously, he could have done a better job." Zedula narrowed his eyes, refusing to give an inch. "The fact that he's former Mossad didn't factor in to his hiring beyond having tactical knowledge and training. However, since you and your associate," Zedula looked at Fennel, "have taken it upon yourselves to focus on that one aspect of Mr. Sambari's life, should I assume it's because whoever broke into my apartment and killed him did so because he had a score to settle? Maybe this has nothing to do with me. Was anything taken, Detective DeMarco? You still haven't answered my question. I need to go inside and check. You can't keep me in the dark. I have rights."

"You said Sambari acted as a bodyguard and security guard. Exactly what were his duties?" Brad asked. "Why wasn't he with you tonight?"

"Mr. Sambari protects my home. I have two personal bodyguards who accompany me on occasion." Zedula glanced toward the other end of the hallway. "Police officers are speaking to them now." He shoved the phone at me. "Speak to my lawyer. You can't deny me access to my apartment."

"Unfortunately, we can. This is our crime scene," Brad said.

I took the phone and pressed the red disconnect button. "Oops."

Deciding we had to compromise, my partner asked, "What do you keep in your safe, Mr. Zedula?"

"Which one?"

"Which one?" Brad practically sputtered, catching himself. "How many do you have?"

"Several. That's why I have a full-time security guard. Earlier this evening, I delivered an Egyptian artifact to the charity auction, which is why two guards accompanied me and why I was delayed in returning home after the breach. That safe is now empty, but the others are not. Now if you'd be so kind." Zedula crooked two fingers, impatiently waiting for me to return his phone.

"We'll need a list of your clients, deals, and anyone who knows what you do and the types of things you keep in your apartment," Brad said. "I'll take you inside, but you can't touch anything. Your apartment is an active crime scene. Do you understand?"

Zedula nodded, and Brad accompanied him into the apartment.

TWO

"I don't like this." Brad tapped his pen on the desk.

"It's not too late. You can ask to transfer back to intelligence. I don't think Captain Grayson's replaced you yet. He can probably expedite the transfer, or you could ask my dad if he can pull some strings or unpull them, since talking to him is what got you into this mess in the first place."

Dropping the pen, Brad leaned forward in his chair. "Liv, I'm not talking about this." He waved his hand dramatically in the air. "I'm talking about this." He stabbed at the report and photos on his desk. "Who stashes crown jewels inside a home safe? That's just asking for trouble. Did you see the rest of Zedula's inventory? Art, swords, chalices, artifacts. Hell, that thing in the corner, it was a dinosaur bone."

"It could be a replica."

"That's not the point."

"It might be. Maybe the rest of that stuff is fake or just worthless flea market junk."

"I doubt it."

I did too. "So why didn't the thief take any of it?"

"Guess he has a one track mind and knew exactly which

hidden safe to target and how to unlock it. According to the manufacturer, it's uncrackable."

"Nothing's uncrackable." A sick thought wormed its way through my mind. "Do you think it's an inside job?" I replayed my conversation with Mr. Zedula over in my head, but the man never showed the slightest bit of remorse or grief over his dead security guard. The only thing he cared about was the missing emerald and diamond tiara rumored to have been worn by some 16th century empress.

"Given what we know, I don't know what else it could be," Brad said.

Sucking in a breath, I reached for the four other case files. "How does that fit in with our other home invasions? You said it yourself, it appears to be the work of the same killer-thief."

"Maybe this one's a copycat. He used a gun. That's new. Rappelling down from the roof might just be his way of throwing us off. Maybe he saw a news report on the recent deadly home invasions and got lucky with his tactics."

"That's not helpful."

Brad chuckled. "I'll work on coming up with a better answer."

"You do that." Catching his eye, I fought to keep the smile off my face.

"So what are you thinking, DeMarco? Impress me with your badass deductive skills."

"If this is an inside job, the guy didn't take any steps to cover his tracks." I flipped through the previous case files. None of the MOs were an exact match. The items stolen varied from a vintage watch collection to a painting to a pile of cash to a programmer's work computer. Each crime resulted in exactly one death. The previous victims included two homeowners, a gardener, and a dogwalker. The method of killing changed each time. The only commonality was the agility and skill needed to steal the items and escape. As far as we knew, none of the victims were connected. "Maybe we're dealing with a professional thief, who doesn't mind killing." I cocked my head to the side, but something didn't feel right.

"Someone could have hired him to steal all these things, including the tiara." Brad thought about it for a moment. "Zedula or someone on his payroll could have given the thief the combination to the safe and told him about the security in place." Brad typed something into the computer. "We'll need backgrounds on Zedula, everyone he employs, and anyone who knew about the location of the safe and what was inside it."

"That could be a long list." I put the roof photos back in the folder and perused the images taken from inside Zedula's apartment. Expensive antiques and artifacts cluttered the display cases and coffee table. Zedula claimed to be a broker, but from what I'd seen, he was also a collector. "A professional thief could have easily doubled his score, but he didn't take anything else, not even the Fabergé egg on the coffee table."

"You're right. That doesn't make sense, unless he thought picking it up might trip an alarm, and he didn't want to risk it. Though, if he didn't want to attract attention, he should have gone back out the window instead of tripping the alarm when he went out the front door."

"Could he have gone out the window?" I asked. "You said you found nylon fibers. Maybe he cut the rope or wouldn't have been able to climb back up without losing his loot."

Brad tapped the file on my desk. "He triggered the alarm after he left the apartment, just like in these other cases. Once out the door, he had ten seconds to escape. To me, taking the elevator down to the lobby and exiting out the front would have made the most sense, but he didn't do that. Why not?"

"He would have had to take off his mask," I said. "At some point, we'd identify him off the security footage. But the roof should have been a dead end. I want to know how he escaped or, better yet, how he got on the roof in the first place. We know he didn't gain access from inside the building."

"I want to know why he didn't take the damn egg. Those are worth a mint."

I cocked my head to the side. "Perhaps he thought it'd break."

"Are they breakable?" Brad asked.

"How would I know?"

He shrugged. "Don't you have knickknacks?"

"Not the same thing." I jerked my chin at his computer. "Google it."

While he waited for the internet to give him an answer, I put in a request for nearby security footage. Our thief must have found a way onto the roof from a nearby building, and I wanted to know which one.

But now that Brad was hung up on that stupid egg, I found myself wondering the same thing. Even if the thief turned killer set out with a specific goal in mind – neutralize the security guard and steal the tiara – that didn't mean he couldn't make a little extra on the score. Unless this wasn't about the tiara. Could this have been a hit? Maybe the theft was a misdirect. Our killer waved a shiny bauble at us, and while we were busy chasing down fences and tracking the jewels, he was getting away with murder.

"I dunno. You might be right, and Zedula keeps replicas on display. Or the thief figured a Fabergé egg is too hard to move and not just because it's an egg, which might break," Brad declared before turning away from the screen. "What is it, Liv? You look like you're on to something."

"Maybe this wasn't a botched burglary. Maybe this was premeditated murder." Picking up the phone, I made a request for a full workup on Ezra Sambari. Due to the nature of his former career and dual citizenship, everything would have to be coordinated through the state department. But we had grounds to make the request. The man had been murdered, after all. It was our job to find his killer. I just hoped Fennel and I weren't getting into the middle of some black ops bullshit.

"I'll check with burglary and see if they can offer any insights as to how our cat burglar made it off the roof without anyone noticing," my partner said. "Worst case, I'll call the FAA and see if any helicopters were flying around midtown without us noticing." A few minutes later, he returned with a list of recent home invasions, burglaries, and robberies. The city had no shortage of crime. But we'd gone through burglary's cases each time we responded to a new deadly home invasion, and we never found any connections between the nonviolent crimes and ours. "CSU's hoping to get something off the nylon fibers, but our killer-thief has mad skills. He would have had to rappel down, position himself perfectly, time the shots, and enter quickly since he couldn't be sure no one would report gunfire or glass breaking. He must have done something like this before. I'll see if any other high-rises suffered broken windows recently."

Nodding, I considered Sambari's previous profession. Until I learned more, I wasn't willing to add this case to the growing stack of felony murders. Sambari might have been a hit. "We could be looking at a team. Our killer popped Sambari, and the thief entered and stole the tiara. Two birds, one stone, so to speak."

"Security footage only caught one person exiting the apartment. Was the second guy invisible?" Fennel asked, playing devil's advocate.

"No, but the accomplice could have gone out the window or never stepped foot inside the apartment. The killer and thief could have worked in tandem. The thief shoots out the window. The killer shoots Sambari. The thief goes inside, and while he's stealing the jewels, the killer escapes."

Fennel didn't buy it. "It's possible, just like an alien invasion."

Normally, I held off on the ridiculous speculating until we were three or four days into the investigation, but this was our fifth scene in less than a month. Even if it wasn't related to the others, we hadn't cleared any of those cases, which meant we probably wouldn't clear this one either if we investigated it in the same manner. We had to make a decision. We could either treat this case like a burglary, or we could treat it like a homicide. And the sign on the door said homicide.

Brad snapped his fingers in front of my face. "Liv," he waited for me to look up, "I don't like it when you go mute.

What are you thinking?"

"Divide and conquer. Pick your target. Sambari or the tiara? You're primary. It's your call."

My partner blew out a breath. "The tiara. Our unsub broke into the apartment with a sole mission – to steal the jewels. If he only wanted to kill Sambari, he could have shot him from a nearby rooftop or popped him on his way home. He didn't have to rappel off the roof or enter the apartment if his only goal was to kill the guard. Plus, a killer wouldn't give a shit about a tiara."

"Even though it's worth millions?"

"So is everything else in that apartment. If our killer just wanted to grab something valuable, he would have taken the items in plain sight, not the thing hidden in the safe. This is about the tiara. It has to be."

"Maybe the killer shot through the window because he wanted the element of surprise. After all, Sambari was ex-Mossad."

"I don't care who you are. You can't protect yourself from an unseen sniper. Plus, if this is some leftover spy rivalry thing, the killer wouldn't want to call attention to his crime. He'd never use a gun. He would have poisoned Sambari or staged a car accident or heart attack. Distracting us from the murder by stealing a tiara isn't the way to go."

"How'd you come up with that?"

"Common sense. That's not what I would do."

I raised a questioning eyebrow. "You served in the military. Is there anything I should know?"

He laughed. "I wasn't on one of the special teams, Liv. The CIA agents I encountered didn't call themselves CIA agents. They called themselves state department officials. But shooting someone and then stealing the crown isn't exactly their style."

"Isn't that exactly what governments do?"

"Now who's been watching too many spy thrillers?" He picked up the phone. "I'll contact the insurance company and see what they have to say. Maybe they know something we don't." He gestured at the other files. "They might have insured some of the other stolen items. We haven't explored that possibility, but maybe that's how these crimes connect. In the meantime, see how much progress has been made on verifying Zedula's whereabouts and checking into his staff. After that, find out who notified Sambari's next of kin. Someone had to tell his wife he wouldn't be coming home tonight." Fennel's tone dropped, and he rested his elbow on the desk, putting an end to our conversation. Normally, we would have made the notification, but while we worked the scene, the sergeant did our dirty work. It made our life easier, but since we had yet to speak to Sambari's widow, following up would be difficult.

Other members of our unit were performing their due diligence regarding Zedula and his staff. They'd let me know what they found. At least that was one less thing on my plate. Preoccupied with my own musings, I went in search of Sgt. Chambliss and collided with another detective who just entered the bullpen. The stack of files he carried crashed to the floor. A few people nearby clapped and whistled.

"Thanks, I'll be here all week. Don't forget to tip the dancers." He knelt down to pick up the scattered pages, and one of the cops stuck a folded single in the back of the detective's waistband.

"There ya go, Jake," the cop said. "So when can I expect an encore? I want to make sure I have a front row seat."

"Soon," the detective replied. "Why don't you hold your breath?"

Confused by the exchange, I bent down to help the detective pick up the fallen files. "I'm sorry. I didn't see you," I said. I just transferred to homicide a few weeks ago. I hadn't even learned names yet, but I didn't recognize this guy. Maybe he worked in a different unit. Based on the way he dressed, he could have come from gangs or vice.

He stopped what he was doing and looked up, meeting my eyes. "I didn't realize I was that hard to miss." A grin pulled at the corners of his mouth. "You're the infamous Liv DeMarco. I wondered when I'd run into you. I just didn't realize it'd be quite so literal." He took the files and pages I collected, placed them on top of the stack, and stood up. "Jake Voletek. I'd shake your hand, but then I'd drop these and there'd be more applause. And I only do one performance a night. Union rules. You understand." His name meant nothing to me, but he said it like it should. "Nice to meet you." I eyed the dollar bill hanging out of the top of his pants. He must work vice.

I sidestepped around him but only made it a few feet before he called out, "You could at least thank me for making the Sambari notification for you."

I turned. "I thought Sgt. Chambliss was handling it."

Voletek squinted, placing the files on a nearby desk. "Yeah, well, I owed him. Anyway, it probably made things easier for you, seeing as how I know what questions to ask." He shuffled through the files, pulling out forms and notes, and placed them on the edge of the desk. "Here's what I got on Sambari, in case you're interested. I told Penny you'd be in touch in the next day or two."

I backtracked to his desk and picked up the pages. "Penny?"

"Penelope Sambari, your vic's wife."

"How did she take it?"

His brow furrowed. He thought I was crazy to ask that question. "Not great. But she didn't strike me as surprised. Hard to tell, though. It might have been shock. People react differently."

"Did Ezra have enemies?"

Voletek shook his head and dropped into his chair. "None she knows about. But she figured it was just a matter of time. The guy's dead, so obviously, someone didn't like him." Voletek swiveled, glancing at my partner's back. "Penny wants to know who killed Ezra, and she's willing to cooperate any way she can. Whatever you need, DeMarco, all you have to do is ask. I'm your guy." He grabbed a highlighter from the cup and marked Mrs. Sambari's phone number on one of the pages. "I'd wait until tomorrow, at the earliest, before you call her. She needs some time to process and grieve. Right now, she's not thinking clearly. You'll have better results once some of that wears off."

"How—"

"Just a trick of the trade. You'll get used to it."

"You're a homicide detective?" I didn't mean to voice the question out loud, but Voletek's presence and attitude caught me off guard.

"Have been for a while. Sorry I waited so long to introduce myself. I've been busy." He reached for one of the files, and I wondered what a restaurant fire with no reported casualties had to do with homicide but decided it was best not to ask. When I didn't immediately disappear, he glanced up at me. "You honestly have no idea who I am, do you?"

"I'm sorry. I don't. Have we met before?"

He laughed, finding this amusing. "No."

"Liv," Brad called, and I spun, "the insurance investigator is on his way to speak to us. He wants to check the scene. And he has some thoughts concerning ways to track the tiara. Only a few local fences could move an item like that."

"How'd news travel so fast?" I asked.

"Apparently, Mr. Zedula's already sought outside help. As soon as we left, he contacted the insurance agency and immediately hired a private consultant to investigate. The body isn't even cool yet, and the only thing Zedula's worried about is getting paid for that tiara." Brad sighed. "I'm pretty sure this is an inside job. It sure as hell looks like one."

"I don't know, but it takes all kinds. Did we get access to Sambari's financials? The first thing the insurance investigator will ask is if Sambari could be involved in the heist."

"Here." Voletek pulled a sheet of paper from the middle of the stack. "That's the account info and authorization."

"Thanks."

"No problem." Voletek nodded to Brad. "How come you never introduced me to your partner, Fennel?"

"Why the sudden interest? Are you planning to horn in on our case?" Brad's brown eyes grew dark. "That better be the only thing you're horning in on, Jake."

Voletek chuckled and turned his attention back to the arson report.

I crossed the bullpen and took a seat at my desk, filing their exchange away to ask about when we weren't so busy. Right now, it was time to get to work.

THREE

"This is it?" Rob Kalen asked. The insurance investigator peered into the empty safe. "This is where the item was kept?"

"That's what Mr. Zedula said." Fennel stared down at the carpet. CSU finished processing the apartment a few minutes before we arrived.

Kalen lifted the velvet-lined tray with gloved hands. Underneath the lights, I could see an outline of the tiara from where it had sat on the material, leaving scuffs in the otherwise smooth fabric. He placed the tray on top of the safe and checked the interior with a flashlight. Fennel and I exchanged a look. Our people already did this. There was nothing to find. The thief didn't pry the safe open. He knew the combination.

Disappointed the killer didn't leave a calling card behind, Kalen returned the tray to the safe, examined the exterior, photographed the marks CSU had noted in their report. "What about the security system? Can you ID the perp?"

"No." The question annoyed Brad.

"Your office already placed a request for a copy of the footage. Once approved, the department will release the video to you," I said. My gaze drifted to the stain on the floor. "The thief came in through that window." I pointed, forcing the insurance investigator to turn around. "It appears he rappelled down from the roof."

"Interesting." Kalen crossed to the window and ran a finger over the sill.

"Do you know of any cat burglars operating in the area?" Fennel asked.

Kalen bit his bottom lip, which emphasized his buck teeth. "A few, but cracking that safe is damn near impossible. If you want to find the killer, I suggest you start by looking at safecrackers. The acrobatics with the window are nothing compared to getting that behemoth open."

"Could the killer have had the combination?" I asked. That had been our assumption.

"I'm not sure." Kalen returned to the safe, sidestepping around the bloodstain. "You see this?" He pointed to a few marks on the front. "I'd say these were made by a stethoscope and other manipulation tools."

"Manipulation tools?" Fennel arched an eyebrow, wondering if I was following along any better than he was.

"There are two ways to open a safe. You force it open with something like a torch, thermal lance, or jam shot. Or you manipulate it into opening by turning the knob and listening to the mechanisms inside." Kalen patted the side of the safe. "This baby is supposed to be top of the line, but with enough time, a professional safecracker could open it." He pointed to a few round marks. "I'd say that's from the bell of a stethoscope. And this," he pointed a gloved finger at what looked like a white scratch, "might be the remnants of chalk. Most pros write down the numbers as they go, especially when dealing with false tumblers which can throw the entire thing out of whack."

"And he erased his work," Fennel said. "So we're looking for a neat freak."

"We need to narrow down Sambari's time of death," I said. We assumed the killer entered and exited in a matter of minutes, but if the insurance investigator was right, the killer could have been inside for hours. "What time did Mr. Zedula leave for the auction?"

"Just after three." Fennel eyed Kalen. "Have you worked

with Leopold Zedula before?"

"Several times. He's a frequent flyer, but this is the first time he's filed a claim."

"Has he ever asked you to insure anything as expensive as the stolen tiara?" Fennel asked.

Kalen nodded again. After walking the scene, he didn't believe Zedula was behind this, which made one of us. "Leo's a broker. Plain and simple. He gets a cut of the proceeds from the sales he makes. He only gets paid when the items are delivered. He insures them to protect himself and his buyers. We authenticate and appraise the items before insuring them and Leo takes possession."

"Why use a middleman?" I asked. "Why doesn't the seller make the deal himself?"

"Most of the items are bought and sold overseas. The owners and buyers have no desire to make the trip themselves. That's why they use Leo. And that's why he uses us. It's to protect all parties," Kalen said.

"Explain that." Fennel pulled the notepad from his pocket and clicked his pen.

"Like I said, we authenticate and appraise before insuring. We've also evaluated Leo's security measures and travel arrangements to ensure the utmost care is taken in delivering the items. We even vet and screen the guards Leo uses." Kalen pointed to the safe. "The news about Ezra is unsettling. He's worked for several of our clients over the years. He was a good man. I liked him."

"You knew him?" I asked.

"Yes."

"Do you believe it's possible someone wanted to hurt him?"

"To get to the tiara, yes."

That wasn't what I asked, but Fennel shook his head. So I backed off.

"Any idea why the thief didn't take any of these other items?" Fennel nodded at the jeweled egg.

"I don't know," Kalen said. "Perhaps he didn't have time. Like I said, this is the Everest of safes. And since the thief broke the window, he must have feared someone would report it. He was on a clock."

Why didn't anyone hear the shot? The neighbors across the hall or even on the floor below should have heard gunfire. It wasn't like the room was soundproofed, and since we were so high up, no one could confuse it with a car backfiring.

"We'll need names of the appraisers and authenticators," my partner said, "and anyone else you can think of who's evaluated Mr. Zedula's security and a list of the other guards and staff he's hired in the past."

"Do you think someone at my firm is responsible?" Kalen asked.

"We need to rule out your coworkers," Fennel said. "The sooner we do, the sooner we'll be able to hunt down the thief and find the tiara."

FOUR

"The insurance agency's clean." I rubbed my eyes and leaned back in my chair. "I contacted Sambari's previous employer. Our vic used to work for an armored truck company which transported valuables from private collections to museums and vice versa. Occasionally, he'd moonlight on the side for those clients. That's how he hooked up with Zedula."

"Anything hinky in Sambari's financials?" Fennel asked.

I shook my head. "He's clean. His wife's clean. I don't think he was involved in the heist."

"Oh, so now our break-in is a heist?"

"With a score that big, yes, it's a heist. I hate to say it, but I think you're right."

"What?" He cupped his hand around his ear. "I didn't quite catch that."

"Too bad. I'm not repeating it."

"C'mon, Liv, you know this is my favorite part."

Ignoring him, I asked, "Do you want me to dig deeper into Zedula?"

"No. He and his staff came back clean, but we'll follow up in a few days. However, I doubt we'll find much. His lawyer's done his best to shut us out. They refuse to voluntarily turn over any information not related to the jewels. But we have the list of guards Zedula has employed over the years and the parties for which he's brokered deals, thanks to Kalen. According to the insurance company, Zedula's been doing this a long time. I put some feelers out, and from the whispers I'm hearing, Zedula also dabbles in black market import/export, which would explain why his lawyer doesn't want us poking around in his client's business."

"What is Zedula moving? Drugs? Guns?" He told me he had a collection of guns, but I had yet to research them.

"Not exactly. Zedula stays on brand and moves art, jewels, and artifacts, which might have been stolen during the war or considered sovereign property."

"Which war?"

"Probably all of them," Brad said.

"Jeez. Do you have proof? Sambari might have gotten wind of this and had to be eliminated." It was an angle I hadn't considered.

"It's just speculation. I placed a call to the Feds and have the guys downstairs shaking some trees to see if anyone knows anything about this. But even if Zedula's shady, I'm not sure that's the reason for the break-in or murder. However, I'm hoping to find a fence who knows something about our thief. After all, our cat burglar has a hot item to unload, and it's not like he can sell it at some jewelry store or pawn it off to a museum without the proper documentation and proof of ownership."

"You're right." My gaze settled on the other case files. Aside from the cash, the thief or thieves couldn't just pawn off the stolen goods. And according to our underground contacts, no inquiries had been made about moving the watch collection, computer, or art. Whoever stole them was waiting for the heat to die down. If this was the same guy, he would probably sit on the tiara too. "Did you ask Mac to monitor the dark web for any hits?"

"Of course, Laura Mackenzie was my first stop. Since she's our favorite computer geek and works for the entire department, not just intelligence, there's no reason we can't enlist her help." Fennel chuckled. "You know, we might be new to homicide, but I do know a thing or two about working a case. You haven't cornered the market on investigations, DeMarco."

I held up my palms. "Sorry. Force of habit. I'm used to taking lead."

Brad leaned in and lowered his voice. "By the way, thanks for dealing with the body. You didn't have to do that. I'll get used to it."

"You shouldn't have to."

"No one should, but that's the job. I knew that when I signed up."

"But you didn't sign up for homicide. I did."

"Liv, don't. I'm a big boy. I can take care of myself."

"Fine. So what should I do now, big boy?"

Before Brad could answer, Lieutenant Winston came up behind us. "You and Fennel should go home. Shift's over, and with budget cuts, no one's getting OT without special permission." He glanced down at our case files. "What is this? Number five?"

"Yes, sir," I said.

"Any ideas?"

"We're working on it." Fennel logged off the computer and tidied his desk. "Burglary's assisting as much as they can. Right now, we're assuming the murders are a byproduct of the break-ins, but," my partner eyed me, "it might be too soon to say for sure. DeMarco's checking into our latest vic for possible suspects, and I'm working the jewelry angle."

Lt. Winston pointed to a printout before Fennel could stow the file and photos. "Is that what was stolen?"

"Yes, sir."

Winston scrunched his nose. "Check with jewelers and pawn shops. A piece like that could be taken apart. It'd be easier to sell off each stone than the entire tiara. And it wouldn't attract nearly as much attention."

"Good call." Fennel reached for his phone.

"Tomorrow, Detective. I'll make sure everyone's on notice, but you do the rest of the work tomorrow. Understand?"

Fennel nodded, but as soon as the LT walked away, he

said, "I don't get it. A killer is at large. We need to find him, especially if he's responsible for all of these crimes. At this rate, he'll strike again in a few days, and I don't want to see that happen." Brad picked up the stack of folders and properly filed them away.

"We will, but Rome wasn't built in a day, right?" I opened my bottom drawer and removed my purse, made sure my gun was holstered, checked for my phone and keys, and turned off my computer.

Fennel shoved his arm through his jacket sleeve. "I'm not used to this role reversal thing. Usually, I'm the one saying we need to take a break." He frowned. "I don't think I like this."

"You'd like it less if you were wearing some skimpy outfit or ridiculous heels."

"Don't forget the makeup and crazy hairstyles." He led the way to the stairwell and held the door for me. "For the record, Liv DeMarco's pretty great on her own, without the disguises."

"What do you want? You're never this nice."

"I'm always nice, but since we're having a *Freaky Friday* moment, you should pick up the check tonight."

"Who says we're grabbing dinner? I could have plans."

Brad snorted as if the notion was ludicrous. "Let's go to Angelo's. We'll split a pie and work on our theories." He nudged me with his shoulder. "That's where all the cool kids hang out. You know you want to."

"Fine, but only because they have the best cauliflower crust pizza in the city."

I followed Brad to Angelo's, surprised to find a parking space so close to the restaurant until I realized the time. No wonder Lt. Winston sent us home. If he hadn't, we probably would have stayed all night without realizing it. Luckily, Angelo's stayed open late.

Since the place wasn't crowded, Brad asked if we could sit in the round booth in the back corner. Neither of us liked to have our back to the door, hazard of working undercover, so this solved that problem. Plus, the round booth was roomier, which we'd need if this dinner turned into one of our typical working dinners.

"How's the packing going?" Brad swirled the straw around in his glass, eyeing the beer taps and liquor bottles across the room.

"I'd be done by now if Emma would stop unpacking and reorganizing my boxes."

He laughed. "She doesn't want you to move out."

"I don't think that's it. She's just afraid I'll forget something and when I go back to get it, I'll never leave."

The server placed our pizza on the table with two plates, not bothering to hide his disdain at the gluten-free, dairy-free abomination. "Anything else I can get you?"

"Go ahead," I mumbled, figuring my partner wanted something harder than sparkling water.

"No, that's all right." Brad shook his head and nodded to the server. "We're good, thanks."

The server walked away, and we didn't speak again until we had devoured half the pie. No longer starving, Brad rummaged in his pockets for a pen and reached for the stack of napkins. Snagging another slice from the pan, he bit off the end and chewed.

"Do you think Winston's right?" I asked. "Could the stones be removed from the tiara without damaging them?"

"Probably, but I'll ask an expert. Kalen gave me some names. But I am sure of one thing."

"What's that?"

"Selling off the pieces won't net nearly as much as selling off the crown."

"Tiara."

"Whatever," he said around another mouthful. He wrote *appraise individual stones* beneath *contact expert*. "This is wonderful and all, but if we're looking at the same guy, then it doesn't appear he's in a rush to cash out and disappear. Honestly, he might just be getting started."

"Do you think it's the same guy?" That question nagged at me since we received today's call.

"That's the first thing we have to determine. If we take each case at face value from a homicide standpoint, I'd say no. We're looking at different offenders since he used a different method of killing each time. With today being the exception, the rest were convenience kills. The offender used whatever means were available. He strangled the dogwalker with a leash. He stabbed a woman with her own kitchen knife. He bashed in that man's skull with," Brad squeezed his eyes closed, "what was it? A candlestick?"

"That's *Clue*. It was a trophy."

"And he drowned the gardener."

"Yeah." I remembered the responding officer's report. He found the man at the edge of the pool, the upper part of his body forced into the water while the rest of him remained on dry land. "Why didn't he cover his tracks on that one? He could have pushed the body into the water and made it look like an accident." A disconcerting thought entered my mind.

"He wanted us to know he did it," Brad said, echoing my thoughts. "Or he wanted Mr. Arnold to know someone got inside his house and stole his cash."

"Tripping the alarm should have tipped him off."

"Alarms can be accidentally tripped. Killing people doesn't happen accidentally."

"I guess not," I said.

"From the looks of that safe, Mr. Arnold might not have noticed his money was gone or bothered to look if he hadn't found his gardener murdered. The guy's loaded. I doubt he even opens that thing except when he wants to put more money inside."

"I don't know. Rich people are weird about their money. He might count it every night like Scrooge."

"Then why didn't the thief wait for him to do that and then kill Arnold and take the cash instead of drowning the gardener?" Brad asked. "Unless Arnold killed the gardener for stealing the money and then hid the cash in order to cover his tracks."

We speculated for days, but Dieter Arnold had an airtight alibi, complete with dozens of witnesses. He didn't kill his gardener, and nothing indicated he hired someone to do it for him.

"It doesn't track." I reached for another slice. "Arnold didn't do it."

"Which means the thief wanted us to know he killed.

Maybe he left the body like that as an obvious threat to Arnold." Using a second napkin, Brad marked down our timeline. The gardener was killed five days ago. We were knee-deep in that case when we got the call today. Six days before that, the computer was stolen and the programmer killed. He'd been clubbed over the head. His boss asked us to retrieve the company laptop from the victim's house, and that's when we discovered it had been stolen. Mac hoped whenever the thief turned on the device, we'd be able to track his location, but so far, we had no hits. Seven days before that, a masterpiece was stolen from a woman's private collection. Responding officers found her dead in the kitchen, a knife in her stomach and the empty frame in her living room. And five days before that, a million dollar watch collection had been stolen from another high-rise. The security company alerted us to a breach, and when we arrived, we found Mr. Starmon's dogwalker dead in the foyer. At the time, we figured the dogwalker surprised the thief, a struggle ensued, and, in his haste to escape, the thief triggered the alarm. Now, I wasn't so sure.

"They have nothing in common," Brad said, "except for the way the killer gained entry. The alarms weren't tripped on the way in, just on the way out. Three of the crimes happened in high-rises, but the killer-thief always gained entry from above. Never the ground floor."

"Right, he used a harness to lower himself down. And another time, the window washer's carriage. Still, each time, he had to do some free climbing and acrobatics to gain access. And with the other two home invasions, the owners had laser grids and sensors. Either our killer is Catherine Zeta-Jones, or he's an acrobat. Or Harry Houdini."

"You always say Harry Houdini," Brad chastised. "He was an escape artist, not a break-in artist."

"Same skill set."

"No, it isn't. Our killer-thief sucks at escaping undetected."

"Only because he wants us to know he's been there." I blew out a breath. "It's the same guy. It has to be. The three safes he cracked, those were all touted to be uncrackable, but he got into each of them. We're looking for someone who's a cat burglar and master safecracker."

"He could have been there for hours."

"It doesn't matter. The point is he cracked them. And he never took the easy way out of the building. He always went up and out. We need to find a connection. If it isn't the victims, then something must connect the stolen items."

"Even the cash?"

I shrugged.

"And what about today?" Brad asked. "He changed his MO. Do you think he's escalating?"

I bit my lip, wishing I had an answer.

Brad slurped down the rest of his sparkling water, nudging the last piece of pizza closer to me, but I shook my head, my appetite gone. "This is the first time he used a weapon he brought with him."

"He had to. Sambari's windows don't open," I pointed out.

"Why didn't anyone hear the gunshots or the window breaking?" Brad paused, the wheels turning in his head. "I bet the bastard used a silencer."

"That wouldn't muffle the sound of glass breaking."

"No, but it might have helped."

FIVE

"Did ballistics come back yet?" Brad asked when he returned to his desk. "Was I right?"

"You know ballistics can't determine if a suppressor was used." I looked up from the victim profiles, dividing them into two categories, killed and robbed. In three of our cases, we had two victims, the property owner and the deceased. So I was building a profile for each of them, just to be thorough.

"I know. But guns go bang, so I want to know what kind of gun it was, if it's been used to commit any other crimes, and whether anyone remembers hearing it. Uniforms were supposed to conduct a second canvass today."

"The report is on your desk." I pointed to the sticky note stuck on top of a file. "No one heard gunfire. So you're probably right, and the killer used a suppressor. The neighbor across the hall was out, so he didn't hear anything, but the woman in the apartment below thought she heard glass break and heavy footsteps. She didn't think anything of it. She says she thought it was the TV."

"Why didn't she tell us this yesterday?"

"You know witnesses."

Brad rolled his eyes. "Yep." He scanned the notes on his

desk. "So we're looking for a nine mill probably with a suppressor."

"We knew this yesterday."

"It's nice to have hard proof to back it up." My partner dropped into his chair. "I spent the last few hours speaking to jewelers and museums. So far, none of our stolen items have surfaced, but Lt. Winston's right. The tiara could be disassembled. The stones could be cut smaller and sold that way. It'd make it almost impossible to link them back to the stolen tiara."

"Great."

"Isn't it?" He reached for the phone. "Our pals downstairs and in the federal building gave me a list of locals who could do the work. My friend in burglary is already checking with his contacts to see if anyone's heard anything."

"Since you're looking into jewelers, don't forget to ask about the watches."

Brad jotted down my suggestion. "In the meantime, I scheduled a meeting with Zedula for later this afternoon. We need a list of private collectors. When I told the Feds what's been going on, they seemed to think the stolen items were taken for a purpose. If that's the case, our killer-thief probably has a buyer or buyers already lined up. Mac's working on it, but she hasn't found anything concrete."

"Assuming that theory holds water, the thief may only meet with the buyer in person to broker the deals. Given what we know, we should assume he takes precautions."

"Which means we're less likely to find him."

"What about pawn shops?" I asked.

Brad held up a finger while he listened to his messages. "Do you want to take a ride?"

I looked down at the profiles. My gut said the victims were connected. I just wasn't sure how, and I'd been dissecting each of their lives since arriving at work. I could use a break. "Sure."

The city didn't have a shortage of pawn shops. The PD kept a file on most of them since at one point or another hot merchandise had been reported or discovered on the premises. Some pawn brokers didn't want trouble, so they shied away from hot merchandise. Occasionally, they'd call us with a tip or have us run a check on whatever someone tried to sell them. I couldn't blame them. They had a business to run and didn't want to deal with confiscated goods and lost profits. However, finding ethical pawn brokers was a little like finding a four-leaf clover. Most of them bought and sold without batting an eye, which is why we had a file. And since criminals weren't usually geniuses, they tended to move guns and hot goods through the same few stores. Patrol usually kept an eye on them and performed random checks, so when Brad and I arrived at the first shop, we didn't get the friendliest of greetings.

While Brad asked questions, I wandered around and peered into the display cases. Aside from a plethora of engagement rings, I didn't see much in terms of diamonds. And with the exception of one shop having a pair of emerald earrings for sale and another having an emerald pendant, the only green in these places was the cash they used to pay their sellers. The stores didn't have any expensive watches or priceless art for sale either. And while there were dozens of laptops, I didn't think any of those belonged to our dead programmer. The only value in that computer was the software, not the hardware, and as a rule, pawn shops wiped the hard drives before putting the items up for sale. This was a waste. If any of the stolen goods were here, they were hidden in the back.

Restless, I approached the counter where Brad was speaking to the last owner on our list. This was the ninth place we visited.

"What about recently acquired weapons?" Brad asked.

"The only things that have come in this week are two hunting rifles and a musket."

"A musket?" I asked.

The store owner shrugged. "It's a rusted hunk of junk. Do you want to take a look?"

I nodded, and he turned his back to us and unlocked the cabinet behind the counter. Inside were the two hunting rifles, several boxes of ammunition, and the musket. He picked it up and placed it in front of me.

"Who brought this in?" I asked. My partner gave me an odd look, but he wouldn't question me in front of a civilian. The store owner looked at me, as if contemplating if he should ask to see a warrant. "What'd you say your name was?"

I put my badge on the counter. "Detective Liv DeMarco, homicide."

He looked down at the insignia, probably memorizing my badge number in the process. He thought for another moment and reached beneath the counter. My partner's hand inched toward his holstered weapon, but the store owner didn't grab a gun. Instead, he pulled out an ancient looking three-ring binder. He flipped to one of the rear tabs and ran his finger down the page.

"Anthony Lovretta. He dropped this off three days ago."

"Is he coming back for it?" Fennel asked.

The store owner shook his head. "I'll hold it the full thirty days in case he changes his mind, but I'm certain he just wanted the cash."

"How much did you give him for it?" I asked.

"$200."

"I thought it'd be worth more," Fennel muttered, but the owner didn't respond. "And you're sure no one dropped off any nine millimeters or attachments?"

"None." The owner stepped to the side, giving us a better view of the rear cabinet.

I put my card on the counter. "If that changes, we'd appreciate a call."

Fennel eyed the guy. "You should know, there's a reward for any information that leads to identifying and capturing the thief."

"A reward, huh?" Pocketing my card, the store owner thought for a few seconds. "I'll let you know if I hear anything."

"You do that." I offered a tight smile before walking out of the shop. Brad and I didn't speak again until we were inside the unmarked cruiser. "What do you think?"

"The guy's ripping off his customers. Guaranteed, he'll polish that musket, possibly fake some kind of certificate of authenticity, and sell it to some Civil War reenactor or enthusiast for five times what he paid for it."

"Civil War reenactor?" Those words caught my attention.

"Yeah. Who else would want a musket?"

"Not that." I reached for the MDT and typed in Anthony Lovretta.

"My ESP must be on the fritz today," Brad tapped his third eye with his pointer finger, "since I have no idea what you're going on about."

"The musket. Zedula said he has a gun collection."

"And he has muskets?"

"I don't know."

My partner sighed. "I hate to be the bearer of bad news, but according to the pawn shop owner, Lovretta dropped the musket off three days ago. That was before the killer broke into Zedula's apartment. Plus, Zedula told us nothing else was taken. I doubt it's his musket."

"I know, but," I pointed to the screen, "Anthony Lovretta has a record for B&E's." I pulled up his address and driver's license photo. "We could pay him a visit." It was a stretch, but solving one crime while working on another wasn't unheard of in our line of work. Though, I had no basis for thinking Lovretta committed a crime, but seeing that musket tripped something in my brain. I just couldn't figure out what it was.

"Okay, fine." Fennel glanced down at the address and switched lanes. "Why don't you phone Kalen and ask if Zedula's filed any other claims in the last twenty-four hours? I'm pretty sure Zedula insures all of his property with that firm. If that's his musket, the insurance firm will know about it."

I dialed and waited to be redirected. After a brief game of twenty questions, I hung up. "Zedula didn't report anything else stolen. But we'll ask him about his gun collection when he stops by this afternoon, just in case."

Fennel parked outside Lovretta's apartment building and turned in his seat to look at me. "What is it, Liv? What's significant about the musket?"

I squeezed my eyes closed, hoping to collect my thoughts. And then it dawned on me. "Dieter Arnold's a history buff, and his father had been a reenactor. I discovered it this morning when I was updating our profile."

"Does Dieter have his own musket?"

"I don't know, but he might have inherited one. His dad passed a few months ago, and Dieter's his only surviving relative."

"He didn't report one stolen?"

"No, but maybe he didn't notice."

Finally on the same page, Fennel added, "Lovretta brought the musket in three days ago. That fits perfectly with our timeline for the break-in and murder of Mr. Arnold's gardener. All right. Let's stay on our toes. Who knows what we might be walking into?"

SIX

"Anthony Lovretta, open up." Brad banged against the door.

"Hold your horses," a voice sounded from the other side. A few moments later, the door opened a few inches, the security chain holding it in place. "What do you want?"

"Detectives Fennel and DeMarco. We have a few questions."

Lovretta rubbed a stain on his wrinkled and dingy white t-shirt. "What kinds of questions?"

"May we come inside?" Fennel glanced down the hall, but Lovretta didn't appear to have any qualms about airing his dirty laundry in front of his neighbors, literally or figuratively.

"What do you want?"

I gave him my practiced, no-nonsense cop stare. "We're curious about one of your recent transactions."

He eyed me up and down. "I'm gonna need a bit more than that, honey. I make a lot of transactions."

I bristled at the *honey* but held my ground. "Sir, it'd be better to discuss this in private."

"Too bad. I know my rights, and I ain't gotta talk to you." He tried to shut the door, but Fennel pressed the toe of his shoe into the crack. "This is harassment," Lovretta squawked.

"We just want to ask you a few things about the musket you recently pawned," Fennel said.

"Are you a collector or something?" Lovretta asked, but neither of us answered. He held up his palms. "Yeah, okay. Just let me take the chain off the door, and you can come in and we'll talk about it."

Nodding, Fennel took a step back, allowing Lovretta to close the door. I heard the click of the lock and then nothing. Brad ran a hand down his face. "Dammit." He knocked on the door again. "Mr. Lovretta, this will only take a few minutes. Please, we need your help. It'd be in your best interest to cooperate."

"Go fuck yourselves," Lovretta mumbled.

Exchanging a look with my partner, I stepped away from the door. Without a warrant, we couldn't make him comply with our request. And no judge would grant one without further substantiation. This was a waste of time.

"Do you want to drop by Mr. Arnold's office?" Fennel asked as we headed for the stairs. "We could ask if he knows anything about the musket. If he says his is missing, that should be enough to force Lovretta to answer our questions."

"We might as well," I said. "Right now, that's probably our best bet."

"Correct me if I'm wrong, but didn't Arnold tell us he didn't own any guns?"

"According to the records I pulled, he doesn't, which probably means this is a wild goose chase. Maybe we shouldn't waste our time."

"Arnold might not have thought his dad's Civil War prop counted as a gun."

"Do you believe the musket connects to our string of deadly B&Es?" I asked.

"I have no idea, but you seem to think so. And that's good enough for me. It might be nothing, but Lovretta has a record. And he doesn't want to talk to us. I dunno. Something's up." Fennel glanced at the time. "We should sit on Lovretta for a few minutes. If he's our killer or connected to our killer, our questions might have made him nervous. Let's see what he does."

I led the way out of the building and back to the car. Lovretta kept an eye on us from his apartment window, so Fennel put the car in gear and headed down the street. I turned in my seat, keeping an eye on Lovretta's silhouette in the window.

At the next intersection, Brad turned, looped around, and parked on the other side, farther away from Lovretta's apartment building. But when I looked up at the window, Lovretta was no longer standing still. Instead, he paced back and forth. Obviously, our presence made him nervous. And as a rule, innocent people weren't typically this nervous.

For the next twenty minutes, we sat in the car. Fennel checked the MDT, but Lovretta had never been convicted of a violent crime. "I don't think he's our killer."

"I don't think so either," I said. Still, there was something about the musket I couldn't quite shake. Fennel checked the mobile data terminal for additional information and made some calls. I stared up at Lovretta's window. He hadn't left the apartment. In fact, he hadn't stopped pacing. Every few minutes, he'd peek outside. "He's anxious. Paranoid. That has to mean something."

"It could mean he stole the musket." My partner glanced up at the window. "Lovretta has a history of B&Es, but he's always been more of a smash and grab kind of guy. According to this, he usually breaks a window to gain entry, whether it was at the back of someone's house or the window on their fire escape. It's also how he's gotten caught every time. And as far as I can tell, he's never cracked anything open that was more complicated than a beer can."

I reached for my phone. "Keep your eyes peeled, okay?"

After Brad agreed, I performed a few searches and called Mr. Arnold. He didn't answer, so I tried his office. His assistant told me he was in a meeting and asked if she could take a message. After leaving my name and number, I checked to see if any of our other victims had gun collections. But I didn't get far in my search before Brad tapped me on the shoulder.

"What do you make of him?" He pointed to a hooded man carrying an oddly shaped duffel bag. The unsub glanced around before ducking down the steps to the laundry room in the basement of Lovretta's apartment building. Lovretta leaned out the window, catching sight of the man entering. A moment later, Lovretta disappeared inside his apartment, no longer pacing in front of the window. "Do you think that's who Lovretta's been waiting for?"

"Could be. Based on his outfit and that suspicious bag, I'd say whoever that man is, he's trouble."

Brad reached across my lap and grabbed the binoculars out of the glove box. However, from here, we wouldn't be able to see into the apartment unless Lovretta or the mystery man stood directly in front of the window. "We need a better angle. Did you notice any interior stairs going down to the laundry room?"

"No, but I wasn't looking. What do you think he has in the bag?" I asked. Due to the shape of the duffel, our potential unsub could be carrying a rifle or musket.

"Let's just hope it's dirty gym clothes." But even though Fennel said it, neither of us believed it. "We need eyes inside, but we don't need to spook him in case he's connected to our case. I'll take the front door. I thought I saw an interior staircase leading into the basement at the back by the mailboxes. I'll keep watch from there."

"Okay. I'll follow the path he took," I said. Untying my braid, I shook my hair loose and combed my fingers through the brown and honey-colored waves.

"Liv, what are you doing?" Brad watched me from the corner of his eye.

"Improvising."

"When has that ever worked for you?"

"It's bound to one of these days. The way I see it, that puts the odds in my favor," I reasoned.

"Tell me you're not going to waltz in there and do something stupid. We need to keep a low profile."

"Don't worry. I got this. I'll just perform a quick pass, make sure the guy isn't packing or trafficking in stolen muskets, and that'll be it."

"Liv," Brad said in that tone I often ignored, "don't do anything stupid."

"I won't." I took off my jacket and unbuttoned my shirt, leaving on the spaghetti-strap tank top I wore beneath it. "Plus, if I'm wrong, no one's going to bat an eye at a woman who spilled coffee on her shirt and wants to wash it before it stains. You can't say the same." Digging into my bag, I put on some lipstick and tucked away my badge and gun.

"I can spill coffee too."

"But you're not dressed for a strip tease. And someone has to stay in the lobby to make sure Lovretta doesn't slip out while we're distracted. For all we know, he called this bozo in the hood, just so he can slip out while we check on his friend with the suspicious package."

Brad glanced down. His solid grey t-shirt and dark jeans meant he didn't have any extra layers to play with. He had changed before we went to the pawn shops in case we needed to blend in while asking questions. "For the record, I don't like this." He alternated his gaze from me to the building. "Are you sure you can handle this?"

I gave him an exasperated look. "What kind of cop do you think I am?"

"Depending on how much more lipstick you put on, maybe a vice cop."

I slapped his arm and tucked away the tube. "Is it that bad?" I flipped down the vanity mirror. "I'm trying to blend in, but if you think this is calling too much attention, I can rethink it." I blotted my lips with a napkin.

"You look fine." He turned his focus back to Lovretta's window. The shadow was gone. "But it's an unknown situation, so I need you to be careful." Though he remained facing the building, I could see the wrinkles deepen across his forehead.

"I always am."

"The hell you are." He licked his lips. "I'm serious, Liv."

"Okay, Mom." I reached for the cold coffee in the cupholder and poured some on my shirt before balling it up in my left hand. It was important to keep my gun hand empty, just in case things went south. A lot of things had gone south recently, but I promised Brad I'd be careful. And this time, I meant it.

My partner mumbled something under his breath that I didn't quite hear. We'd both been on the job long enough to know this wasn't a coincidence or misunderstanding. Nine times out of ten, our instincts were right, which meant the guy in the hoodie with the suspicious duffel was up to no good. However, that could mean anything. "I'll text you if something changes." He reached for the radio to inform dispatch of our location. Afterward, he met my eyes, an amused expression on his face. "It's scary how you go from business to casual in seconds. Just find out what's what, and let me know if you need help."

"The same goes for you." I glanced at the intel still displayed on the MDT. Lovretta wasn't a cat burglar or safecracker. But criminals normally associate with other criminals. If Lovretta knew the guy with the suspicious bag who ducked into the laundry room, all bets were off.

I opened the car door. Tingles traveled down my spine. It was game time.

Trudging down the exterior steps, I noticed a brick held the basement door open. Carefully, I entered, expecting to be greeted by the laundry room. Instead, I found myself in a narrow hallway. I looked around until I found a staircase on the other end, which presumably led upstairs to the main floor of the apartment building. The first door on the left was locked and labeled maintenance. Halfway down the hall, on the other side, were two double doors. I pushed down on the handle, keeping one eye on the open door across the hallway.

The double doors opened into a dark room, and I fumbled against the wall until I found a switch. Storage, just like I suspected. Several bikes were chained around a support pillar. The locks were meant to deter thieves. Against one wall was a net of sorts, holding several lawn chairs and Christmas decorations. Aside from that, there were boxes, dusty white sheets over various pieces of furniture, some long-forgotten baby toys, and a few damaged appliances. This room might be of later interest, depending on what turned up on Lovretta and the musket. After making a mental note, I turned off the light and continued toward the next room, unable to shake the smell of dust and mildew.

Unlike the storage area, the open door provided a warm, inviting light. I stepped inside, the scent of detergent and fabric softener competed with the musty smells inside my nostrils. Four washing machines covered one side of the room. A folding table stood in the center, and four dryers took up most of the back wall. A few chairs were pressed against the empty wall, but no one was inside. Where did he go?

Curiously, I went to the washing machines and lifted the lids but found nothing inside except clothing. No duffel bag. No man. And I wasn't about to search four loads of laundry for a dark-colored hoodie. Reaching for my phone, I dialed Brad.

"Room's clear," I said. "No sign of him or his bag."

"No one's gone past me. He must already be on an upper level inside the building. Meet me near the mailboxes."

"I'm on my way." I checked behind the machines, but I didn't spot anything except a few mousetraps. Maybe this case was getting to me. Why the musket? Why did I believe that was significant? On my way up the stairs, I remembered. It wasn't the musket; it was what the musket represented. "I may know how our vics are connected."

"How?" Brad asked.

"An estate auction."

"What? Whose?"

"I'm not sure yet. I need to check a few things." A commotion sounded from somewhere above us. A man and woman screamed at each other, but their words were garbled. After a few seconds, the voices quieted.

"I'll check that out," Fennel said, not giving me room to argue. "Stay here."

While I waited, fearing the situation my partner just walked into, the hooded man came up the same staircase I took only moments earlier. How did he get behind me? The duffel remained slung over his shoulder. He kept his face down as he unobtrusively slinked up the stairs. *Oh, hell no*, I thought, forcing myself to count to five before following him. The hooded man didn't stop on the second floor; he kept going. So I followed, keeping my eyes on him. My phone buzzed in my pocket, and I checked Brad's message with one eye while keeping the other glued to our unsub's back.

Run-of-the-mill argument. Apparently, someone didn't rinse the dishes before putting them in the dishwasher.

The hooded man stopped suddenly at the opening to Lovretta's floor, and I busied myself with sending a text to Brad. Nonchalant, Liv. Nonchalant. After informing my partner of what was going on, I tucked my phone into my pocket and moved past the man, circling to the next flight of steps. "Hey," I mumbled as I passed.

"Hi." His response was common. Perfunctory. By the time I was three steps up, he had vanished down the hall toward Lovretta's apartment. I waited a beat, wanting to follow but afraid of attracting more attention.

A moment later, Brad jogged up the steps. He caught my eye and continued down the hallway to Lovretta's apartment. I waited a few more seconds before going down the steps and after my partner. "Any movement at Lovretta's?" I whispered, finding Brad pressed against the wall across from Lovretta's door.

"Someone's still inside. I assume it's Anthony. But I didn't see the hooded man. You're sure he stopped on this floor?"

"Positive."

Fennel squinted, straining to hear. "Someone's moving around inside." He pointed to the changing light patterns beneath the door.

"Do you think Anthony Lovretta has company?"

"I can't see inside, Liv. I'm not Superman."

"You should work on that."

Brad chuckled. "I'll add it to my to-do list."

Stepping closer to Lovretta's door, I felt it before I saw or heard anything. Call it cop instincts, but I knew, even if I didn't realize it. Two seconds later, a shriek sounded, followed by breaking glass. The door swung open, nearly banging into me, and a man in a dark hoodie bolted from Lovretta's apartment. He flew past me before I even had time to process what was happening. He had a misshapen duffel shoved over one shoulder, and as he sprinted past us, something fell out of the bag with a clatter.

"Stop," I yelled. The suspect continued to flee, never slowing or even acknowledging me.

"I got him," Brad said.

Just as I turned to see what fell out of the duffel bag, a loud bang sounded from Lovretta's apartment. Pulling my gun, I stepped around the dropped evidence and pressed my back against the wall. Glancing over my shoulder, I peered into the apartment. The blinds hung askew. One side pulled all the way to the top while the other fell almost to the floor.

"Police," I announced, but no one was inside. Carefully, I cleared the apartment, but it was empty. The end table in front of the broken window had toppled over, probably making the bang. A thick, nylon rope was tied around the bottom rung of the table, extending out the window. Edging closer, I shoved the blinds out of the way and peered out, catching just a glimpse of someone shimmying down the building and landing on the sidewalk below.

Requesting backup and all available units to my location, I ran out of the apartment and after the escape artist. As I raced down the steps, Fennel met me on the landing with Anthony Lovretta in cuffs.

"Asshole's getting away," I said, not slowing. "Evidence is still on the floor. Grab it and secure the scene."

My partner shouted something after me, but I didn't hear him. Bursting through the front door, I ran to the left, but I didn't see the escape artist. He had to be here. A man couldn't just scale a building and vanish. I slowed for half a second, searching for him.

Spotting him, I sprinted in his direction. "Hold it right there," I yelled.

He didn't look back. He didn't slow. Instead, he darted across the street just as the *Don't Walk* sign illuminated. Horns blared and brakes squealed, but he made it across. A truck drove through the intersection, and I momentarily lost sight of him.

I darted through traffic, but I didn't spot him anywhere. By the time I reached the sidewalk, he was gone. For the next ten minutes, I searched everywhere. I even asked pedestrians if they'd seen him, but the guy vanished. When a patrol unit rolled up, I gave them a description, sent the information over the wire, and trudged back to the apartment building.

"DeMarco," Fennel said when I made it back to Lovretta's apartment, "did you get him?"

"No."

"Dammit." He rubbed a hand over his mouth as he stalked the space in front of Lovretta's apartment door while a patrol officer sealed off the area. "Our killer got away."

"How do you know he's our killer?" I asked.

Brad reached for the evidence bag and pulled out a broken jewelry box. It was the same kind I had when I was little with a wind-up ballerina inside. But instead of storing an assortment of jelly bracelets and plastic barrettes, the box contained three of Mr. Starmon's stolen watches.

"Where's Lovretta?" I asked. The uncooperative asshole better have answers and be willing to talk. I was no longer in the mood for games or playing nice.

"Waiting in the back of the car. An officer's watching him." Fennel eyed me. "At least we know we're on the right track. Come on, let's go get some answers."

SEVEN

I rubbed my face and dropped my head to my desk. Anthony Lovretta wasn't talking. Since he possessed the stolen watches at the time of his arrest, he was facing murder charges. I'd spoken to ADA Logan Winters, and the DA's office was on board to offer a deal if Lovretta gave up his accomplice – the unknown hooded man we'd followed into the apartment building. However, Lovretta insisted no one else had been inside his apartment, that the hoodie he wore was his, and he denied knowing anything about the watches or how they came to be inside his duffel bag. His attorney even posited that perhaps the watches were never in the bag but had been in the hallway all along, and Fennel had no grounds to make an arrest.

"This is bullshit," Brad grumbled. "Francis Starmon identified the three watches we found as part of his collection. The serial numbers match. We know where those watches came from."

I lifted my head off the desk and made sure no one was within earshot. "Do we?"

"What the fuck, Liv?"

I held up my hand, hoping to calm Brad's temper. "We

know the watches were inside the jewelry box that fell out of the duffel bag. But we don't know where the jewelry box came from. Starmon didn't recognize it."

"So what? It could have come from anywhere. That's irrelevant. Lovretta dropped the box out of the bag when he attempted to flee. That means he had the watches."

"I know," I said patiently, "but is that his duffel bag? I'm not even sure that's his hoodie. He made a point to tell us it is, which makes me think it isn't." My gaze dropped to the phone. "Hopefully, the judge will sign off on letting us analyze the hoodie, but you and I both know the unsub was wearing something just like it, and when we knocked on Lovretta's door, he only had on that stained t-shirt."

"But you said the man who rappelled down the building was also wearing a dark hooded jacket. Why would they switch?"

"I don't know. Why would our killer leave his duffel bag and a six-figure score with a nobody like Anthony Lovretta?" I rubbed the bridge of my nose. "Lovretta knows who the killer is. He must have called him the moment we left the apartment. I sent officers back to the pawn shop to pick up the musket. It must connect." I reached for the files. "Our five victims were collectors — antiques, art, watches, the kinds of things one would find at estate auctions."

Brad pointed to the photos on the board as he went. "Okay, so Zedula has enough antiques to open his own exhibit. The dead woman had an art collection. Starmon had his watches, and we know Arnold inherited his father's Civil War memorabilia. What did the programmer collect? Computer games?"

"Antique chessboards." I flipped a crime scene photo around and pointed to the built-in bookcase. The upper portion had been divided into nine separate square compartments, each containing a handcrafted, antique chess set.

"But the thief didn't steal those," Brad protested.

"Not that we know of. But since he killed the programmer, we can't be sure he didn't take another set that wasn't on display."

Brad took the photo and tacked it to the board beneath the profile we had for that victim and crime scene – Kevin Maser, programmer, bludgeoned. Brad stared at the crime scene photos. The trophy used to kill Kevin sat just feet away from the beloved chess sets.

"I thought the connection might be the safes." He scratched out the notation he made since the personal security systems had been installed by different companies. "Our stabbing victim had laser grids and sensors protecting her valuables. However, her safe wasn't broken into, but the killer thwarted her alarm system in order to take one of the paintings. And he took the watches and tiara," Brad said, following my train of thought, "but we don't know for sure about the chess sets or the musket. Have you spoken to Arnold yet?"

"Mr. Arnold said it's possible something else could have been stolen in addition to the cash. He's on his way with the certificate of authenticity. That should clear this up."

"I'll see if any of Mr. Maser's friends or coworkers know if any chessboards or collectibles are missing from the apartment." Brad made some calls while I checked on our progress and waited for Mr. Arnold to arrive.

After some preliminary questions, I learned Arnold placed most of his father's belongings in storage but had a few unopened boxes in his garage. Since his father only passed a few months ago, and the loss was still new, Arnold was dealing with bigger issues and hadn't had much time to go through all the junk.

"I brought this," Arnold held out an inventory of items from his father's estate and several certificates. "I don't remember seeing a musket, but according to this, he owned three." He pointed to the list of items and their assessed value. "The last one was recently acquired, only days before he died. If it had been delivered around the time of his death, it probably got redirected to my house and has been sitting in the garage ever since."

"Did you happen to notice if anything else in your house looked disturbed?" I asked, reading the number and matching it to the musket on the table.

Arnold laughed. "Detective DeMarco, right now,

everything is disturbed, even me."

"We'll do our best to find the person who murdered your gardener and stole your money."

"And my father's musket." Arnold picked up the tarnished firearm from the table, examining it closely. Evidence collection dropped it off in the conference room after they finished examining it and dusting it for prints. "If this is my father's musket."

"According to this certificate of authenticity, it is." I leafed through the pages he brought. "You're right. He just acquired it. Do you mind if we hold on to it a little longer?"

"Don't rush. I don't need more useless junk in my house." But he lovingly stroked the grip before gently placing it on the table. "Regardless, my dad would have loved this. Rust and all." He chuckled. "He would have said it added character. It's probably why he bought it. It's a shame he never got a chance to enjoy it."

"I'm sorry for your loss, your losses." After reminding him to call if he thought of anything, I showed him to the door and returned to my desk.

"Maser's boss just e-mailed me this photo." Brad pointed to my monitor. "I forwarded it to you. It turns out Kevin Maser recently bid on a crystal chess set. He kept the knight on his desk at work."

I looked at the photo and whistled. "That must have set him back a pretty penny. You said he bid on it." I waited for an elaboration.

"That's all I got. I'll have someone do a more thorough evaluation of his financials, but I don't remember seeing anything about an auction."

"Maybe he used PayPal or bitcoin."

"Could be, but right now, everything is pointing to estate sales and auctions. I just got off the phone with Zedula's insurance company. Kalen confirmed some of Zedula's valuables have come from estate sales."

"What about the tiara?"

Fennel nodded, digging through the file for the proper form. "Zedula acquired it from Agnes Archibald's private collection. According to the transfer information and the news stories I found, the news broke days after the

Archibald estate went up for auction. Agnes died, leaving three heirs who had no interest in anything other than money. They auctioned off everything and split the proceeds."

"Any chance one of them changed her mind and is stealing back family heirlooms?" I asked, already searching records to see if the other items taken had come from the Archibald estate. No dice. The painting the thief took didn't come from that estate sale. However, a small sculpture the art collector owned did. "Okay, I found a link between our stabbing vic and the Archibald auction."

It didn't take long before we discovered each of our victims had purchased something from that estate sale, even Maser, who, according to his bank, paid using an aggregate. However, only our female victim and Mr. Arnold's father attended the auction in person. Kevin Maser bid online using an alias to procure the crystal chess set rumored to have belonged to a member of the royal family. And Mr. Starmon sent a proxy to act on his behalf. However, the pocket watch he procured remained safe and sound at his house. The thief didn't want it. Aside from the tiara, the chess set, and possibly the musket, the painting and watch collection didn't come from that auction. So the thefts weren't about reclaiming parts of the Archibald estate. They were about something else.

"The auction must be how our killer-thief chose his victims, not how he chose his score," I said. "I'll get in contact with the auction company and get a list of buyers. One of them might be next."

"Check out the company's employees and the auctioneer too," Fennel said. "I'd bet my badge someone present at the auction is our killer."

"I thought we had the killer in custody," Lt. Winston said, sneaking up behind me.

My face contorted in annoyance, and my partner's eyes danced in amusement. Unlike Capt. Grayson in the intelligence unit, Lt. Winston didn't treat me like the golden child, which meant I was just another grunt to pick on. Forcing my expression into something more neutral, I turned in my chair. "Lovretta's not our killer, but he knows who is. Lovretta provided a distraction while the man we believe to be the actual killer escaped."

"You let him escape," Winston said matter-of-factly.

"Sir," I began, but he shushed me with a wave of his hand.

"It happens. So now you have to do things the hard way. You need to break Lovretta. His attorney's hoping to get his client sprung as soon as possible. He's challenging our rationale for making the arrest." Winston looked from Fennel to me. "The clock's ticking. We have forty-eight hours before we have to charge him with something. And unless he gives up the real killer, we'll take him down for the murders."

"Sir?" I asked, but the lieutenant didn't even bother to acknowledge my question before walking away.

"Maybe he was joking." My partner glanced at the set of desks closest to ours. "Hey, Jake, is there anything we should know about the LT?"

"Winston's a hard ass," Detective Voletek spun in his chair to face us, "but his bark is worse than his bite. He talks a big game, and bluffs like no one I've ever seen. He could scare a choir boy into snitching on his own mother."

"Lovely," I muttered.

Voletek scooted his chair across the walkway until he was sitting perpendicular to Fennel. "He thinks it gives us incentive to work harder, and if not, it gives the crooks incentive to go above and beyond to assist us. The way Winston sees it, it's a win for the department either way."

Brad and I exchanged a look. This wasn't the way to do things, but when you dealt with homicides on a daily basis, it was easy to see how the ends might justify the means.

"Anyway, since the two of you are still pretty new around here, I got you a little something. You guys might want to take a look at this." Voletek reached for Brad's keyboard and mouse, waiting for my partner to relinquish control of the computer. "I got a buddy, used to be a cop but now he's a private dick. Leopold Zedula hired him to recover the tiara. Anyway, since my pal's already helping me out on an arson thing, I figured it wouldn't hurt to ask him what he's uncovered on your jewelry thing." Voletek typed something in, and Brad's eyes grew wide.

"What is it?" I asked.

"A lot more than what we had before," Brad said. He turned to the other detective. "Jake, is any of this legal?"

"I don't know how my pal, Renner, stumbled onto it, but since he gave it to us, you can use it however you want. Cross Security has a lot more resources and pull than we do. Just don't tell Lucien Cross I said that. The guy already thinks he's above the law. I'm guessing he probably hacked private security feeds and found relevant footage. I don't know what will hold up in court, but since we didn't pull the footage, it's clean on our end."

"Maybe you should check with Winters before we proceed," Brad said as I came around the desk to see what the two men were looking at.

Footage from a neighboring building caught sight of a cloaked figure practically flying off the roof of Zedula's apartment building before landing on a nearby rooftop, climbing down a pipe, and disappearing over the other side, probably jumping to another building or rappelling down from there. "We could be looking for an urban climber," I said.

"Or a traceur," Voletek said.

"A what?" I asked.

"A traceur."

I glanced at Brad, wondering when the conversation stopped being in English.

"Yeah, I've seen the movie," my partner said, "but that's not this guy. This guy's a climber. He uses equipment. We might want to check into BASE jumpers, former military, even gymnasts." Brad pointed to the screen. "It's hard to see, but that might be a wing suit or even some type of pulley system. Human beings can't move like that, unless he's part flying squirrel."

Narrowing my eyes at the screen while the two men debated, I reached for the mouse and sent a copy of the footage to Mac. She'd settle the debate, but until she got around to it, I zoomed in, watching the way our killer soared from one roof to the other, maintaining almost the same position the entire time. "It's a zipline," I said. "See?

And whatever anchor he used to hold it in place, he retracted. That's why we didn't find anything on the roof when we searched."

"We need to check these other buildings." Brad pointed. "And we need to expand our search perimeter."

"Glad I could help," Voletek said, sliding back to his desk.

"Thanks, Jake." Consumed, Brad didn't even look up.

"We owe you one," I said to Voletek.

"Oh yeah?" Voletek asked.

"You shouldn't have said that," Brad whispered as he clicked keys. I arched a confused eyebrow at my partner, but before I could ask why that was a bad idea, Voletek grinned at me.

"Buy me a drink after shift, Liv," Voletek said. He glanced at Fennel. "Your partner can't afford another night like the one we had two weeks ago."

Now I knew there was a story between Brad and this homicide detective. "Something you want to tell me, partner?" I asked.

"Jake drinks like a fish. He said one drink. Hold him to it." Brad glanced over at Voletek. "And just so you know, Liv carries pepper spray and isn't afraid to use it. Oh, and fair warning, her roommate's a bit overprotective and has a thing for castration."

"Sounds like a party," Voletek said. "Does she eat like you do?"

"Worse," Brad replied.

"Gentlemen, I can hear you."

"Oh, I'm aware," Voletek grinned, "and I'm definitely looking forward to tonight."

That's when I realized even though I never agreed to buy this scruffy homicide detective a drink, I was somehow now indebted to follow through on a promise I didn't make. I glared at Brad and took a seat behind my desk. "Before you leave work, you're going to tell me everything you know about Jake Voletek," I hissed, relieved Voletek had taken a call and left the bullpen.

"Don't worry, Liv. You can handle him. Hell, you'll probably chew him up and spit him out. Anyway, unless we actually find some leverage to use against Lovretta or we finish running down these new leads, no one is leaving tonight."

"You think Winston's going to let us stay past our shift? Yesterday, he seemed pretty adamant about denying overtime."

"That was yesterday. Today we let a killer slip through our fingers." Brad swallowed and dove into the profile head first.

EIGHT

"Where are you on Anthony Lovretta?" Fennel asked.

"Most of his associates are serving time. The few who aren't alibied out for this afternoon," I said.

"Any cat burglars in the mix?"

"Nope."

"Violent offenders?"

"Plenty, but like I said, most are currently incarcerated. Patrol checked alibis and passed along additional leads, but it doesn't look like Lovretta's ever worked with our killer before."

Fennel leaned back in his chair, absently reaching for the baseball he kept on his desk. He tossed it up in the air a few times. "What about former military? Ezra Sambari was Mossad. Did anything shake loose on that?"

"The state department hasn't gotten back to us yet, but I spoke to Penny Sambari. She said Ezra was just a pencil-pusher. He severed ties with his old life twenty years ago when they moved here. But based on Sambari's build, I don't necessarily believe he pushed pencils, unless they weighed a few hundred pounds, but we've checked everything. Nothing indicates he was still active in the spy game or that anyone from his former life was gunning for him. I spoke to the FBI and DHS, but they haven't heard anything. Based on the connection we've found among our vics and the Archibald estate auction, I'm willing to bet Sambari just happened to be in the wrong place at the wrong time. Our thief didn't kill any other trained assassins, so I don't think this is a hit or contract. It appears everything links back to the Archibalds."

Fennel listened, nodding as I spoke. "I agree, but we need to keep in mind that our killer possesses the skills needed to zipline off a building, rappel out a window, and vanish into thin air."

"The guy's a fucking magician."

"Don't start with the Harry Houdini schtick again, Liv. You know I prefer David Copperfield."

I stuck out my bottom lip in a pout. "Anyway, since we've ruled out Sambari's former enemies and we're still waiting to hear back about the Archibald auction, I checked into Anthony Lovretta's non-jailbird contacts, figuring maybe he knew a few guys who served or were former Olympic gymnasts."

"And?"

"No gymnasts, but according to his friends list on social media, he knew plenty of guys from high school who enlisted. Ninety-five percent of them don't have records."

"We should check them out anyway."

"This could take forever." I shot a look at the LT's office. "And we don't have that kind of time."

"So we'll narrow it down to people he's recently been in contact with. The paperwork came through, so we have his phone records and internet history. That gives us a nice starting place."

"Mac's on it. She already scoured his social media accounts and ran the subsequent background checks on Lovretta's less upstanding friends." I handed Brad the list of names. "Again, we have a nice mix of potential suspects, but none of them appear promising."

He scanned the list. "Dammit."

"Did you track the killer's escape route after he left Mr. Zedula's apartment?" I asked.

"I'm still waiting on the court orders for nearby surveillance feeds, but CSU checked the roof again. They found a small hole and a scrape from where our killer-thief anchored the zipline. CSU found a similar spot on the adjacent building where he landed. From the video footage, it's safe to assume the zipline's how he gained access to the penthouse in the first place. He came across from the roof of the other building, lowered himself down to the window, shot it out, killed Sambari, stole the tiara, and left using the same zipline that got him across. From there, I don't know where he went."

I drummed my fingernails on my desk. The auction company agreed to provide a list of employees and staff involved in the Archibald estate sale, but until they received a copy of the warrant, they refused to give us a list of the attendees and buyers. Once the judge signed the paperwork, they'd comply, but compiling the information would take time. We wouldn't get it until tomorrow afternoon.

"Do you think the killer will go to ground?" I asked. After the close call this afternoon, that would be the smart thing to do.

"It depends."

"On?"

"Why he was at Anthony Lovretta's apartment." Brad returned the baseball to its stand and rubbed the scruff on his jaw. A thought flashed across his face. "Do you think Lovretta's a fence?"

"An hour ago, I verified the musket Lovretta pawned came from Mr. Arnold's house. We know he moved the stolen musket. And it would explain why he had the watches, but it doesn't explain why he took the loot and ran."

"He didn't know we were outside his door. He thought we drove away, remember?" My partner stared at me. "Lovretta's scared of our killer. I don't think he was running to get away from us. I think he was running to get away from him. Did we get anything back on the clothes he was wearing when we brought him in?"

"We found traces of blood on his sleeve. It's not his. So it could be our killer's or one of the victims. DNA takes time to process, so right now, all we have is blood type, which doesn't match Lovretta."

"You think they tussled?" Brad asked.

"Could be."

"Do you want to hear my theory?"

"Go ahead," I said.

"I think the killer brought the musket to Lovretta to fence and decided to unload a few of the watches. Lovretta probably knew the killer was on his way, and that's why Lovretta was in a rush to get rid of us. Either Lovretta acted squirrely, tipping off the killer that something was wrong, or the killer made us after he arrived and figured he'd get rid of the loose end. Remember, we heard sounds of a struggle coming from inside, and when Lovretta ran out, he didn't even care we were there. He just kept running."

"The killer heard us announce, and that's why he went out the window."

"Probably," Brad said.

"He must keep his gear with him at all times. When I spotted him, he had a bag over his shoulder. At first, I thought he had Lovretta dress up like him to throw us off his scent, but now, I'm not so sure." If this case got any more complicated, I'd scream.

"One thing's for sure," Fennel said, "Anthony Lovretta is more afraid of the killer than he is of us. That's why he's not talking. He's probably more than willing to take the blame if it means he remains breathing. Prison and police custody might be the two safest places for him."

"Maybe we can use that to leverage him to cooperate. We could offer him witness protection."

"Yeah, but before we do that, we need proof he wasn't involved in the murders, and right now, aside from the mystery man we've barely glimpsed, we can't prove any of it. Lovretta hasn't offered us anything in his own defense. And he won't talk. He's hoping what we have is flimsy enough to let him go or strong enough to hang him. At the moment, it could go either way. Perhaps, he's hoping the longer we keep him, the easier it will be to convince the real killer that he didn't give him up."

"That's a lot of guesswork."

"Until the information we requested comes in, there's

nothing else we can do. The rest will have to wait until tomorrow, Liv."

"I hate this."

"Me too."

NINE

He stood across the street, watching the detectives leave the precinct and head to the bar. Congratulations were in order. They may have caught a killer.

Frankly, he wasn't surprised Anthony Lovretta got caught. Lovretta had a sheet a mile long. He remembered hearing stories about the loser from a police sergeant. But supposedly the thief had turned over a new leaf. He just wondered if anyone believed it.

However, Lovretta's arrest complicated matters. He approached Lovretta for a singular purpose. He needed Lovretta to do one thing. Just one. It's why he gave Lovretta the musket. To bait his hook. But the fish didn't bite. Not yet. But that would change. He'd collect more intel and steal more valuable items. Plus, he still had the tiara. He could try another approach. He just needed to find another way in. There were plenty of possibilities. And he wouldn't give up until he found the perfect opportunity.

He'd been planning this too long to let a nobody like Anthony Lovretta get in his way. And since Lovretta was arrested with the watches, the loser might even go down for the five murders. But was that a risk worth taking?

*   *   *

"Brad was right. You are worse than he is." Despite his words, Jake Voletek held the same charming, yet slightly mischievous, grin. "So tell me, Liv, what do you drink when you feel like getting into trouble?"

"Tequila shots."

His grin turned into a full-blown smile. "Woman after my own heart." He spun his beer bottle on the table, keeping an eye on our surroundings. "I'm just wondering what would happen if I showed up to your apartment with a bottle of Patron and a bag of limes."

"You might face stalking charges."

"Ouch." Jake clutched his chest and took another swig of beer, but the smile didn't waver. "So let me make sure I got this straight. You don't consume grains of any kind, or refined sugars, or processed oils, unless you're undercover."

"Right."

"But you're not vegan?"

I shook my head.

"Did you go to college in California?"

Laughing, I reached for my wine glass. "No, Voletek."

"Jake," he corrected. "So why do it? I get Brad has an aversion to the things he had to eat while in the military. MREs, blah." Jake shuddered and made a gagging sound. "And he just took that to an extreme, but you don't have the same excuse."

"Why the twenty questions?"

Voletek brushed off my question with another of his own. "That's why you and Brad are partners, isn't it? No one else in the department would put up with your healthy food obsession. Grabbing lunch would be a disaster. It'd take you hours to find a place to eat, and by then, shift would be over." He made a tsk sound. "Seriously, homicide has the best pastry selection out of all the units. You're missing out. Flour, white sugar, cheap oil, yum yum."

"I doubt it."

"Doubt what?" Brad asked, dragging an extra chair up to the table before taking a seat.

"That my life would be better if I ate the pastries in the break room," I deadpanned.

"That's not what I said," Jake insisted. "What about restaurants? Do you eat at restaurants?"

Brad snorted and sipped a tropical concoction loaded with rum and not much else. "Are you trying to ask my partner something? The direct approach would work better and save us all some time."

"Just getting some facts straight," Jake said, but the wheels turned in his head.

"All right, enough chit chat." I leaned forward and lowered my voice. It wasn't uncommon to discuss a case in public, but I normally didn't do it somewhere this crowded, even if ninety-nine percent of the people inside were fellow cops. "It's time you come clean, Jake. Why are you so invested in our case?"

"I help where I can. The LT hasn't given me much to do lately since he's been so busy breaking you two in. So I've been looking into an arson investigation with my friend, Bennett Renner, the P.I. I told you about."

"Renner," the name rang a bell, "didn't he take early retirement after getting shot?"

"You remember that?" Voletek asked. "Isn't that before your time?"

"Actually, I was in uniform when that happened, but I remember my dad telling me about it."

"How is the great Vince DeMarco?" Voletek asked.

"Fine." I sensed some hostility, but I wasn't sure why.

Brad put down his glass. "So a former cop turned P.I. turned us on to the footage after he discovered it because Mr. Zedula hired him to find the tiara. I'm just curious, if we find it first, is Renner going to take credit in order to claim the reward money? Or did he turn the footage over to us out of a sense of loyalty to the badge?"

"Does it matter?" Voletek asked. "Cops are exempt from accepting rewards. Someone recently pointed that out to me. And as far as Renner's motives, it's tough to say for certain. He just does his job to the best of his ability. He's happy to have it after getting kicked off the force."

"Regardless of Renner's motives, we appreciate the

assistance, but he's a civilian now. He needs to be careful not to interfere in our investigation," Brad said.

"He won't," Voletek said. "He just wants to find the tiara. Identifying the killer is all on you. But some of his leads might prove helpful. So I thought I'd get what I could out of him and pass it along."

"Why are you helping us?" I asked.

Voletek stared at Brad, who suddenly found the drink menu on the table fascinating. "You really don't know who I am, do you, princess?"

"Should I?" I asked.

Voletek laughed again, the flirtatious grin from earlier returning. "Let's see. Where do I begin?" He glanced at Brad again. "You seriously never mentioned me, man?"

"Liv, Jake and I worked a case in gangs together before I transferred to intelligence. He was my partner on that big joint op we ran. We also play on the precinct's softball team together."

"You play softball?" I asked, wondering how I didn't know this.

Unlike most cops, Brad didn't tell a lot of stories. But his time with gangs was short-lived. I knew he took down a major player and was transferred to another unit for his own safety. If Jake had been his partner, they might have been under together, but I couldn't be sure. And Brad obviously didn't want to talk about it.

"I can't believe you never bothered to mention me. Even after the two of you joined homicide, you still didn't say a word or introduce us," Jake teased. "I'm hurt, man. Really hurt."

"Do you know Bennett Renner too?" I asked Brad.

He shook his head. "No, Renner worked homicide with Jake."

"Yep," Jake confirmed. "But I still don't know why you kept me a secret. Are you afraid I'll steal Liv away from you?"

"From what I hear, it wouldn't be the first time you've done something like that," Brad retorted. His phone buzzed, and he pulled it out of his pocket. The corner of his lip curled, and he leaned back in his chair, suddenly much cockier. I knew what that look meant. Carrie just texted him. He shot off a reply and finished his drink. "I should take off. Liv, I'm sorry I didn't introduce you to Jake, but I'm guessing before you leave the bar, you'll understand why." Brad turned his focus to Voletek. "Don't piss off my partner. You mess with her, and you mess with me. Got it?"

"I thought we were bros," Jake said.

"We are, but Liv takes priority."

I hated when Brad pulled the weird macho shit. "We have a long day tomorrow," I said to him. "Don't stay out too late."

"Back 'atcha."

"Oh, that's not a problem." I narrowed my eyes. "Have fun. Blow off some steam, but just remember what I said about screwing us."

"Imagery, Liv." Brad cringed. "I've told you before I don't need that kind of imagery." I slapped his arm as he pushed away from the table.

Jake silently watched our exchange but didn't comment. Instead, he finished his beer and debated getting another. "Do you want another glass of wine?"

I shook my head. "So you're upset I didn't know you worked with Brad?"

"No. Frankly, I understand why Brad didn't introduce us." Jake leaned in, brushing his fingers against my forearm. "He didn't want me to ask you out."

"I got that."

"Well, now I'm curious. Is that a yes?"

I laughed. "You got some balls on you."

Jake shrugged. "Dating is a number's game. I just keep trying until I find one to stick."

"Dating in the department is frowned upon, even more so within the same unit."

"So you don't date cops?"

"I don't really date anyone. Who has the time, especially with weeks and months spent undercover? Not to mention, who do we meet besides other cops and crooks?"

"That's a shame. You need to get out more." Voletek leaned back. "So you and Brad aren't a thing?"

I nearly choked. "No."

He scrutinized me for a moment, and I saw a flicker of what he must be like inside an interrogation room. "Don't worry, I believe you."

"So if you knew Brad never mentioned you, why did you think I should know who you are?"

"Well, princess," again the odd nickname left his lips, irritating me, "you just knocked me down several pegs. I assumed my reputation preceded me, just like yours precedes you. But apparently, I was wrong. After all, one should never assume."

"What reputation?" Was this about the gangs bust? Maybe I should ask about it, but doing so would feel like betraying my partner. If I wanted to know, I'd ask Brad.

"I'm a legacy. Police royalty. Just like you."

"Voletek." I let his last name roll off my tongue. "Your father's Manny Voletek. He works out of HQ, doesn't he?"

"Yeah, he works for the commissioner. And both of my brothers are cops at different precincts. It's a lot to live up to."

"Shit."

"Isn't it?" Voletek flagged down the bartender and pointed to his bottle. "So trust me when I say I understand the kind of crap you've dealt with."

"Add being a woman to that list."

Voletek winced. "First, let me start by saying I'm sorry. You've had it way worse than me." He excused himself from the table and returned with another beer and a second glass of wine for me. "Second, Lt. Winston's a dick. Plain and simple."

Even though I didn't want the wine, I thanked Jake anyway. Now that I put an end to his advances, he didn't seem like such a bad guy. And he had gone out of his way to help our investigation. "Earlier, you said he wasn't that bad."

"He's hardnosed and no-nonsense, like most of the old-timers. He's all about justice and law and order. Dun, dun," Jake mimicked the iconic sound. "He's a good cop, but he's still a dick."

"Is that why you've been helping us out?"

"No, I'm helping because I can and because Renner

wants to help. He worked homicide. You can take the man out of uniform, but you can't take the uniform out of the man."

"What?"

"I dunno. It sounded better in my head." Jake grinned. "It also sounded a little inappropriate, which might be why I liked it so much."

"Is that what you do? Push boundaries?" I knew the type. Jake's family connections would keep him out of trouble. Unless he broke the law or majorly overstepped, the worse that would happen would be he'd get a slap on the wrist. He knew he was untouchable within reason, and it sounded like he knew it and took advantage. The few times I called my dad for a favor I always regretted it, even though I'd done it in order to get additional resources or assistance on a case. It had always been in the name of the greater good, but it was abuse of power and a slippery slope. And I always felt icky about it afterward.

"We're catching killers, Liv. And just so you know, I'm not dirty. If you don't believe me, ask your partner. But no matter how good we are or how amazing our clearance rates are, we'll always be stuck trying to fill impossibly large shoes. I just thought it'd be nice to get to know one another. Not many people on the force can commiserate with our plight. Most people think I'm just bitching about my good fortune. They don't realize the pressure, stress, and unfair biases I deal with day in and day out. Your father is touted as being the best police captain to ever run our precinct. I'm sure plenty of officers have given you a hard time because of it, thinking you've received an unfair advantage. And from what I've seen, you work harder than almost everyone else, probably because of it. I just wanted to tell you that your hard work does make a difference."

"Thanks, I appreciate that. I just wish the LT realized it."

"He will. Solve this string of murders, and he'll take notice. He's a cranky, old bastard, but he's not blind. This is your first big case. Multiple victims, multiple crime scenes. It's terrible, but it might be just what you need to show him you aren't police edition Barbie."

"Is that what he called me?" I asked. Suddenly thirsty, Voletek focused on drinking his beer, which answered my question. "And I thought it was bad when everyone thought I was getting preferential treatment since my commanding officer used to be my dad's partner."

Voletek snorted. "The grass is always greener, isn't it?" He took another swig and put the beer down. "I'm just curious. How many strings did you have to pull to make sure you and your partner were transferred together? You do know that never happens."

"I didn't pull the strings. Brad did."

"Shit," Voletek laughed, "I guess I had it wrong. On the bright side, at least one cop knows you're something special. Well, make that two."

TEN

Arriving at my apartment, I rubbed my eyes. I shouldn't have stayed out so late. Jake Voletek was trouble. Sure, he could be charming with his smooth words and expressive eyes, and it didn't hurt that beneath the scruff he wasn't exactly bad looking either. But he was a player. Everything was a game to him. I just hoped he took his job and my investigation more seriously than his dating life.

Emma's car wasn't outside, but it wasn't uncommon for an ER nurse to pick up an extra shift. Then again, with the hours I'd been keeping, I lost track of Emma's schedule. Was she back to working nights?

I trudged up the steps to our apartment, ready to crash into bed and not move until it was time to leave for work. Unlocking the door, I immediately noticed a stranger going through the cabinets. The couch cushions sat in disarray. Obviously, he'd already ransacked the living room and had moved on to the kitchen.

Silently, I inched forward, my gun in hand. He kept his back to me. I cautioned a glance into my bedroom, but I didn't see anyone inside. Hopefully, he was alone.

"Police. Put your hands in the air." I edged closer. My gun aimed at the center of his back.

"Oh, is that what we're doing now? I thought we were

still doing the naughty nurse bit." He laughed, closing one of the cabinets. "Do you want to play with my nightstick?" He reached down, but the island blocked my view. "You should probably cuff me since I've been a bad, bad boy. Let me guess. You want me to assume the position and spread 'em."

"Let me see your hands. Turn around slowly."

Not listening to a word I said, he spun around and jumped back in surprise. "Whoa." He held up one hand, the other frantically zipping his junk back into his pants. "Who the hell are you?"

"Police," I repeated. "Who the hell are you, and what the fuck are you doing in my kitchen?"

"Your kitchen?"

"You picked the wrong apartment to break into, perv."

"Liv?" Emma rushed out of her room, pulling on her robe as she ran toward me.

"Em, stay back. Call 9-1-1."

"No, Liv, it's okay. He's with me. You can put that thing away." Emma pushed past, standing between my gun and the pervert in the kitchen. "This is..." Her face flushed. She couldn't even remember his name. She glared, angry that this situation highlighted her reckless behavior, as if it were my fault.

"Oh." I holstered my weapon. "Sorry, I'm Liv. I'm Emma's roommate. And you are?"

"Eric," he said, making sure his naughty bits were zipped up before offering a smile. He tucked a loose strand of brown hair behind his ear that had fallen free from the elastic tie. He had one of those haircuts where the sides were buzzed and the top was long. And his blue-gray eyes looked spacey enough to make me think he was on something or incredibly aroused, but based on the tent in his pants, it was probably the latter. From the look on his face, you'd think he just won the lottery. "You didn't tell me you lived with anyone, babe," he said to Emma. "Is she the surprise you were telling me about?"

At this moment, moving day couldn't come fast enough. Emma turned an even darker shade of crimson. "Liv, I forgot to text you."

"Yeah." I stepped backward toward the door. "I should go."

"Wait," Eric said. "A naughty nurse and a sexy cop, and it isn't even Halloween. Damn, this is sweet. What do you say, girls? I'm down if you are."

Where did she find this one? The set of a porno? I gave her a look, but she wouldn't meet my eyes. Shuffling backward, I grabbed my dropped purse and keys. "You got this situation handled, Em?"

"Uh-huh."

"Oh, come on," Eric wheedled, "we could always use an extra set of handcuffs."

"I...uh...yeah. I'm gonna go. Sorry about the...uh...," I waved toward the kitchen, "whatever. Carry on."

"Liv, you don't have to," Emma said, but I was halfway out the door. "You can stay. You're only gonna be here a couple more nights anyway. I don't see what the big deal is."

"Seriously, Em?" I pulled the door closed behind me and leaned my back against it. My heart pounded in my chest from adrenaline and embarrassment. Emma normally texted to let me know if she was bringing home a houseguest, which made me wonder if everything was okay. But from her last statement, she obviously wanted me gone as soon as possible. But just in case things weren't as consensual as they appeared, I sent her a text before moving away from the door.

She responded a minute later, adding in our little codeword so I'd know she was actually safe. And then she launched into a ten-message long rant about how rude I was to her guest and threatened to kill me. That was Emma.

Unsure where to go or what to do, I thought about calling Brad to see if I could crash on his couch, but then I remembered he was with Carrie. At this rate, I probably should have gone home with Jake since everyone else was hooking up. Apparently, it was the thing to do.

I drove to the precinct. We had a lot of work to do, and I'd be able to get a jump on it as soon as the intel came in. But after checking my messages and the progress that had been made, I settled onto the couch in the break room. It was the middle of the night, and while the police had tons of things to do, I did not. Closing my eyes, I hoped we'd find a way to get Lovretta to talk before our killer-thief struck again.

Hours later, someone entered the room. "Liv? Are you asleep?"

"Not anymore." Blinking, I noticed the sun coming in from outside. "What time is it?"

"A few minutes before eight." Jake set the two plastic containers he was holding on the table beside a drink carrier. "What time did you get in?"

"Two."

"You slept here all night?"

I shrugged.

"When you left the bar, you said you were going home. Alone. I remember a certain emphasis on that part. I didn't realize you lived here." He looked around the empty break room. "I like what you've done with the place. Is this commercial chic or functional minimalist?"

I laughed, sitting up and combing my fingers through my knotted hair. After untangling it as best I could, I slipped the hairband off my wrist and put my hair up in a ponytail. "Something came up."

"You could have called me. Was there a break in your case?"

"No."

He looked confused. "I hope you didn't feel you had something to prove by burning the midnight oil. If I offended you last night, I didn't mean to." Voletek pulled out one of the chairs from the small table. "Let me guess, you were waiting for the breakfast pastries to arrive since I made them sound so delicious."

"You caught me."

"Seriously, what's going on, princess?"

"For starters, stop calling me princess, unless you want to dress up and parade around here like a court jester."

He held up his palms. "Done. What else?"

"Nothing. It's fine. My roommate had company and didn't give me advanced warning. Usually, I'd find somewhere else to crash." Like with my parents. "But she forgot, so I came back here. Thought I'd get a jump on things, but nothing came through." I stretched, eyeing the bullpen through the open doorway. Brad wasn't at his desk, not that I should be surprised. If he was here, he would have woken me up.

"In that case, I must be psychic." Voletek removed the lid on one of the coffees and placed it in front of the empty seat across from where he sat, beside the second plastic container. "Since you don't do pastries or donuts, I brought you breakfast."

"Why?"

"Because that's just how I roll." He opened his container. "Most people would say thank you. Plus, this new restaurant opened near my apartment that I've been dying to try. And you gave me the perfect excuse. They do only whole foods. They might be paleo. I'm not sure, but I figured it was right up your alley. Even the coffee is organic and fair-trade certified." He nudged the container with the tip of his fork. "Since you slept here last night, you obviously haven't had breakfast. You should dig in before it gets cold. I don't know how well it will reheat. And you need your energy. You have a big day ahead of you."

"Yeah, okay. Thanks."

Jake grinned. "That's better." He watched as I opened the container. "Veggie scramble with breakfast sausage on the side and fresh fruit salad. You said you weren't vegan, but I didn't know if you had a problem with eggs or if you're kosher. The fruit should be safe, unless you have some kind of aversion to sliced bananas or an allergy to strawberries."

"Wow. You put a lot of thought into this."

He gestured with his fork. "Dig in."

So I did. While we ate, Voletek prattled on about the restaurant, its menu, and the owner's story. I tried to pay attention, but aside from being grateful to have coffee that didn't come from the burnt pot on the counter, my mind remained on catching a killer.

A few uniforms entered while we were eating, helping themselves to a box of bagels and croissants. Briefly, I wondered when the pink pastry box arrived. I must have been zonked out not to have woken up when it was delivered.

"That was delicious," I said, wiping my mouth.

"It was." He eyed the box of donuts as it entered the break room. He waited for the officer to leave and leaned in conspiratorially and said, "For the record, this was way better than any donut or pastry. You're not missing anything."

"Now I know you're full of shit. You're practically salivating at the sight of the box."

"I am not."

I quirked a questioning eyebrow, but before I could come up with a clever remark, I spotted my partner. I cleared off the table and met Brad at our joined desks. He eyed me suspiciously.

"You wore that yesterday," he said.

"Yeah, I need to go downstairs and change. Maybe shower too."

Fennel picked up his phone and checked the notifications. "Did I miss a message? Did something happen?"

"Not here."

"Where?" Fennel's gaze darted toward Voletek's desk, and he noticed the detective had the same logo on his coffee cup as the one that I held in my hand. Brad turned back to me, scrutinizing my appearance. "You look tired. Did you even go home last night?"

"I did, but Emma was entertaining. So I came back here."

"I would think, considering how overprotective she is of you, that she'd have more common sense when it comes to her own safety." He logged onto his computer and checked the time. "From that sour note in your tone, I'm guessing you don't approve of this one either."

"She didn't even know his name. And he asked me to stay for a threesome."

Brad rubbed his mouth, doing his best not to laugh. "Did you shoot him? Tell me we don't have another homicide to deal with this morning."

"I didn't shoot him."

Brad eyed the cup in my hand but didn't comment. "You realize what this is about, right?"

Bewildered, I gave him a confused look. "I'm one fine piece of ass?"

"Yes, Liv," he said patronizingly, "but given Emma's history, you moving out has brought up some abandonment issues, so she's acting out and looking for another close human connection."

Rolling my eyes, I took another sip of coffee and put the cup on my desk. "I don't want to deal with Emma throwing a tantrum right now. We have too much to do."

"Nothing's come in yet. I'll cover for you if you want to go home for a bit to get some sleep, get changed, or grab some coffee that doesn't match Jake's." He raised an eyebrow, but I didn't volunteer any additional information. "I thought coffee was our thing."

"Did you bring me coffee?" I asked.

"Well, no."

"Then how is coffee our thing?"

Brad clicked a few keys. "Usually, if we go out drinking, you bring me coffee or a smoothie the next day."

"That's enabling. Plus, didn't Carrie make you coffee this morning?" I nodded at the unfamiliar travel mug on his desk.

"Yeah, but yours is better."

"That's what the guy last night thought too."

"Liv," Brad scolded, his eyes wide.

I held up my palms and shrugged innocently before taking a seat and logging into the system. After finding nothing of value, I glared at the screen. "What is taking these auction people so long? Don't they realize this could be a literal matter of life or death?" I angrily reached for the phone and stabbed at the digits, but Brad pressed down on the switch hook, disconnecting the call before I even placed it.

"Take a breath. Go get cleaned up. I'll see if Mac's come in yet and ask where we are on acquiring additional nearby security footage."

I stepped away from my desk, noticing the laidback way

Brad was handling things. Obviously, he and Carrie must have had a good time last night. And for once, he didn't come in with bloodshot eyes and an obvious hangover after the bad day we had yesterday. Blowing off some steam must have helped. Perhaps I should cut Emma some slack. When I got to the locker room, I sent her a text, asking if she was still alive, a morbid joke of sorts, and apologized for interrupting. Then I dug around in my locker for the emergency work attire I kept on hand, grabbed my shower caddy, and hurried through my morning routine. After dressing and brushing my teeth, I pulled my wet hair into a tight bun, checked my appearance in the mirror, and went upstairs. By then, Emma had replied. She was safe and sound at work. Eric didn't raid my underwear drawer or rob us blind, so that was a nice added bonus.

ELEVEN

Security footage from around Lovretta's apartment turned out to be a bust. A few cameras glimpsed our unsub, but he got lost in the throng. We didn't know where he went or how he arrived. He was good. Too good. He had to be a professional. Thief or killer was the question we still couldn't answer.

"He works alone," Fennel said after he watched the footage from the night of the Zedula break-in. "Our unsub doesn't have a team. No spotters. No safecrackers or sharpshooters. No lookouts. Nothing. It's just him."

"You're certain?" I asked.

"Ninety-nine percent."

"It's always that damn one percent." Exhaling, I slid out from behind my desk and stood in front of the murder board. "So we're looking at a lone wolf, probably. He kills and steals. Did burglary have anything helpful to add?"

"At this point, we don't know enough about our unsub to rule anything out. But based on the stealth kills and high-end thefts, none of their open cases fit the bill, unless we're missing something." Fennel got up and stood beside me, resting his hips on the side of my desk and hoping the change in angle would give him a new perspective. It did not.

"We still need to figure out the killer's MO. How does he choose his victims? Why did he steal those items? What makes them significant to him?" I asked.

"Maybe it's not the items or even the victims. Maybe it has to do with the one person who connects all of our crime scenes."

"Agnes Archibald?"

"Or just the Archibald estate. Agnes' three children wanted nothing to do with their mother's antiques, which is why they went up for auction. But according to the auction information, the art, jewelry, and other antiques have been privately held by the family for years and envied by buyers for centuries. As if anyone could trace their family lineage back that far."

"It could be bullshit." But since the Archibalds possessed the tiara, a sculpture, an antique chess set, pocket watch, and the musket, it probably wasn't bullshit. "Let me guess, the Archibald family came over on the Mayflower."

"It wasn't the Mayflower, but you're close," Brad said, continuing to read the printed pamphlet. "Given what we know, I contacted the only living Archibalds."

"Any chance one of them is our unsub?"

"Nope. They're all fifty-something women. Two of them live outside the US and haven't set foot in this country in the last six months. The third, Marilyn, is local but has done an excellent job deferring our questions to her staff."

"Staff?"

"Maids, butlers, personal assistants, publicists." Fennel flicked the blown-up photo of a good-looking woman with frosted blonde hair. Based on the plumpness of her cheeks and lack of crow's feet and frown lines, she'd had work done. Or she'd inherited some amazing genes. "Marilyn Archibald is one of the richest women in the city."

"Which makes her a prime target for our killer-thief," I said.

"I already sent plainclothes officers to keep an eye out, but Marilyn refused our protection. She has her own team of bodyguards. She doesn't want our help, so we're keeping watch from a distance."

"Does she have any idea who might be behind this or why they are targeting buyers from her mother's estate sale?"

"She does not." Fennel returned to his chair just as an officer entered with a box of files. The uniform looked lost, but Fennel spotted the name and numbers scrawled on the side. "Are those for us?" he asked.

The officer came over, reading my partner's nameplate. "Yes, sir."

My partner signed the form and opened the lid. "Looks like the auction company finally sent over the info you requested, Liv."

"Great. Do you want to run background on the remaining auction house staff and employees?" I asked, lifting the relevant files out of the box. "Or do you want to run down the bidders and buyers?"

"Since I started this yesterday, I'll stick with the employees."

I handed Fennel the relevant folders and cleared off my desk. Somewhere in this mess was our killer's next victim and, hopefully, our killer.

When Fennel finished making a list of potentials from the auction employees, he moved on to building a more detailed profile on Marilyn Archibald, her staff, and security. Based on the security footage of our unsub, our techs were positive our killer was male between 5'9 and 5'11. That eliminated Marilyn, and based on his acrobatic skills and agility, we assumed he couldn't be over fifty. Again, not Marilyn. Though, the AARP might disagree with our ageist assessment.

Since Brad was hunting our killer, I worked on victimology, hoping to gain insight into who off the bidder and buyer list might be next. Why did the unsub steal those items? They appeared random. The watch collection he stole didn't even include the pocket watch Starmon acquired from the estate auction, and the musket wasn't the only thing he took from Arnold's home. Our killer-thief also emptied Arnold's safe and took a pile of money, probably since the musket wasn't worth much.

Additionally, we didn't even know the musket had been taken when we performed the initial walkthrough because Mr. Arnold treated it like junk. More than likely, he never would have realized it was missing or reported it stolen had I not stumbled upon it in the pawn shop.

"That's why he passed it off to Anthony Lovretta to pawn," I mumbled to myself.

"Huh?" Fennel looked up.

"I don't think unloading the musket was about money. Our killer wanted us to find it, just like he made the gardener's murder blatantly obvious."

"He's playing with us. He couldn't be sure we'd make the connection, but he knew we'd scour pawn shops and jewelry stores after he took the tiara." Fennel drummed his pen against the desk. "I don't like this. That means he led us to Anthony Lovretta. He wanted us to find his patsy. But why? Shouldn't his goal be to get away without a trace?"

"That would make sense," I said, "except nothing he does makes any sense." And that's when I saw it. "He didn't accidentally trip these alarms or get caught in the act and have to kill in order to escape. You remember when we went to Mr. Arnold's and found the gardener dead? He could have dumped the body into the pool and made it look like an accident to cover his tracks, but he made it obvious."

"We thought it was so Arnold would know he'd been the victim of a burglary," Fennel said.

"Yeah, but why?"

"He wanted to fuck with Arnold."

"Perhaps, but look at these others. With the exception of Ezra Sambari, whose entire job it was to protect Zedula's valuables, I don't think our thief would have had any problem slipping in and out undetected. He knew how to get inside without tripping the alarms, and he never set off the interior sensors or laser grids while conducting the heist. He only triggered the alarms when he was ready to leave. He must have scouted the locations and knew the occupants' schedules."

"That bastard. He's thumbing his nose at us, and he killed those people on purpose." Brad cursed. "This has to stop. What do they have in common?"

I didn't know. Nothing connected them. They didn't travel in the same circles, visit the same coffee shops, or take the same train. They weren't even in the same social classes. The dogwalker and gardener were hired help, but the gardener didn't even live in the state. He lived an hour and a half away while the dogwalker lived in a tiny studio apartment with his college roommate. The programmer and art collector might have been in the same tax bracket, but one would never know it based on their lifestyle and interests. Nothing overlapped. Nothing connected. The only common thread among them was the Archibald auction, which meant any one of the names on my list could be the killer's next victim. "The auction."

"That connects the thefts, not the vics," Brad said.

"Yeah, but the vics were in the vicinity of former Archibald estate items. It's all we have to go on."

"That's going to make it tough to narrow. How many names do you have there?" He jerked his chin at the folder.

"227."

Fennel whistled. "The department doesn't have the resources to protect all of them at once. We need to figure this out."

"No shit."

"All right, Liv. Since all the victims purchased something at the auction, let's just focus on actual buyers and not those who bid." He looked down at his own stack of auction employees. "Maybe our killer only had access to the people who made sales or had items delivered." He made a note to start with the employees who possessed the buyer's personal information. Then he reached for the phone and requested paper on the delivery companies the auction house used. When he hung up, he looked at me, the brilliant deduction lighting up his brown eyes. "Our killer knew the layouts, the alarm systems, and how to get in and out of each location. My money is on someone from the delivery service." He shuffled through the pages on his desk. "According to this, the auction house uses several different services. Do you see any notation on which service delivered to our victims?"

I scanned the columns. "Nothing's here. What about in the employee records?"

"Delivery was contracted out. I'll call every service they've used and see who handled the Archibald estate sale. Once we get that, we'll be one step closer to finding our killer."

"Call Zedula," I said. "I bet he knows who delivered the tiara." While Fennel did that, I phoned Arnold and Starmon and asked the same question. Within ten minutes, we had our answer – Speedy Delivery Service.

"I'll get on this," Fennel said. "In the meantime, go through the list of buyers and start making calls. We need to speak to anyone who accepted delivery from Speedy."

"On it."

While I made call after call, adding names and addresses to a list of potential victims, one thought nagged at me. The killer knew we'd canvass pawn shops for the stolen tiara. We did it with the stolen laptop and watches too, but nothing shook loose. This time was different. He didn't get sloppy. He wanted us to find the musket, timed Lovretta's drop off just right, and knew by killing Sambari with a gun, we'd also ask about firearms. That was the only way to make sure we didn't overlook one glaringly obvious piece of evidence. Our killer was leaving a trail of breadcrumbs for us to follow. And those breadcrumbs led to Lovretta.

There had to be a reason. I just didn't know what it was. But what worried me even more was his familiarity with our methods and procedures. He orchestrated this for our benefit. To get our attention. He must have known we missed the musket. But how?

Grabbing a blank notepad out of my drawer, I wrote a few questions to ask Anthony Lovretta. Round two of interrogation would begin shortly. We didn't go at him first thing this morning because we needed to learn as much as we could, and even though our investigation was still full of question marks, we were on to something. I could feel it. Lovretta had to cooperate, or we'd find a way to convince him. He had the answers we needed.

After jotting down the stray thoughts that came to mind,

I returned to the task of narrowing down potential future victims. Out of the 227 bidders, only sixty-three of them actually won the auction and made a purchase. Five of them had already been targeted. Percentage wise, I didn't like the odds. After I placed two dozen calls, half of which went unanswered, Brad confirmed Speedy Delivery handled the entire Archibald estate sale. That didn't help matters. As I made call after call, I asked the buyers about the deliverymen and driver.

Not surprisingly, no one remembered any names. I asked for descriptions, which varied greatly. No one paid attention to the deliverymen. They saw the uniform and truck and not much else. Most of the deliveries had been scheduled. Some of them went to offices, museums, and charities. Others were delivered to residences. So far, the killer-thief only struck private dwellings, so I color-coded our potential future victims based on a threat assessment. Since it worked for meteorologists, I figured it was good enough for the police department.

Dozens of calls later, I ran out of individual names. Only half the buyers answered, which meant I'd have to try later or send a patrol to perform a wellness check and ask a few basic questions. While I determined how I wanted to proceed, I moved on to the remaining buyers. LLCs and private holdings made up the remaining seventeen purchases.

I dialed down the list but found most of the phone numbers went to automated mailboxes or answering services. Why couldn't this be simple? Checking the time, I passed the list of unanswered buyers off to patrol. Twenty-six names spread out amongst the patrol units shouldn't take too long. In the meantime, I ran the businesses through the database, found the owners' names and numbers, and made more calls.

The second to last name on the list stopped me in my tracks. I stared at the result on my monitor. Axel Kincaid – private club owner, reformed car thief, and the bane of my existence. I spent months undercover inside his club, only to have my cover blown and to learn the DEA flipped him, using their leverage to turn him into an asset.

As if that wasn't bad enough, I'd asked for his help on my last intelligence case. After that, Axel cleaned house. Several prominent members of his club vanished, and no one had seen or heard from them since. I didn't know what happened to them, but Axel told me it was best not to concern myself with the details. That didn't leave me feeling warm and fuzzy. It left a gnawing guilt in my gut. Sure, they were scum who probably got what they deserved, but I didn't know exactly what role Axel played in it or how much of that might have been my fault. He claimed to be a friend of law enforcement. He told me we were on the same side, that he wasn't one of the bad guys, but here he was again in the center of one of my investigations.

"DeMarco?"

I looked up from the screen, realizing Brad wasn't at his desk. "What is it?"

"Detective Fennel wanted me to tell you Anthony Lovretta and his attorney are waiting for you in interrogation room one."

"Thanks," I said.

The sergeant looked at me for a moment. "Is everything okay, DeMarco?"

I nodded.

"You sure?" he asked again. "You look upset."

"I'll be fine."

TWELVE

When I went down the hall to interrogation, I spotted my partner speaking to Lt. Winston in the hallway. He was giving our commanding officer a progress report. Though we didn't have proof yet, we were now working under the assumption our killer worked for Speedy Delivery. It would have given him access to the apartments and houses, a look at the security measures in place, and some idea as to where the owners kept their valuables.

"Okay. Finish up in here, and if necessary, reinterview the thief's previous targets. Let's see what they remember. From the reports I read, Arnold had video surveillance. See how long he saves the footage," Winston said.

"Shit," I cursed, seeing the huge hole Winston just blew in our theory.

"What?" the two men asked, turning to face me.

"I don't know if the musket was delivered to Mr. Arnold's house or his father's."

"I'll check. If it went to dear old dad, I'll see who packed up his father's belongings and trucked them over to Arnold's. With any luck, maybe it was Speedy Delivery." Winston jerked his head toward the door. "In the meantime, get us some answers. Lovretta knows who our killer is. Convince him to give us a name and put this thing to bed, Detectives. I'm tired of some asshole making a mockery out of my unit."

"Yes, sir," Fennel said.

Winston walked away, and Brad and I stepped into the observation room to size up our suspect. Anthony Lovretta and his attorney, Chris Gildan, sat quietly. Lovretta stared straight ahead, directly into the two-way mirror. Gildan flipped through the pages in his folder, a briefcase on the floor at his feet. His greasy, slicked back hair, too big off-the-rack suit, and thick ostentatious tie told me everything I needed to know about him. Though, like Lovretta, the attorney's reputation also preceded him.

In the last five years, Gildan had filed over three dozen suits against the city for misuse of power. He wasn't a crusader. He was just a glorified ambulance chaser, so desperate to make a buck, he'd file as many complaints as possible in the hopes one of them would stick. No wonder the validity of Lovretta's arrest had already been called into question.

"Gildan had the audacity to ask if I mirandized Lovretta before questioning him," Fennel said. "Can you believe that?"

"What'd you say?"

"I told him I did. And then he asked if anyone else was around to witness it." Fennel glared at the attorney through the glass. "Lovretta needs to give us a name, but I doubt Gildan will let him say a word."

"Go get started. I'll call Winters. Since Lovretta's entitled to have his attorney present, we might need counsel of our own."

After convincing ADA Logan Winters to come to the precinct in the event we managed to strike a deal, I stepped into the interrogation room. Fennel didn't look up when I entered, but Mr. Gildan did.

"Detective DeMarco, homicide," I said, taking a seat. "What did I miss?"

"Nothing," Fennel mumbled.

Gildan smiled wolfishly. "I was just telling Detective Fennel this is harassment. My client didn't do anything wrong."

"He pawned stolen property," I said.

"I didn't know it was stolen," Lovretta said. "I didn't steal it. I found it."

"Where?" Fennel asked.

"In a garbage can."

"Let me guess. It was just sitting there." The doubt obvious in my partner's voice.

"Yeah, that's right. You know what they say about one man's trash." Lovretta wouldn't give an inch.

"Why didn't you report it to the police?" Fennel glanced at the attorney. "I'm sure your attorney would have instructed you to turn over the firearm to the authorities."

"It's an antique," Lovretta argued.

Gildan didn't even look at his client. He kept his eyes on me. "Based on the reports I've read, the item in question wasn't used to commit any crimes. Definitely, not any homicides. Frankly, if you want to pursue that path, I'll insist on seeing proof the alleged firearm is even capable of being fired."

"Oh, I'll give you proof," Fennel muttered.

"That's not the point," I said.

"Then why did you arrest my client? You're homicide detectives. Obviously, you intend to charge him with murder, but I don't see any basis for that claim. So let's hear it." Gildan leaned back, crossing his arms over his chest, a smug look on his face.

"You know why we arrested him," Fennel spat. "Anthony Lovretta was in possession of three stolen watches at the time of his arrest."

"The watches that conveniently fell out of a bag he was carrying after you chased him," Gildan said.

It was Lovretta's turn to look smug.

"We weren't chasing him," I said, the full force of my cop stare coming to rest on Lovretta. "Were we? You were running away from the man inside your apartment."

"What man?" Gildan made a show of looking at the file. "I don't see anything here to substantiate that claim."

"In that case, your client is facing five counts of murder, along with several other crimes." Fennel made a show of getting ready to walk. "The musket and watches were taken during two different deadly home invasions. We've linked three more to the same perpetrator. According to forensics, the only prints found on the watches belong to your client."

Lovretta swallowed but kept quiet. He turned his focus to his attorney.

"Since you've been through the system, you know how this will play out," Fennel said, staring at Lovretta.

"You're fishing," Gildan said. "Just because he touched the watches doesn't mean he stole them, and it certainly doesn't mean he killed anyone. You have nothing. Unless you're ready to file charges, we're walking out of here, or I'll add claims of unlawful imprisonment to the list of complaints I plan to file."

Ignoring the attorney, I appealed to our suspect. After all, it was his ass on the line. "Mr. Lovretta, you have a record. That will weigh against you. And I'm sure Mr. Gildan can attest to the department's need to close active homicide cases as quickly and efficiently as possible." I glanced at the attorney, hoping to use his previous attempts to sue the city against him. "Right now, you're our prime suspect. Quite frankly, our only suspect. Unless you tell us about the man inside your apartment, you're gonna go down for this. We just want to know about the other man, the one who rappelled out your window. He's who we want. We get him, and this goes away. All we want is a name. We don't care about the musket or the watches. We just want the guy who brought them to you. Who is he?"

Lovretta opened his mouth as if to yawn, then worked his jaw for a moment, and shut his mouth. I wasn't sure what to make of that. Was he teasing us? Or was he close to cracking?

"You're afraid of him," Fennel said. "That's why you don't want to talk to us. That's why you wouldn't speak to us when we knocked on your door to ask about the musket. Did you call him after we showed up? Or was he already on his way?" A thought crossed Fennel's mind. "Once we access your phone records, we'll find out, anyway. But it'll be better for you if you cooperate. Save us some time, and we'll help you out of this mess."

"Who exactly do you think this alleged mystery man is?"

Gildan rolled his eyes and made rabbit ears with his fingers. Though from his timing, it was obvious he didn't understand exactly how to use air quotes.

Fennel ignored Gildan and locked eyes with Lovretta. "We know he's killed five people in the last month. And we know you can identify him," Fennel said. "If I were you, Mr. Lovretta, I'd be afraid too."

"But we can protect you," I said.

"What are you offering?" Gildan asked.

"Protection. Immunity. It depends on how much your client knows and how willing he is to cooperate." I looked at Gildan, suddenly getting the feeling the sleazy, ambulance chaser schtick might be an act.

"I'll need some time to confer with Anthony in private." Gildan glanced over at Lovretta, who appeared paler than he had a few seconds earlier. "May we have the room?"

I nodded, getting up from the chair.

Fennel held the stone-cold glare for a moment longer before pushing away from the table. "Our job is to stop a killer by any means necessary, got it?"

Neither man said a word, and Fennel met me at the door.

After it shut, I turned to him and snorted. "What was that?"

He shrugged. "It felt right in the moment."

"And now?"

"Now, you're making me feel self-conscious. Stop doing that."

"Sorry, I can't. Part of the job," I said.

Fennel rocked back and forth on his heels, the beginnings of a smile creeping onto his face. "There's only one reason for them to confer. Lovretta wants to deal."

"Don't jinx us."

But we'd done this job long enough to see the writing on the walls, and no matter how hard Fennel tried, he couldn't keep the smirk off his face. I gave him a look, hoping he'd stop, but instead he said, "Face it, Liv. Your partner's a bad boy."

I cringed. "Please don't sing the song."

Instead, he hummed it loudly, and the officer stationed

outside the interrogation room joined in. Hopefully, we weren't misreading the situation, and Lovretta was about to give us what we wanted. But unlike Brad and Officer Jenkins, I wasn't going to celebrate until we had a signed statement and our killer in custody.

I slapped Brad's shoulder. "Stop that. People are staring."

He laughed but sobered. "C'mon, Liv, for the first time since we caught this case, I actually feel good about this. I think we have something here." I sighed, and the smile fell from his face. "What's wrong?"

"Axel Kincaid's on the list."

"He bought something from the estate auction?" Fennel asked.

I nodded.

"What'd he buy?"

"A crystal chandelier and coordinating candelabras."

"Rich people." Fennel rubbed the stubble on his cheek, something he did to buy time to think. "Why is this a problem?"

"I don't know that it is. But it's Kincaid. When is he not a problem?" I looked down the corridor, but I couldn't see Winston's office from here. "We still don't know much of anything. Right now, we're coasting on a lot of assumptions. We could be wrong. Our killer might not be a delivery guy or someone from the auction house. I just don't think we should celebrate yet."

"Yeah, but if Lovretta talks, which is what we've been hoping for, it won't matter. He'll give us a name, and we'll get the guy." Fennel ran a hand down the upper part of my arm and lowered his voice, even though Jenkins seemed to have lost interest in us and was now humming the newest pop song. I wondered if he even realized he was doing it. "Look at me, Liv. We have one of our killer's associates in custody. We're gonna nail this guy to the wall."

I nodded, taking a breath. "Okay." But something continued to nag at me.

The door to interrogation creaked open, and Gildan poked his head out. "We're ready to deal. But I want everything in writing. You're not screwing over my client.

Frankly, if it were up to me, I wouldn't waste my time. I'd just file complaints against the two of you and call it a day, but he wants to talk."

"Good to know." I gave Gildan a hard look. "The ADA's on his way. I hope whatever your client has to say is worth the trip."

Gildan stepped back into the room. Fennel grabbed the door before it could close, turning to look at me. "I thought we were supposed to be nice," he whispered.

"I'll be nice to Lovretta, but Gildan rubs me the wrong way."

"From where I'm sitting, he'd be more than happy to rub you any way he can."

"Ugh." I followed my partner into the room and took a seat across from Lovretta.

"Okay," Fennel said, "so before we agree to anything, we need to know what we're dealing with."

"My client is willing to give up what he knows about the man in question in exchange for police protection and full immunity for any crimes in which he might implicate himself," Gildan said.

Fennel nodded. But before we could get underway, someone knocked on the door. I got up to get it, assuming Winters had arrived to join the party. Instead, the watch commander stood in the doorway. He jerked his head into the hall, and I followed him out. A second later, Fennel joined us.

"What's going on?" I asked.

"You requested patrol conduct twenty-six wellness checks," the sergeant said.

I nodded, realizing I might be in trouble for wasting resources and diverting so many units at once. "Yes, I did."

"One of them interrupted a crime in progress. They rolled up on a townhouse and found the back gate open. The lock was broken and so was one of the rear windows. It looks like they rolled up on a B&E. The suspect jumped out the third floor window to escape."

"Sounds like our killer's MO," Fennel said. "Is the suspect in custody?"

The sergeant looked uncomfortable. "We're still

investigating."

"Have units lock down the crime scene. We'll check it out," Fennel said. "Lovretta will just have to wait."

THIRTEEN

"Detective DeMarco, this is Dr. Kapinos. He owns this place," the patrolman said.

I stepped closer to the sidewalk and nodded to the thin man with the thick coke bottle glasses. "I'm Detective DeMarco." I gestured toward my partner, who was crouched down near the bushes where the suspect allegedly landed after jumping out of the window. "That's my partner, Detective Fennel. We just have a few questions to ask."

"I have a question." Kapinos pushed his glasses up on his nose. "Why were officers at my house?"

"Where were you this morning?" I asked.

"Teaching a class in applied physics at the university." He glanced nervously at one of the officers. "I already gave him my schedule. My TA can vouch for my whereabouts."

"No need," I said. "I tried calling you to ask about a purchase you made a few months ago at an estate auction. When you didn't answer, a unit came to perform a wellness check. That's when he spotted the broken latch on your gate and the window."

"Hell of a thing," Kapinos said. "How'd he get up there? Do you think he climbed that tree?"

"Probably."

"I should have those lower branches cut down."

"Sure, but in the meantime, I have a few questions about the Archibald estate auction." He pulled a pen out of his breast pocket, and I found myself slightly disappointed he didn't have a pocket protector. "Yes, I bought some early printings of Isaac Newton's books. Is there something wrong with them?"

"No, but I have some questions about the delivery."

While I questioned him, Fennel finished his assessment and joined us. Unfortunately, Dr. Kapinos didn't remember anything about the delivery truck or driver.

"Would you mind checking inside to make sure nothing was taken?" Fennel asked.

Kapinos grew ashen. "Do you think someone came to steal my Newtons?"

"We don't think the thief had time to take anything," I said, gesturing toward the front door, "but we need to make sure." Officers had already checked the house. At least we didn't find any bodies this time.

"He's worried about cookies?" Fennel whispered to me, and I shook my head. Confused, Brad followed Dr. Kapinos inside and straight to the bookcase in his study.

"No, they're here. Perfectly safe and sound." He pointed to the glass case containing the treasured volumes.

"Okay, good." I looked around. The room was practically floor to ceiling books with an occasional model or scientific instrument breaking up the monotony on the shelves. Since the room was intentionally cluttered, anything missing would stick out like a sore thumb. But the same couldn't be said for the rest of the house. "Would you mind checking everything else? The man we're looking for is an expert thief."

"And safecracker," Fennel added, gently tapping one of the planets on the model of the solar system and watching them spin around the center piece.

Kapinos' expression soured, but he resisted the urge to berate my partner. "I don't have a safe. I don't see any reason to hide valuables away."

For the next thirty minutes, we followed Kapinos

through his house while he methodically checked every single item he owned. We peppered him with questions about the auction and why someone would want to break into his house. His answers were of little use, but as far as we could tell, the thief had been stopped in the act. Dr. Kapinos would have to file a report and needed to get the window repaired, but that was of little consequence compared to what could have happened.

"Thank you for your time. We'll beef up patrols in the area to make sure the thief doesn't return," Fennel said as we left the house.

Before we made it to the car, two patrol officers stopped us. "You're the detectives working the serial home invasions?" one of them asked.

"Yeah, what do you have?" Fennel asked.

"Some neighbors spotted a guy snooping around the house. They're pretty sure they saw him running away after we pulled up. We got a description. White guy, early twenties, heather grey sweatshirt, black track pants with white stripes down the sides, and a blue baseball cap."

"Get a sketch artist down here and see what else they remember." Fennel studied the broken branches and the nearly destroyed hedge from the thief's hasty escape. "You said they saw him running away from the house?"

"Yes, sir."

"So he didn't get hurt in the fall. Lucky bastard." Fennel turned to survey the area. "Did anyone see which way he went?"

The officer pointed down the street. "When backup arrived, we sent them to search the neighborhood. Those neighbors," the officer pointed to the townhouse at the end of the row, "thought they saw a guy matching that description getting into a black two-door. They didn't get a plate."

"This is a nice neighborhood," I said. "It's not exactly gated, but since everyone's hedges are all the proper height, I'm guessing someone's keeping a close watch around here."

"Like a neighborhood watch?" Fennel asked.

"Maybe. Let's find out."

It didn't take long to locate the head of the HOA and ask some questions. But without video surveillance, I didn't think we'd be able to locate the thief or his vehicle. Patrol would follow up with the neighbors and knock on a few more doors. We were close, just not close enough.

"We almost caught him in the act," Fennel said as he whipped the car around and headed back to the precinct. "It looks like his luck is finally running out."

Something about the situation didn't sit right. "I'm interested to see what Lovretta has to say."

Based on the text I'd received twenty minutes ago, Winters was waiting for us, and Gildan and Lovretta were getting antsy. Lt. Winston took over in our absence, but it'd be best if we asked the questions.

"Kapinos doesn't have anyone taking care of his house. No pets. No babysitters. No gardeners. And according to his schedule, he wouldn't be home until six. We got the call at three. How long do you think our killer typically waits around after he breaks in?" I asked.

"Maybe he wasn't planning to kill this time. Maybe he just wanted a book," Fennel suggested, "or something else Kapinos has. Frankly, I'd be more interested in stealing some cookies than old scientific publications. But that's just me."

"Those books could buy a lot more than cookies. They're worth five figures easy," I said.

Fennel glanced at me from the corner of his eye to make sure I wasn't joking. "Like I said before, rich people. I just don't get it." He blew out a breath. "Based on TODs of our previous vics, they were all killed within a few hours of when we received the calls. It's too close to narrow, so we don't know how long the killer hangs around, but it seems to me he does his homework. He must in order to get inside so easily. He has to have the occupants' schedules memorized. You know what else I just realized?"

"You missed lunch?" I teased.

"Besides that. Every one of the killer's targets lives alone. No spouse, no partner, no roommates."

"Do you think it's significant?"

"At this point, everything's significant, but it's just an

observation. It must make gaining entry undetected a lot easier. Less moving pieces."

"You call dangling from the roof, thwarting a security guard, or climbing a tree easy?"

"No, but you know what I mean. He bypasses security without a problem, well, without a problem until today."

"Which is why we think he works for Speedy Delivery."

"Yeah, he'd have prior access to the property and time to plan out his crime. Speaking of, did Kapinos let the delivery guy into his house?"

"No."

"See," Fennel pointed out, "that might explain the discrepancy. But I'm not sure I buy it. Someone spotted our unsub leaving. That's never happened before."

"Except yesterday, when I spotted him just as he jumped out of Lovretta's window. According to what we know, the description Kapinos' neighbors gave fits our profile. If we get a usable sketch, I think we should show it to Lovretta and see what he has to say."

"You don't think our killer broke into Dr. Kapinos' house?" Fennel asked.

"I don't know. This case has me double-guessing everything. But who else could it be? Our killer targets buyers, and Kapinos is a buyer. Plus, since it's been a few days since he killed Ezra Sambari and stole the tiara, it's about time for him to strike again."

"Let's just hope once Lovretta identifies him we'll be able to bring him in before he racks up another kill."

"Yeah, but if he's smart, he'll go to ground. He's had two close calls in two days. He's making mistakes, which means he's getting desperate. I just hope he doesn't escalate."

Fennel pressed down harder on the accelerator and darted around traffic. At least in the unmarked, motorists were less likely to slow to a crawl. It was time we got a name and picked up this piece of shit. Lives depended on it.

FOURTEEN

"This isn't a name." Fennel slammed his palm against the table. "We need more. A lot more. How do you get in contact with him?"

Anthony Lovretta looked from the paper to his attorney to ADA Winters. Gildan nodded, so Lovretta said, "He found me at work. When I told you I found the musket, I wasn't lying. He left it."

According to our file, Lovretta worked in waste collection. Basically, he picked up garbage and litter at the park and near the waterfront. Given his record, most businesses didn't want to hire him, but since there wasn't anything to steal outside, he'd gotten a job with the city as part of their second chance program. For an ex-con, he made decent money and had good benefits, just the right kind of incentive to stay on the straight and narrow. At least until the killer threw a wrench into Lovretta's plans.

I picked up the notepad and read the alias – Wild Bill. Not exactly the name I'd give our cat burglar, but no one asked me. "Is this his phone number?"

Lovretta nodded. "Yeah, but that's all I know. I swear."

I doubted it.

Fennel jerked his chin toward the door. Silently, I left

the interrogation room, updated Lt. Winston, who'd been watching from the attached observation room, and ran a reverse lookup on the number. It came back as an untraceable VoIP. Perhaps Mac could work some magic, but the calls and texts had been routed all over the world. I didn't think even she could pull off this miracle. And as predicted, the number went to an automated voicemail box which did nothing to help our case or track our killer.

When I returned to the interrogation room, a sketch artist was sitting with Lovretta. Fennel paced back and forth, his hands stuffed into his back pockets. "How did you get the watches?" my partner asked Lovretta.

"Wild brought them over," Lovretta said, not looking up from the sketch. "His eyes are a little closer together."

"What color?" the sketch artist asked.

"I don't remember," Lovretta said.

"Did Wild bring them over before or after we knocked on your door?" Fennel asked.

"After." Lovretta leaned back in his chair. "He called earlier that day, wanting to know if I felt like making some easy money. He said he had some other things to unload and thought I could help him out."

"Did you give him a cut of the musket sale?" I asked.

"No." Lovretta didn't appear to be lying, but it was hard to tell. "That was a gift. Like I said, I found it while at work."

"Where was it?" Fennel asked.

"Inside one of the garbage bins. When I pulled out the bag to dump the trash, I found it. It's old. I didn't think it could be used to hurt someone."

Gildan glared at us. "The police have yet to demonstrate that's the case."

Winters opened his mouth, but one look from me shut him up. This wasn't the time or place to debate whether the antique musket should be considered a firearm.

"So, Wild told you he'd drop by with something else for you to pawn?" Fennel asked, cringing at the use of our killer's alias.

Lovretta swallowed uncomfortably.

"Deal's been signed," Winters reminded him.

"Immunity, remember?"

"Right." Lovretta took a deep breath. "He wanted me to fence the watches. I still have some connections from my old life. He promised me a cut and said if I did a good job, he'd throw a bit more work my way. Something real nice. But I don't have fences exactly, more like a few pawn brokers who always gave me a fair shake, so I figured sure, what's the harm."

"And then we knocked on your door," Fennel muttered.

"Yeah, well, now you see why I didn't want you coming inside," Lovretta said. He looked back at the sketch. "His hair's shorter and a little darker, like he shaved his head a few weeks ago and it's starting to grow back."

"How'd he find you?" I asked.

Lovretta looked straight at me. "What?"

"You heard me. How'd he find you? Did you work together in the past?"

"No."

"So answer the lady's question," Fennel said.

"I dunno. Seriously. I don't. I found the musket in the park, so I held on to it, figuring it might be worth something. Hell, maybe it got left by accident, and someone would offer a reward. A big group of old timers had a picnic a few days before. I thought maybe it belonged to one of them, like they were a reenactor group or something."

"Uh-huh," Fennel mumbled, unconvinced.

"You realize if you're not honest or refuse to cooperate then the deal's off," Winters reminded him.

"I know." Lovretta glared at him. "I'm cooperating. Just give me a chance to think. Jeez." He let out a huff. "Later that afternoon, when I got back to my car, I found a note. Okay? You happy now? That's how I knew who left the musket." Lovretta crossed his arms over his chest and stared at us.

"Do you still have the note?" I asked.

"Nope."

"Of course you don't." Fennel swung a chair around and straddled it, leaning forward and staring at our witness. "Do you remember what it said?"

"Just that the musket was a gift, and he'd be in touch." Lovretta watched the sketch artist put the finishing touches on the mockup.

"Did Wild Bill sign it or leave a phone number?" Fennel asked.

"No."

"So how'd you know who it was from?" I asked.

"I didn't."

"You seem awfully chummy with Wild Bill, but you're telling us you never worked with him, that you knew nothing about him prior to when he approached you, which would mean he shouldn't know you either. But he left you a musket in the trash. Obviously, he knows where you work, what you drive, and where you live. Care to explain that?" I asked.

"I can't." A sheen of sweat developed on Lovretta's forehead, and a panicked look filled his eyes. "You gotta believe me."

"So how'd Wild Bill get your phone number?" I asked.

Lovretta paled. I was on to something. And whatever it was made him nervous. "Social media? The internet? I don't know."

"When did Wild Bill first introduce himself?" Fennel asked.

"Right after I dropped off the musket." Lovretta gulped. "As I was walking out of the shop, my phone rang. The call came up unknown, but I answered anyway. He asked if I had any problems unloading the musket and wondered if I had any interest in unloading more antiques. I said sure."

"Just like that?" Fennel asked.

"Yeah. He said he heard about me and since he's new to the game, he thought we could help each other out. He figured I might need some pocket money since I've gone straight." Lovretta wiped at his brow. "How long do you think Wild's been following me?"

Fennel and I exchanged a look, but before either of us could ask the next question, ADA Winters asked, "Is this on the level?"

"Yes. Absolutely." Lovretta stared at the black and white image the sketch artist created. "Before Wild Bill came to my apartment, I'd never seen him before. I never worked with him. As far as I know, we never crossed paths. I don't know how he found me or why he chose me to help him out. All I know is it was an easy payday. I didn't know for a fact the musket was stolen. And I thought it best not to ask. I've stayed clean since I got out. I don't want to go back. I didn't do anything wrong." He emphasized the last part.

"So Wild Bill didn't directly contact you until you pawned the musket." Fennel reached for the notepad where Lovretta had written every detail regarding his encounter with Wild Bill. "And that's when he introduced himself and tells you he has more items for you to move. Did he tell you what they were?"

"No. That first conversation was brief. Maybe a minute. You can check my phone records."

"We will," Fennel said. "So I take it he called a second time."

"Yeah, the morning you two came knocking on my door." Lovretta glanced from Fennel to me. "At first, I thought maybe he wanted to set me up. He told me he had some limited edition watches to move, and twenty minutes later, the cops knock on my door."

"Did you give Wild Bill your address after he told you about the watches?" I asked.

"Yes. Maybe. I can't remember. I just remember I thought it was strange he wanted to meet at my place. Since he had the goods, he should have set the location for our first meet somewhere he'd be comfortable," Lovretta replied. "Someplace safe for the both of us."

Fennel turned around to look at me. "Wild's careful. He didn't want to risk Lovretta selling him out."

"You can't blame him, if they never had dealings before," Winters said.

Fennel spun back to face Lovretta. "So after we left and Wild Bill entered your apartment, what did he say? What did he do?"

"It's all right there." Lovretta pointed at the paper. "He came in with a big duffel bag and asks if I'm a guy who can move things. I told him it depends on what kinds of things. He digs a jewelry box out of the bag, shows me the watches, and says there's more where that came from, if I do a good job." Lovretta gulped down some air. "Next thing I know, he's going through my apartment, like he's looking for something. He shoves a hoodie at me and tells me to put it on. Then he grabs my gym bag from the closet, puts the jewelry box in it, and tells me to run. I thought he was crazy. I'm like 'Dude, this is my apartment', but then he pulls a gun. So I ran."

"Right into us," Fennel said.

"From the look in his eye, he would have killed me if I didn't do what he said. And I'm sure he won't like that I'm talking to you. You have to protect me," Lovretta practically begged. "I don't know where he got the name Wild Bill, but the dude's crazy. Wild doesn't even begin to describe it. You can see it in his eyes."

Winters tapped on his phone and read. "Gambler, gunfighter, spy, soldier, scout." He kept reading. "Lawman."

"What are you looking at?" I asked.

"Wikipedia."

"This isn't the Wild West," Fennel mumbled, tuning out the ADA. "Mr. Lovretta, is there anything else you haven't mentioned? Maybe you know this guy by reputation or know someone who might know him? A friend of a friend? A former associate?"

"No. As far as I know, Wild Bill didn't exist when I was in the game. He said he's new or new in town. That's why he wanted my help. After the musket, I asked around, but no one's heard of him. No one recommended me. That's it. That's everything I know, I swear," Lovretta said.

"My client cooperated. He's given you a name, a phone number, access to everything you've asked for. He can't tell you what he doesn't know, but you will hold up your end of the agreement," Gildan said.

While Gildan and Winters bickered, an officer knocked on the door. I opened it, glad to have an excuse to step away for a moment. The officer held out a copy of a sketch. I took it, quirking an eyebrow.

"Is this from the Kapinos' break-in?" I asked.

"Yes, ma'am." The officer stepped back, ready to return

to his duties.

Taking it, I turned to find Fennel standing behind me. He took the sheet from my hands and compared it to the sketch the artist just finished of Wild Bill. Then he showed it to Lovretta. "Is this Wild Bill?"

Lovretta studied the new sketch carefully. "I guess. Same eyes and chin. His cheekbones look more pronounced here than what I remember, and his face is a little thinner. But it could be him. It's close enough."

Unlike the sketch we were just handed, the sketch created from Lovretta's description made Wild Bill look like a stereotypical villain with narrow, beady eyes, a permanent scowl, and his face smushed together in what Fennel referred to as "the pug", with his forehead furrowed and his eyes deep set beneath pronounced brows and a dark hood. Conveniently, Lovretta couldn't remember Wild Bill's eye color, just that he looked crazy.

"Great." Fennel nodded to the sketch artist seated beside Lovretta. "I need a copy of that too."

"No problem, Detective." The sketch artist collected his materials and left the interrogation room.

"I'll get Lt. Winston in here to work out the logistics, but we'll keep you safe," Fennel promised. Then he and I left the interrogation room. "Liv, I'll bring these to Mac and have her run them through facial recognition to see if we get a hit. In the meantime, search for the alias Wild Bill. See what you can find. And expand your previous search and check to see who did time with Anthony Lovretta or anyone suspected of being in his crew. That might be how Wild Bill got Lovretta's name, even though the former thief denied it."

"On it," I said. "But shouldn't we check with Speedy Delivery to see if they recognize the man in the sketch?"

"That's where I'm headed as soon as Mac scans the sketches. I'll make a few calls and see if we can get access to the security cameras in the park from the day in question. Let's see if we spot anyone leaving the musket in the trash. That might give us a better description of this guy than the crap Lovretta gave us."

"Are you sure you don't need backup?" I asked.

"If we divide and conquer, we'll find him faster. Since it looks like we just thwarted Wild's latest heist, he's preparing to strike again. I can feel it."

Nodding, I marched to my desk and got to work.

FIFTEEN

Your search returned 0 results. I stared at the message on the screen. According to the police database, that alias had never been used in connection with a crime, at least not in the last 150 years. Sighing, I typed Anthony Lovretta and waited for the details to populate.

We already knew Lovretta had been arrested several times for B&Es. For a thief, he was sloppy. He also worked alone. Smash and grabs didn't involve extensive choreography and planning. Though, if Lovretta had put some thought into his plans, he might not have gotten caught on five separate occasions. But I wasn't naïve enough to think those were the only five crimes he committed. He probably committed a lot more that we didn't know about.

After reading his arrest record and transcripts, I didn't have any doubts left that Lovretta worked solo, but he needed some way to unload the stolen goods. And since we never pinged him for trafficking stolen items, he must have a damn good fence he refused to give up. But in case I was wrong, I made a note to call the area pawn shops again and ask them to check their records since that's how Lovretta claimed to have moved the hot merchandise.

Something bothered me, and I scribbled down the wayward thought. Lovretta said Wild contacted him immediately after he left the pawn shop. It could be a coincidence, but that seemed unlikely.

The computer dinged, and I scanned the prison records. Lovretta had served a few stints here and there. The last being his longest, so that's what I focused on. No names stuck out, which wasn't surprising. Any one of these men could have pointed our killer right to Lovretta. But I had no basis for knowing who might be responsible. We'd already checked with burglary and the Bureau to see who could fence high-end merchandise, and we followed up and performed our due diligence, which led to more dead ends. None of the high-end fences had heard of Wild Bill or his recent scores.

I made a few calls and asked our colleagues to check again, this time for a connection to Anthony Lovretta. But I knew the results wouldn't be different, even with the new parameters. Did Lovretta know a guy we didn't? Somehow, I found that hard to believe.

"DeMarco," Laura 'Mac' Mackenzie bounded toward my desk, "where's Fennel?"

"He's running down a lead. What's going on?"

She held out a tablet with several small DOT photos. "That sketch from your crime scene today came back with some results. I narrowed it to include men in the estimated age range who also own black two-doors."

I looked at the array of similarly featured men. "Okay, compile a few six-packs. I'll run them by Dr. Kapinos and his neighbors and see if any of these men stick out."

"Copy that."

Picking up the phone, I dialed Fennel and updated him on Mac's progress. "Are you still at Speedy Delivery?"

"Yep." From his tone, things weren't going well.

"All right. I'll have Mac send you the possible matches. With any luck, someone will recognize this guy."

"I wouldn't count on it."

Before I could ask what was wrong, Fennel hung up.

Jotting down a few quick notes on my progress, so I'd know where to pick up once I returned, I grabbed my coat and took the printouts Mac handed me. Then I called Kapinos to make sure he was home and hadn't come in to give a statement and drove to his townhouse. I kept my fingers crossed he'd ID one of these men as the Speedy Delivery driver. Mac told me none of them had criminal records, but based on what little we knew about Wild Bill, I wasn't surprised. With any luck, he finally screwed up and we were about to catch him.

Kapinos ushered me into his house the moment I arrived and locked the door. Obviously, the break-in made him nervous. He studied the array of images. "You think one of these men broke into my house?"

"I don't know. Do you recognize any of them?"

"They all look the same, but I guess that's the point."

He stopped on one of the last images, his brow furrowed. He put the photo aside and examined the rest. I waited. When he was finished, he returned to the one he pulled out. "Do you know this man's name?"

"Greg Johnson."

Kapinos' eyes grew wide. "He's in my class on the practicality of theoretical physics."

"Does he have any reason to want to harm you?"

"I don't think so."

"Have you ever had any arguments?"

"Last week we had a discussion about his mid-term. He thought he deserved a higher score."

"Does he know about your Newtons?"

"Yes, my students know all about them."

Bragging never led to anything good. "Would he have any reason to know where you live?"

Kapinos grew even more uncomfortable. "At the beginning of the semester, I invited the graduate students over for dinner as a meet and greet. We're a small department, Detective."

"So he's been here before?"

"Yes."

"Okay."

After making arrangements for officers to bring Greg Johnson in for questioning, I went across the street and spoke to the eyewitnesses from earlier. They, like Dr.

Kapinos, identified Greg Johnson as the man they saw fleeing the scene. When I got back to the car, I radioed ahead and asked for a full workup on Greg Johnson and an arrest warrant.

On my way to Johnson's apartment, I updated my partner on the situation. He theorized that the physics training might have prepared our suspect to zipline from building to building and perform nearly superhuman feats.

"I guess he never learned the law of gravity," I said.

"Based on the destroyed shrub outside Kapinos' place, he mastered it earlier today."

"Did anyone at Speedy Delivery ID him?" I asked.

"No, but that doesn't mean shit. These yahoos have no earthly idea what's going on around here or who's making deliveries. I'll head back to the precinct and dig into the university's records and see what I can find on Greg Johnson."

"I'm heading to his place now."

"Liv," Fennel warned, "do not confront him. We think he killed five people, one of which was a fucking Mossad agent. Don't do anything without backup. Do you hear me?"

"Yeah."

"I'm serious. I need you to be careful. Maybe I should meet you."

"Brad, I'm fine. I won't do anything. I'll cruise by to see if I spot his vehicle, and then I'll just sit on him until tactical arrives. Okay?"

"You better."

Rolling my eyes at my partner's overprotective nature, I let the GPS lead me to Greg Johnson's apartment. I'd been inside this building before. The apartments were small and dated. A lot of college and graduate students rented units due to the price and location. Nothing about this place screamed out killer-thief. But appearances could be deceiving.

After I found Johnson's car, I parked on the opposite side of the street, checked the area for signs of the man, got out of the car, and peered into his vehicle. No sparkly jewels or stolen antiques in sight. I didn't see any climbing gear, weapons, or blood either.

I returned to my car, wondering if Johnson was even home. Thirty minutes later, my radio chirped. Units were on the way, so I waited. They rolled up. No lights. No sirens. We wanted to do this quietly to keep him from rabbiting. This guy had already outrun us twice. I'd be damned if I let him do it again.

"Set up a perimeter. I want eyes on all the exits. Get someone up on the roof. This guy's a fucking magician. We're not letting him go poof again," I instructed.

"Yes, ma'am."

Once all possible escape routes were covered, the tactical unit moved in. I brought up the rear, hoping we hadn't missed anything. The officer in the front knocked and announced. We waited, but Johnson didn't answer the door.

"Open it up," I said.

The officer nodded, and within seconds, the door flew open. "Police. Hands in the air."

Greg Johnson stood in the middle of his living room, a bowl of steaming ramen noodles on the cluttered coffee table in front of him. He held both hands up. He didn't move, still wearing the track pants and hoodie he had on earlier.

"Clear," a team called from the bedroom, returning to the main room.

"Greg Johnson, you're under arrest," I said as the officer frisked and cuffed him, "for breaking into Richard Kapinos' house." The rest could wait until he was booked.

The officer who cuffed him read Johnson his rights and brought him out to the car. Our arrest warrant didn't include a search, but anything in plain sight was fair game. So we looked around, but we didn't find anything damning.

"Are you sure you got the right guy, DeMarco?" the officer asked.

Honestly, I was starting to have my doubts.

SIXTEEN

"That's him?" Fennel asked as the officer dragged Greg Johnson down the hall.

"I don't know. That's why we're putting him in a lineup." I didn't feel good about this. Arresting Johnson had been too easy. He didn't resist. He didn't have any contraband out in the open. I didn't even spot a duffel bag. Our eyewitness from today's burglary interruptus was waiting in the conference room, and Anthony Lovretta remained in holding while Lt. Winston finalized arrangements on the safe house.

"Let's see what happens." Fennel got up from behind his desk and followed the officer down the hall.

It didn't take long for Kapinos' neighbor to positively identify number four as the man who jumped out the window. That was easy. An officer escorted our witness out of the room to handle the rest.

Fennel eyed me. "One down, one to go," he said.

We repeated the lineup again for Lovretta and his attorney. Lovretta didn't identify anyone.

"Do you want us to run through them again?" Fennel asked.

"It doesn't matter. Wild Bill's not there, but nice try,"

Lovretta said.

"Shit." Fennel punched the side of his fist against the wall. "Are you absolutely certain?"

"Yep," Lovretta said, clearly relieved we hadn't actually caught the killer.

Fennel glowered at the two-way glass and silently cursed, his lips forming the words. Finally, he rubbed his mouth and stared at me as if to ask *now what.*

"Mr. Lovretta," I rested my hips on the table as the men filed out of the room and number four, Greg Johnson, was taken to an interrogation room, "I have two more questions for you."

"Make them brief," Gildan warned. "My client's cooperated so far, and the police department's done nothing to safeguard his well-being."

"That's not true. He is in protective custody," Fennel pointed out.

"He's in a holding cell," Gildan snapped.

"Yes, but it's his own private holding cell. No one can get to him there." This turn of events had left Fennel in a worse mood, and he was itching for a fight.

"Brad, go." I jerked my chin at the door. "Get back to what you were doing. This won't take long."

He let out a huff and stormed out the door.

"I'll be brief," I promised, "but Mr. Lovretta, I need to know what you did with the items you stole."

"Allegedly," Gildan piped up.

I glared at him, regretting telling Fennel I'd handle this. "Did you have a regular fence or a pawn shop you liked to frequent? How'd you turn the stolen goods into cash?"

"It varied. If I heard someone was looking to buy something, I'd make that my focus. It's easier that way. Supply meeting demand. The basic untraceable stuff I sold online or pawned," Lovretta said. "I told you I don't have a guy. I'm not sure who you think I am, Detective DeMarco, but I wasn't the greatest crook. It's probably why I got pinched so many times. Honestly, I don't know why someone like Wild would come to me, given what you've said about him."

"It doesn't make any sense," I agreed, giving Lovretta

the full force of my hardened cop stare. "That's why I find it hard to believe you."

"That's enough, DeMarco," Gildan warned. "Anthony Lovretta's rehabilitated. He's a productive member of society. How should he know why some lunatic reached out to him?"

"Then why are you more than willing to throw away everything you've achieved by helping Wild Bill move stolen goods?" I asked Lovretta.

"You don't get it," he said. "He didn't give me a choice. He left the musket. That meant I owed him."

"So because you pawned the musket instead of turning it into the police, he came to collect on your debt by giving you more opportunities to make money." I snorted. "That's messed up."

"That's just how it works. It's an unspoken agreement. Something I learned in prison. A favor for a favor." Lovretta sighed. "I wish I never picked up that musket or found the note on my car. I didn't ask for this, and for the couple hundred bucks I got, it wasn't worth it."

"You're afraid Wild Bill still wants to collect on that favor?"

"I'm certain of it." Lovretta fought against a shudder. "He's watching me. I can feel it. I bet that's how he knew to call as soon as I pawned the musket."

"We'll keep you safe," I said, "but if you know anything else, now's the time."

"I don't."

Gildan cleared his throat. "You're repeating yourself, DeMarco. Anthony's cooperated and will continue to do so, but I expect him to be moved into less hostile accommodations tonight."

"It'll be taken care of." Opening the door, I nodded to the waiting officer to escort Lovretta back to holding, and then I went in search of my partner.

Fennel stood in front of the murder board. To anyone who didn't know him, it looked like he was deep in thought. But I knew better. The only thoughts going through Brad's head were how badly we screwed up.

"DeMarco, Greg Johnson's waiting in interrogation

room three," someone said.

"I'll be there in a minute." Taking up the spot beside Brad, I sighed loudly. "On the bright side, we stopped an actual crime in progress and caught the thief. That counts for something."

"Stopping a pissed off grad student from vandalizing his professor's house isn't exactly what I hoped to accomplish today."

"The day's not over yet," I said. "And we don't have time to throw a pity party."

"That's not what I'm doing." Fennel plucked Kapinos' photo and the corresponding info off the board and tucked them into a file folder before handing it to me. "You'll need that."

"What happened with Speedy Delivery?" I asked, leafing through the file to make sure I had everything I'd need before confronting Mr. Johnson.

"No one recognized the man from either sketch, though now that point is moot." Fennel narrowed his eyes at our suspect's depiction. "My gut says someone at the delivery service is lying or covering. I'm not sure which, but I bet they're afraid to be honest because it might open them up to a lawsuit."

"Why?"

Fennel snorted. "Since we have access to Speedy Delivery's employee manifest, I spoke to some of the delivery guys. A few of them told me if they need to be out or have too much to deliver in one day, the boss doesn't care how it gets done, just as long as it gets done. It has something to do with the company's guarantee."

"Like thirty minutes or less?" I asked, and though the question was stupid, Brad cracked a smile.

"I see I'm not the only one with food on my mind." He stepped away from the board and took a seat at his desk. "Anyway, it doesn't matter who they get to fill in, just as long as someone does. And when Speedy's really swamped or the scheduled deliverymen can't get any of the other employees to pull their shifts, they ask a friend or a friend of a friend to do it. If that doesn't work, they hire someone on one of those assistant apps to fill in and pay them seventy-five percent of what they'd make that day."

"Did you find out which apps they use?"

Fennel nodded. "I passed it along to the techs when I got back, but there are so many users, I doubt we'll get a hit. But since Speedy doesn't have any real checks in place and the guy in charge doesn't even know who's making the deliveries, if our killer did gain access through the delivery company, he might not even be an employee, which brings us back to square one."

"Dammit." I hoped to find an answer somewhere on the board, but I didn't see one. "I asked Lovretta who he uses as a fence, but he's sticking with his story that he doesn't have one. Burglary and the Bureau are looking again, just in case. But I'm actually starting to believe him."

"So we still don't know how Wild Bill found Lovretta. How far did you get on Lovretta's fellow inmates?"

"Far enough to know it could be any of them or none of them. Even the ones still inside have contact with the outside world. They could have passed the intel off to someone else who passed it off to Wild Bill." I cringed. "Have I mentioned I hate that alias?"

"So do I." Fennel reached across and grabbed the stack of files off my desk. "Finding Lovretta and convincing him to cooperate was supposed to assist the investigation, not confuse it."

"Do you think that's intentional?"

"No." Fennel scratched the stubble on his cheek. "I don't know. Maybe we need to go back to before we picked up Lovretta and see if we missed something. How about I check your work and you check mine?"

"Fine, but let me wrap things up with Mr. Johnson first."

Brad laughed. "That's a good idea, to wrap up Mr. Johnson."

"Shut up." I went down the hall and entered the interrogation room.

The patrolman who caught Johnson in the act sat beside me at the table. After I asked Greg Johnson a few questions, he confessed to breaking into Dr. Kapinos' house. Greg hoped to find his professor's computer log-in and password information and change his grade. Greg was under pressure to maintain a certain GPA in order to keep his scholarship and grants. As it was, the university was paying him a stipend on top of covering his tuition, but last semester his grades lagged as he stopped focusing on classwork and spent most of his time researching his thesis.

Once I was satisfied Greg Johnson wasn't our unsub and had no idea who Wild Bill was, I signed off and gave the patrolman the collar. Since the kid didn't have a record and didn't actually steal anything, he'd probably get off easy. However, I didn't know what the university would do or how forgiving Dr. Kapinos would be. But that wasn't my problem. The kid just learned a valuable lesson about keeping things in perspective. A lesson Brad and I needed to be reminded of on occasion.

When I got back to my desk, Brad had finished going over my notes and had phoned the rest of the businesses that I hadn't had time to reach out to this morning. He left one name highlighted on a post-it. Before I even sat down, he shoved his files onto my desk and reached for his jacket.

"Where are you going?" I asked.

"Jake and I are meeting Bennett Renner for drinks. I'm hoping to get more details out of the P.I. concerning Mr. Zedula's tiara and what exactly our victim wants Cross Security to do about it." Fennel jerked his chin at the sticky note. "Talk to Axel Kincaid. If anyone has surveillance footage of the delivery guy, it'd be him. Plus, we know one of his holding companies owns a pawn shop. Who knows what else he might be able to tell us?" Fennel met my eyes. "Do you want me to take care of it?"

"No, I'll do it."

SEVENTEEN

"To what do I owe the pleasure, Detective?" Axel Kincaid lounged in the center of a large round booth in the VIP area of his club. He held a stemless martini glass in one hand while the other slid off the thigh of the woman seated beside him. I didn't read a lot of fashion magazines, but I was nearly certain she'd recently been on the cover of all of them. "Have you finally decided to stop by for a drink?"

"This isn't a social call, Axel." I glanced at the woman with the perfect legs that went on for miles. "Would you mind giving us a few minutes?"

She nodded, climbing to her feet. Even without the spike heels, she'd easily tower over me. Kincaid frowned, annoyed by her sudden retreat.

"What do you want now?" Straightening, he knocked back the rest of his drink in a single gulp and put the glass down. "I warned you last time, the next favor's gonna cost you."

"This isn't a favor."

"No?" His ice blue eyes held a challenge, but I didn't back down. "Well? What is it?" He waved his hand, urging me to get to the point.

"You recently bid on a chandelier and some

candelabras."

Kincaid stared at me as if I had three heads. "And?"

"I need you to tell me about them."

He jerked his chin skyward. "Feel free to take a look."

I turned, spotting the chandelier hanging over the dance floor. "And the other pieces."

"The matching set of candelabras are upstairs in my loft." He narrowed his eyes. "Care to come upstairs and see them? I'm sure there are plenty of other things up there I could show you that you'd find a lot more interesting."

"More antiques?"

"I'm not that old, Liv." He smirked and patted the seat beside him. "Unless you're planning on pulling out the handcuffs, sit down. You're making my guests nervous. You know, Spark does have a dress code."

"I'm well aware of Spark's dress code, but you extended an open invitation to me. You said I could drop by anytime I wanted to have a drink." Dealing with Kincaid always required a bit of a dance, but I wasn't letting him lead this time.

"In that case," he gestured to Mindy, one of the waitresses I'd worked with while undercover inside his club, "what'll it be?" He waited. The smug know-it-all look barely concealed. He expected me to say I was on duty, which is why I showed up after shift.

"Pineapple mojito."

"Really?" he asked, surprised. I shrugged as if to say *why not*. "One pineapple mojito, hold the simple syrup." He held out his empty glass. "And another martini. Very cold. Very dirty."

"Yes, Mr. Kincaid." Mindy turned, scowling at me as she made her way back to the bar. Just another person convinced I was nothing more than a wolf in sheep's clothing.

"That's the way you like it, right? I remember you have an aversion to all the guilty pleasures in life. Sugar. Fun. Everything Spark stands for. I'm surprised just being here doesn't make you break out in hives, Detective."

I didn't respond. Axel Kincaid wasn't a good guy, which is how I ended up investigating him and Spark. As far as he was concerned, that meant I betrayed him. He tended to ignore the fact that before he landed on the PD's radar, the two of us had never crossed paths. But he didn't let little things like the truth or evidence deter him. Kincaid had come from a life on the streets, stealing rare and exotic sports cars. His juvie record indicated a history of violence, but as far as anyone was concerned, he was now a legitimate businessman. Although, that viewpoint had a lot to do with the number of government officials who held a membership to Spark.

Though I never had enough to build a case against him, a lot of illicit things went on inside the exclusive, members-only nightclub. If Kincaid was as squeaky clean as he claimed, the DEA never would have been able to leverage him to assist them on a major drug bust. I didn't buy his holier-than-thou act. I also didn't like the way he leered at me.

Our drinks arrived, and Mindy placed them on sparkly coasters and disappeared. Axel leaned forward, scooping mine off the table and handing it to me. "Drink up," he said. "I promise it's not poisoned."

I took a sip, knowing he wouldn't talk until he felt like it. And he wouldn't feel like it until I did something to prove I was off duty and being honest. He had trust issues, not that I blamed him. "That's good," I said.

He smiled and held his glass up before taking a sip and relaxing against the cushions. "So why are you really here, Liv? Trying to pin another crime on me? Or did you want to show me some gratitude for helping you out with the human traffickers?"

"I already thanked you for that."

He arched an eyebrow. "You did not. But I'll let it go."

Rolling my eyes, I took another sip of the mojito. "Any particular reason you decided to invest in candelabras and that pricey chandelier?"

"As you know, I enjoy beautiful things." He took a sip of his drink and held the rim of the glass with his fingertips. Holding it up to the light, he inspected the glass before picking out the olive and sliding it off the toothpick with his teeth. He watched me as he chewed, making it clear he had no intention of speaking without provocation. This was going to be a long night.

"Did you know Agnes Archibald?" I asked.

"You mean the old biddy who used to own these trinkets to which you are so fascinated?" He thought for a moment. "No, I don't believe we ever had the pleasure."

"What about any of her heirs?"

Something flashed in Axel's eyes. Gently setting the glass on the table, he looked around the room. "I miss watching you dance."

I glared at him, spotting one of the empty cages where I'd been locked for hours at a time to entertain the patrons on the nights Spark was short-staffed or the regular dancers called in sick. "Mr. Kincaid, please, answer the question."

"Only if you answer mine." He nodded at the empty cage. "Do you miss it? Being the center of attention? The envy of the other women and desired by all the men?" He grinned. "And might I add, a few of the women too?"

"No. I hated being objectified like that."

"Really? You never acted like you disliked it. You could have told me. I would have had another waitress fill in. I made that clear the first day you started working here. I never force anyone to do anything they don't want to. This isn't a hostile work environment."

"I couldn't risk blowing my cover."

"That's what it was?" Axel asked. The smarminess made me want to punch him. "It seemed to me you always enjoyed it."

"What I enjoyed was having the opportunity to keep my eyes on you."

He chuckled. "I can see why you'd find that enjoyable."

I let out a disgusted scoff. "Answer the question, Axel."

"Marilyn Archibald is a dear friend, but I don't see what that has to do with anything." He finished his drink, the second one since I sat down. At this rate, he'd pass out before I even got to the point. But he didn't ask for another drink. Instead, he nudged his chin at my half empty glass, waiting for me to finish the mojito.

After swallowing a large gulp which burned the back of

my throat, I said, "Buyers from the auction are being targeted. I need to know more about the auction and how the items you bought were delivered."

He stood, politely gesturing me out of the booth. "Let's take this upstairs."

For the briefest moment, I wondered if Axel roofied me. But he was too smart to do something that dumb. So being the fearless cop that I was, I followed him across the crowded club to a locked door which led to a hidden staircase. Even undercover, I had only glimpsed the loft he kept above Spark once, but I heard plenty of stories about his hedonistic nights and the walks of shame that followed the next morning, though I never personally witnessed any of them.

Unlocking a second door at the top of the steps, Axel pushed open the door and flipped on the lights. While my eyes adjusted to the sudden brightness, he locked the door and strode across the room to the built-in bookshelves.

"Here's one of the pieces." He held it out, and I took it from him, surprised by the heft. This would make an excellent murder weapon. Hopefully, our killer hadn't come to the same realization. "On rare occasions, I have a piano downstairs and I like to dress it up with one of these. It gives things a nice Liberace feel."

"Why'd you buy two?" It wasn't relevant, but I was curious. Based on the auction house's records, they cost several grand each. "Why waste the money if you only needed one?"

"They came in a set," Axel replied, as if that made perfect sense. "And it's the same metalwork as the chandelier." He took the heavy silver object from my hand and returned it to the shelf. "So you said buyers are being targeted? By whom?"

"We don't know."

He studied me for a moment. "You transferred out of the intelligence unit. You and your partner work homicide now, right?"

"How do you know that?"

"I have friends in high places." The wheels turned in his head. "Do you think someone wants to kill me?"

"I'm sure plenty of people want to kill you."

"So you dropped by to protect me?" He moved to the taupe, oversized sectional and took a seat.

"No, I came here to ask you about the auction and the delivery." This was the third time I'd said it, but he derailed me each time. I wouldn't let him do it again. "Let's start at the beginning." I perched on the edge of the sofa, removed a notepad and pen from my jacket pocket, and flipped to a clean page. We needed access to Axel's security footage, but asking him outright would lead to a quick denial. Hopefully, if I eased him into it and explained why the footage was important, he'd be more willing to comply. "How'd you first learn about the Archibald estate auction?"

"Marilyn mentioned it. She was stressed. Distraught. She and her siblings had a tenuous relationship with their mother after their father's passing. And since none of them wanted to carry on the Archibald dynasty in the same old-world fashion, they thought it best to unload the old biddy's belongings, divvy up the proceeds, and go on with their lives."

"So Marilyn didn't have any sentimental attachments to any of the items in the house?"

"No."

"In what capacity do you know Marilyn?"

Axel snickered. "Are you jealous?"

I clicked the pen. "Are you lovers?"

His brow furrowed. "Tell me why it matters? Why do you care so much about my relationship with Marilyn Archibald?"

Even though she wasn't considered a person of interest, we didn't know enough about her to rule out her connection to the killer. Perhaps she hired him to commit these crimes and retrieve the purchased items. But given her money and reputation, the idea seemed ludicrous. "Does she have any enemies?"

"I don't know."

"What do you know about the Archibalds' staff? Either Marilyn's or Agnes's?"

"Liv, tell me what's going on." He pointed an accusatory finger at me. "And don't feed me that bullshit that this is an open investigation. You came here to question me. And you didn't want anyone to know about it. So tell me the damn truth for once in your life."

"The department knows I'm here. Our investigation led us to contact the buyers from the auction. One of your holding companies was on the list. Did you personally attend the auction?"

"No, I had a proxy."

"Who?" I asked.

"Fox."

Of course he had his general manager go in his place. Fox would do anything for Axel. I didn't think there was a line the GM wouldn't cross. "Did he manage the delivery too?"

"No, I was here for that, but George let the guy in." George worked security and doubled as Spark's doorman.

"Do you still have the security footage from the day of the delivery?" I asked.

He slid across the cushions until he was beside me and grabbed the pen out of my hand. "Liv, against my better judgment, I've answered your questions. But that stops now. What is this about? I won't continue to incriminate myself or my employees to satisfy whatever vendetta the police have against me."

"We're not against you. This isn't even about you. We're trying to catch a killer." And against my better judgment, I told Axel about the five murders and asked him about each of the previous victims. He remained silent, ignoring my questions as if he were a statue. But I knew that look. He was deep in thought. "Mr. Kincaid," I snapped my fingers in front of his face, "do you know any of the victims?"

He grabbed my hand and pinned it against the couch cushion. "Is it true you don't have any idea who's doing this?"

I swallowed, and he squeezed my hand harder before realizing what he was doing and released me. I didn't answer him because I couldn't give up our only witness and lead, especially not to Axel Kincaid. He ran a hand over his mouth, but I saw something in Axel's eyes that I'd only seen once before. I just couldn't be sure what it was.

Desperation or fear? It could go either way.

"That's why we need your security footage. We need to get a look at this guy. Once we identify him, we can stop him. We can put an end to the killing." A part of me worried Axel might take matters into his own hands again, but with any luck, the gruesome details I'd given him would keep him from enacting his own form of justice.

"Do you have any idea who he'll target next?" Axel asked.

"Someone off the list. That's why we've notified buyers and beefed up patrols. We're hoping to deter him."

"I doubt a few extra police cars will do much to stop a man with those skills." Axel crossed the room and hit a latch, releasing a hidden door. "Do you believe Marilyn may be in danger?"

"That is a strong possibility. We offered her protection, but she refused. She has her own security. She trusts them more than us."

"Not that I blame her," Axel muttered, opening the door to a tiny closet-sized room full of security monitors and computer equipment. "Do you remember what day I supposedly took possession of the chandelier?" I gave him the date, and he keyed it in. I moved to get a closer look, but one glance from him halted me in my tracks. "What's your e-mail address?" he asked. After I told him, he pressed a few more keys and slid the hidden door back into place. Again, it appeared to be nothing more than a solid wall. "I sent you the footage. Do with it as you like. If you want something more official or additional access, get a fucking warrant. And for the record, Detective, this means you owe me. And I will collect."

EIGHTEEN

"Is that all Axel Kincaid said?" Fennel leaned over my chair, watching the footage from Spark.

"Pretty much." I froze the screen, but the only thing we could see from this angle was the deliveryman's chin. The cap he wore obscured the rest of his face from the security camera. "I spoke to George, Kincaid's doorman, but he didn't remember anything about the guy. And Fox said he didn't remember anyone or anything odd at the auction."

"Or so they say," Fennel said. "Do you think he's sleeping with Marilyn Archibald?"

"Kincaid?"

"Who else?"

"I dunno. When I walked in, he looked like he was about to close the deal with some model. You know, the one who's been on the front of all the magazines these past few months. But Axel isn't exactly a one woman type of man."

"I don't think Marilyn is interested in anything monogamous either. I'll see what I can dig up. Drop a copy of that into my inbox. I'll watch it again when I'm bored."

"The techs are evaluating it for clues." But I sent him the file anyway. "What did you learn from the private investigator?"

"Aside from the fact Cross Security pays a hell of a lot

more than what we make, not much. After we left Leopold Zedula's apartment, he immediately contacted Cross Security to request they locate the tiara. He offered them a twenty percent finder's fee."

"That's steep. Isn't the standard finder's fee ten?"

"Yeah, but nothing about this is standard. One," Fennel ticked the points off on his fingers, "Cross Security is supposed to be the best, so they charge more. And two, Zedula asked them to put a rush on it. Apparently, he already had a buyer on the hook for the piece. Now that it's gone, Zedula's in a jam. He wants it fast, and he's willing to pay through the nose to get it back."

"Does Renner have any leads?" I asked. "Who's Zedula's buyer? He didn't mention anything about this to us."

"Renner claims he doesn't know who the buyer is, but I don't know. I think it's weird Zedula's working against us. But according to Renner, Zedula's been in the game long enough to know that if we find the tiara first, we're going to keep it as evidence in our homicide investigation. So that's supposedly why Zedula won't cooperate."

"We won't keep the tiara forever," I protested.

"No, but longer than Zedula would like, which is why he went to an outside source. He wants to recover his property and complete the sale. The delay is hurting his reputation, and if word of the theft gets out, it could ruin him."

"That seems awfully dramatic."

"I agree. However, you and I might be the only voices of reason left in this crazy world. Not everyone prioritizes identifying and stopping a killer over making a high six-figure sale."

"Is Renner willing to throw us a bone?" I asked.

"Hell if I know, which is why we need to figure this out first, starting with Zedula's buyer. As far as I'm concerned, that person has the biggest motive for stealing the tiara."

"And if it isn't the buyer, it could be someone who wants to screw with the buyer."

Brad tapped his nose with his pointer finger. "The one glaringly obvious problem with that is our killer only targets people who made purchases from the estate auction. I'm not sure how Zedula's buyer connects to them."

"Maybe Zedula outbid someone else at the auction, and that person offered him a better price on the tiara." I picked up the master list of buyers, but I didn't see an easy way of figuring out who contacted Zedula about making a purchase. "What did Kalen and the insurance company have to say? Did Zedula or any third party approach them about the tiara's authenticity or insuring the piece?" Those words caused a slight glitch in my brain. "Wait a minute. Since the tiara is insured, why is Zedula so desperate? Wouldn't he come out on top either way?"

"One would think, but Renner said the buyer was offering thirty percent more than the estimated worth."

"Why would someone do that?"

"Desperation."

"Are we sure this isn't a scheme Leopold Zedula cooked up in order to get paid twice? Like you've pointed out, the MO from the Sambari murder was different. The killer brought his own weapon. He didn't use something at the scene."

"Yeah, but you saw the video, Liv. And even though Zedula looks damn formidable and absolutely regal, he doesn't match the thief's profile, and we've already evaluated and ruled out all of his security personnel and staff. Plus, if he stole the tiara himself, he wouldn't waste his time or money on Cross Security. He'd just file the claim, sell it under the table, and call it a day."

"You're right." I had fallen down the rabbit hole. It was time I got back on track.

"Plus, Kalen said no one's reached out or made any inquiries. I called Zedula and asked him point blank, but he denied Renner's claim."

"It's bad enough when suspects don't talk, but when the victims won't even answer our questions, what are we supposed to do?"

"Work harder." Fennel took the master list from my desk, removed the staple, and divided up the pages. "Let's make some calls and see if anyone expressed an interest in purchasing priceless jewels."

Before picking up the phone, I dug out the list of bidders

and the inventory. The few items that didn't sell were scratched off the list, including a diamond and emerald earring and necklace set. "Wait a second, Brad. Look at this. What goes better with diamonds and emeralds?"

"More diamonds and emeralds." He called the auction house to get additional details on the bidders and why the item didn't sell. When he hung up, confusion etched his face. "Get this, the jewelry was pulled last minute. The auctioneer was told to say an online bidder outbid the attendees, but Marilyn Archibald had the items pulled. She said those had been mistakenly added to the manifest."

"I thought she and her siblings didn't want any of their mother's things." I looked at the appraised value determined by the auction house. $75,000. Nothing to sneeze at, but also on the cheaper end when compared to most of the other items up for bid.

"Maybe she changed her mind. The auctioneer and a few of the assistants recall the flub since they had to scramble to cover it up, so they'll send me a list of the bidders they remember. But I think we should talk to Marilyn again."

"I agree." The trick was getting Marilyn Archibald to talk to us.

On the way to her office, I phoned her siblings. Despite the time difference, they took my call, told me they were aware Marilyn kept the jewelry, and she wrote them each a check for twenty-five grand, making them even. Considering their individual net worths, that seemed petty, but I didn't say as much. What did I know about business or their family dynamics?

"Okay, so Marilyn kept the jewelry. Do you think there's any chance she's in the market to add a tiara to the set?" Fennel asked.

"That would be my guess." But we'd soon find out.

Marilyn Archibald kept an office on the top floor in one of the prestigious downtown buildings. Even after running a background and looking into her, I still didn't fully grasp what she or her company did. The details I read were obscure. However, her security and staff knew exactly what it was they were doing.

"Detectives Fennel and DeMarco," Brad and I badged the man sitting at the desk, "we'd like to speak to Ms. Archibald."

"Do you have an appointment?" the man asked.

"No, but it's important. We just need a few minutes. C'mon, man, you must know what it's like to have your boss breathing down your neck to dot the 'I's," Brad said.

"Sure," the man jerked his chin at the center of the room, "take a seat. I'll see if I can squeeze you in between appointments."

Fennel pressed his palms together and bowed his head. "Anything you can do."

When we were out of earshot, I nudged Brad in the ribs. "Is that some Jedi voodoo?"

"No, but I've seen some big shots do that from time to time. I bet Mr. Security has too. It's about time someone showed him that kind of respect."

"What is it supposed to signify? Bowing to greatness?"

"Why do you always bust my balls? Wouldn't you like to find another hobby?"

"No way. This one's too much fun." I winked and went to stare out the floor to ceiling windows, watching the reflections in the glass as Archibald's staff bustled about. Without turning around, I clocked the security guards. They didn't remain stationary or hidden in an office or behind a desk. They maintained a constant patrol. "Do you think they follow a pattern, or are their movements random?"

Fennel stood beside me, facing the opposite direction while feigning interest in the sculpture on the other side of the room. It was metal, modern, and a monstrosity. "Let's hope we're not waiting here long enough to find out." He tapped me on the shoulder and pointed at the art. "What do you think of that?"

"It's probably a nude. Or people having sex."

He snorted. "One of these days, I'm taking you to an art opening."

"I'm not holding my breath." But something about the metal sculpture made the wheels turn in his head. "What is it?" I asked.

"I'm just thinking that is nothing like the painting stolen from the woman's apartment."

"No, it isn't."

"It's not even the same kind of art or the same era."

"Or materials."

"The two would clash," Fennel said.

"Uh-huh. Apples and elephants."

"What?"

"It's like comparing apples to elephants," I repeated.

"Detectives," the man at the desk called, "Ms. Archibald will have a few minutes to speak to you after her overseas call. I suggest you have your questions prepared. She won't have a lot of time before her next meeting."

"Thank you." Again, Fennel did what I decided was a namaste bow. Removing his notepad from his pocket, he flipped through the pages to get his priorities in order, but since we didn't work like rookies, the gesture might have been more for the assistant's benefit.

Five minutes later, the assistant cleared his throat. "She'll see you now."

"Are you ready to meet the great and powerful Oz?" I whispered. Until now, Marilyn Archibald had done an excellent job avoiding us.

Fennel led the way across the room and opened the door. He held it, gesturing me to go inside first. I stepped into the office, which looked like an extension of the waiting area. More modern art, along with modern furniture, and no desk or workstation in sight.

"Ms. Archibald, I'm Detective DeMarco. This is Detective Fennel. We have a few more questions about your mother's estate auction."

"Sit down." Marilyn Archibald was a strikingly beautiful woman, thin, with expertly applied makeup to hide any signs of her age, and a smart but feminine dress that demanded respect without compromising her sex appeal. "I don't have much time. If this is about the offer for protection, again, I'd like to remind you that I do not need city employees watching out for me. I can take care of myself."

"We understand that, ma'am," Fennel said. He found a

spot on a chair or ottoman, some kind of metal framed object with a seat cushion, and clicked his pen. "This is actually in regards to the necklace and earrings you had pulled from the auction."

"They were never meant to go up for sale. They belong to me. I acquired those years ago and allowed my mother to borrow them. Mistakenly, she believed them to be a gift, and I never corrected her. But since she's passed, I see no reason not to reclaim what was mine."

"I see." Fennel made a show of crossing something out on the page. "Do you know Leopold Zedula?"

"He's one of the bidders, no?" Marilyn asked, not wasting time playing games or asking why we wanted to know.

"Yes, he bid on a jeweled tiara." I perched on the end of a Z-shaped chair, grateful when it didn't tip over.

"Was he in attendance?" she asked.

"No ma'am," Fennel said. "Mr. Zedula bid on the item over the phone. But we were curious if you've had any interactions with him?"

She assessed us, a cold, calculating look in her eye. "You already know, so why bother asking?"

"Humor us," Fennel said, not giving anything away.

"Fine. Yes, I did inquire about borrowing the tiara from Mr. Zedula after the sale, but it's far too ostentatious, even for the Met Gala." She glanced at her watch.

"The Gala?" I asked.

"Yes," again her eyes zeroed in on me like a predator finding its prey, "I'm sure you've heard about this year's theme. But thankfully, I came to my senses. I'd hate to end up crucified or heralded on Page Six. Either way, you can't escape the photos once they're printed."

"I see," Fennel said again, channeling his inner psychiatrist. "Are you aware Mr. Zedula already had another buyer in place for your mother's tiara?"

"I didn't know that," Marilyn said. "Are you sure?"

"That's what we heard. We just wondered if you heard the same thing." He flipped to another page. "So after Zedula rejected your request, what happened?"

"Nothing," Marilyn said. "I checked out the rest of his

inventory and told him I'd be in touch if anything caught my eye."

"Did you contact him again?" I asked.

She shook her head.

"When did all of this occur?" Fennel asked.

"Right after the auction. I approached Mr. Zedula immediately after the auction house shared the invoices with me. I guess you could say I panicked, a delayed reaction to losing my mother and watching her things be sold off to total strangers."

"Did you have any other fond attachments to the other items sold?" I asked. "Maybe you were sentimental about some artwork or a chess set you admired as a child?"

"No, not at all." Marilyn stood. "I'm sorry, but that's all the time I have today. Should you have additional questions, please phone ahead. I'm sure someone on my staff will be able to assist you."

"Just one final question, Ms. Archibald," Fennel climbed to his feet, blocking her path, "who else knew you inquired about the tiara?"

"My assistant and the members of my security team who accompanied me to Mr. Zedula's. Now, if you don't mind," she stuck out her chin, doing her best to stand toe-to-toe with my partner, "I have work to do."

"Thank you for your time." Fennel moved out of her way.

Marilyn glanced at his retreating back, but her focus remained on me.

"Ma'am." I nodded in her direction.

She blinked. "Just a second, Detective." Fennel spun, but she wasn't talking to him. She marched up to me, scrutinizing my dark jeans, white button-up blouse, and leather jacket. "I know you from somewhere."

"I don't think so," I said.

"No, I'm sure of it. I never forget a face." She circled. "Spark."

She swallowed. The color drained from her cheeks. "You must be mistaken."

"I don't think so," I said. "Just so you know, Axel had only the loveliest things to say about you."

NINETEEN

"What the hell was that, Liv?" Fennel asked. "We want her to cooperate. Why are you poking the bear?"

"Marilyn Archibald isn't a bear. And based on her reaction, it's clear she doesn't want people to know she visits Spark. I just don't know why, but I'm guessing it's for obvious reasons. Hanging out with Axel Kincaid can't be good for a rich socialite's reputation, especially when she prides herself on proper decorum."

"Everyone who goes to his club is a rich socialite," Fennel argued. "I think she's sleeping with him."

"Do you want to go back inside and ask?"

"Kind of, but that's not gonna get us anywhere. What we need to do is find out how many other buyers Marilyn contacted after the auction. Do you think she had seller's remorse and that's why she tried to get the tiara back from Zedula?" Fennel asked. "I'm not buying her story that she wanted to borrow the piece to wear to the Gala. She's rich. If she wanted to keep the tiara, like the necklace and earrings, she should have. And since she didn't, she could probably have a replica crafted. She has the money to waste."

That part of her story didn't make sense to me either,

but I figured she freaked and suddenly wanted to reclaim some of her mother's beloved possessions, like she said. "Maybe it was seller's remorse."

"But Zedula denied her request. Maybe she got someone from her security detail to get the piece back through any means necessary."

"Okay," I was willing to buy that, "and maybe the same could be said for the musket and chess set, but the killer didn't reclaim the pocket watch or the sculpture. So doesn't that destroy our theory?"

Fennel fidgeted with his sunglasses. "Why didn't Leopold Zedula tell us Marilyn wanted to buy back or borrow the tiara when we questioned him? That's a material fact."

"All right, let's confront him about the crap he's been keeping from us and see what he has to say for himself." I stared up at the high-rise. On the one hand, Marilyn might have told Zedula to keep these damning details to himself for fear she would become a suspect, but on the other hand, if she wasn't behind the thefts and murders, she might be the killer's next victim.

"Were any of the other victims members of Spark?" Fennel asked.

"No, I don't think so." I opened the car door and climbed in.

"Now I'm curious. Has Kincaid spoken to Marilyn since the estate auction?"

"I can't say for sure, but my gut says Marilyn or her people have spoken to Kincaid about the items he purchased since the auction, but I'll give him a call tonight and double-check." I watched Brad slide the key into the ignition. "Do you think the killer might go after Kincaid?"

"Is that even possible? He's Axel fucking Kincaid. He believes he's untouchable, and as of yet, no one's proven him wrong. Not even us." Checking the mirrors, Fennel studied our surroundings, not ready to pull away from the building just yet. "This is why knowing where he and Marilyn stand might be important. Lesser detectives might even consider that a clue or at least vital information. His relationship to her, if there is one, may be the impetus to stave off an attack or encourage the killer to strike even faster."

"All I know is Axel didn't answer my question. He's cagey, especially when it comes to his private life, but he seemed genuinely concerned for her safety. That tells me they're close. Well, as close as someone can get to Axel Kincaid."

"Maybe he'll convince her to accept police protection," Fennel said.

"Yeah, right. Kincaid's the last person who'd ever vouch for us. Marilyn doesn't want protection. And we can't force it. Plus, from the looks of the armed guards inside, she should be okay without us. Unless one of those guards is the killer."

"Frankly, I'm not convinced she's not behind the thefts and murders. She's done her best to avoid us up until now, and the fact that she associates with Axel Kincaid doesn't bode well for her alleged upstanding citizen status."

"So where do we go from here?" I asked.

"Hell if I know, Liv. The only thing we can say for certain is Marilyn isn't committing the crimes herself, but her trip to Zedula's might have given the actual killer a chance to get another look at Zedula's place, specifically which safe held the tiara and possibly even a glimpse at the combination. We need to check with Arnold and Starmon and find out if Marilyn or anyone from her team paid them a visit too."

"Yeah, okay. I'll make some calls."

But Brad didn't start the car. Instead, he scratched his cheek. "Something else is bothering me."

"Lovretta," I said. Our cooperating witness appeared helpful on the surface, but we didn't get a hit through facial rec. And given how careful the killer had been, it struck me oddly that he'd expose himself to a total stranger.

"Everything about Anthony Lovretta bothers me," Fennel said. "But I can't put my finger on the precise problem. Obviously, you feel it too. Any idea what it is?"

"The killer made it too easy for us to find Lovretta. And then Lovretta just gives him up. Why would the killer screw up like that?"

"Misinformation?" Fennel suggested. "The guy Lovretta described is just your average Joe with a buzz cut. And when we showed him the sketch of Greg Johnson, he acted like it could be Wild Bill, but he wasn't certain, like he'd never seen the guy's face. But he was still willing to agree to it. Plus, how does a killer-thief with a ridiculous nickname like Wild Bill not get a single ping in the system? That doesn't make any sense either. Yesterday was nothing more than a circle jerk."

"You're right," I said. "But we know three things. Lovretta pawned the musket. When we arrested him, he had Starmon's watches in his bag, and someone jumped out the window and climbed down the building before escaping."

"They're working together, Lovretta and the unsub. Or at least they were before we caught Lovretta. Are we sure Lovretta's not a killer? Lt. Winston liked him for it."

"I checked Lovretta's alibis. He was always at work when the crimes went down. But he has to be working with our killer. I'm sure of it."

"The LT's not going to be happy about that considering we have Lovretta stashed in a motel as a cooperating witness," Fennel said. "But I agree. Lovretta's an accomplice. I just don't know to what extent, but the intel he's given us is meant to confuse and delay the investigation. That asshole's doing it on purpose. I just don't know what his endgame is."

"We need to expand our scope and look at the prison guards and Lovretta's PO. Prisons are tiny, and sometimes, guards are corrupt. One of them might have tipped our killer to Lovretta's rap sheet. Maybe that's how the killer and Lovretta hooked up since we know the killer isn't someone from Lovretta's former life and we've already dug through everyone he's met both in and out of prison."

"Perhaps some unknown party heard about Lovretta, got the facts wrong, and hooked him up with the killer. Maybe that's why Wild Bill, or whatever the hell his name is, thought Lovretta had a high-end fence on speed dial," Fennel said. "Maybe that's why he led us to Lovretta and let us capture him. The killer wanted payback for being played."

"That's too risky. And our killer is careful." We shouldn't be speculating, but the more intel we gained, the more complicated the case became.

Fennel snapped his fingers and pointed at me. "Shit, Liv, I think you're right. The only people who could pinpoint Lovretta's whereabouts, know where he worked, his schedule, his address, and his phone number are his parole officer and his boss. We should start there since the best lies always start with the truth. I saw the footage from the park. A hooded man dumped the contents of a zippered golf bag into one of the trash bins the same day Lovretta said he found the musket. I don't think that was a lie. I think the rest of his story might be but not the beginning."

"You realize we're just making this shit up as we go," I warned.

"We're professionals. This isn't shit. These are educated guesses." Fennel licked his lips. "What do you think the chances are Anthony Lovretta knows Marilyn Archibald?"

"Slim to none."

"Yeah, but we should probably ask anyway." Fennel pulled up the details on Lovretta's parole officer and entered the address into the nav system. "Since we haven't matched the sketch of Wild Bill to anyone in facial recognition, the LT's thinking about setting up a hotline and running it on the news, but he's worried it could compromise our investigation. So he's holding off. But in the event we're on to something here, we should let him run it. It'll convince the killer we're way out in left field and it might give us an advantage."

"First things first." I reached for the radio to get the ball rolling on the Marilyn Archibald front. More than likely, the killer connected to her and Anthony Lovretta. If we could find the one common denominator, we'd have our killer, so I was keeping my fingers crossed.

While Brad drove across town to the parole office, I phoned Francis Starmon and Dieter Arnold. Neither of them met or spoke to Marilyn Archibald, but they said someone from her staff reached out after the auction to make sure they received the items they purchased. They didn't remember precisely who called, and no second home visit was made, but that didn't mean the killer didn't moonlight for Speedy Delivery and still hold another job with Marilyn Archibald. I checked with the auction house, but they did not conduct the follow-up. In fact, they didn't know anything about it. The follow-up was orchestrated by Marilyn or one of her people. Now to find out which one.

After phoning the precinct and requesting someone contact the rest of the buyers to find out if Marilyn's staff reached out to any of them, I hung up and stared out the windshield. This was a mess. We needed to get Marilyn Archibald into an interrogation room, but until we had something solid, that wouldn't happen.

On a whim, I called the university and asked to speak to Dr. Kapinos. Luckily, the professor had office hours and took my call. I asked about Marilyn's staff, but he didn't remember anyone calling about the books he purchased.

"It looks like Marilyn's people didn't reach out to everyone," I said to Fennel.

"That's the first bit of good news we've gotten today. It might mean only the buyers Marilyn's office spoke to are targets. This is exactly what we need to stop our killer before he strikes again." Fennel held up his palm for a high-five, but I ignored it.

"Yeah, if the pattern holds," I said. "Which also means someone close to Marilyn is our killer. And if she's not behind it, then her life's in danger too."

"Update the LT and see if he can assign some people to keep a lookout. The more eyes we have looking for a connection between the Archibalds and Lovretta, the better. Frankly, I'm dying to know how someone in Marilyn Archibald's world crossed paths with a low-level loser like Anthony Lovretta."

"Bad choice of words," I scolded. "Don't put that out into the universe. Jake already told me no one else in the department would want to partner with me because grabbing lunch would be disastrous. So I need you to stay alive."

Brad laughed. "Sorry. I take it back. No dying. I

promise, Liv."

"You better." Then I did as my partner asked, hanging up just as we arrived outside the parole office.

TWENTY

Like most parole officers, Officer Deagan was overworked and underpaid. When we showed up, asking about Anthony Lovretta, he immediately pulled out the forms.

"We're not here to violate him," Fennel said.

"That's a first." Deagan shoved the forms off to the side and reached for his half-eaten sandwich. "Is he dead?"

"No, sir."

"So what brings two homicide detectives traipsing down here to my neck of the woods?" Deagan asked.

"Has Anthony Lovretta ever given you any problems?" Fennel asked.

"Just the usual shit. Nothing major. More like whining about transitioning, but I pulled some strings and got him hooked up with a decent prospect. Did he fuck up over there?"

"No," I said, reading the open case files upside down. "Have you placed anyone else in the same job?"

Deagan put down the sandwich, wiping his mouth on the back of his sleeve. "They just had the one opening. Did you come down here to ask for a favor for a recent release?"

"How'd you find that job for Lovretta?" I asked.

Deagan snorted. "Guess you don't like answering questions either, huh, cutie?"

"No, baby doll, I don't," I hissed.

Deagan cracked a wide smile. "Take it easy. I mean no harm." He held up his hands. "Anthony's just a screw-up. But he likes being outside. He didn't realize it until he got stuck in the joint with no windows. So I figured the best chance for him to stay on the straight and narrow was to get him a job in a place he'd like to be. The work's just demanding enough to keep him occupied and hopefully out of trouble. But since he crossed paths with the two of you, guess he found trouble anyway. Anything I should know?"

"Have you followed up with his boss?" Fennel asked. "Made sure he shows up to work?"

"Anthony brings me his time sheet every two weeks. As far as I know, he doesn't associate with criminals. He's making his rent, paying his utilities on time, just being a good boy."

"Have you done a home inspection?" Fennel noted the certificate of achievement hanging, crooked, on the wall.

"I've checked up on him to make sure he is where he says and that he's keeping his nose clean, but I'm not his momma. Man's gonna do what he's gonna do, no matter what I say." Deagan pointed at the plaque. "That's for doing my job. You got a problem with something?"

"My partner does, but we'll let that slide," Fennel said. "I just need a list of people who you've spoken to about Anthony Lovretta."

"Like his landlord?" Deagan asked, lumbering up from the chair and sliding open a drawer in the filing cabinet.

"Landlord, employer, other cops. Anyone." Fennel crossed his arms over his chest and waited.

Deagan grabbed a pen and legal pad off the top of the cabinet and, balancing the folder over the top of the open drawer, copied down a list of names. "Do you want the people I check in with or the people who check in with me?"

"Yes," Fennel said.

Deagan stopped writing, cocking his head to the side to look at us. "Yes to which?"

"Everything."

"Yeah, fine. I got no problem helping you out. You want the list of places he applied or got fired from before he found the one job that stuck?" Deagan asked.

"Yes, please," I said.

He turned and winked at me. "Sure thing, cutie pie." But this time, he said it as a joke, and since he was cooperating, I let him keep his teeth. He finished copying down the intel, giving us names, numbers, and addresses. "Anything else I can do for you?"

"Any violent offenders on your roll right now?" Fennel asked.

"More than I'd like," Deagan said. "Any one in particular you're interested in?"

"Any killers?" Fennel asked.

"No, but I got a couple attempted and a few rapists." Deagan made it sound like we were playing cards or placing an order. "Let me guess, you want to see the files."

Fennel and I exchanged a look. "Well, since we're here," Fennel said. We didn't bother reading the jackets unless the photo and physical description matched the shrouded image from the video feeds or my recollection of the man who escaped out Lovretta's window. "Did Lovretta affiliate with any of them?"

Deagan shook his head. "Nope, unless they crossed paths in the hall on their way to meet with me."

Even though Fennel and I browsed the files, none of the men fit the height, weight, and age of our unsub. And none of them even came close to resembling the possibly bogus sketch Lovretta provided. "How about safecrackers or cat burglars?" I asked.

The parole officer chuckled. "You realize it'd be easier if you told me why you want to know this information."

"We're fishing," Fennel said. "The wider we cast our net, the more likely we are to catch a whale."

"Well, I can say none of my parolees are that smart. I got a few kids who got pinched for smash and grabs and knocking over liquor stores, but that's the extent of it."

"All right," Fennel scanned the info Deagan had given us, "we've taken up enough of your time. In the event you think of someone else who might have shown an interest in Lovretta, let me know." He took a card out of his pocket and placed it down beside the sandwich.

"Yeah, I'll do that. And just so you know, in case you guys change your mind and want to violate some of my guys, no hard feelings. That'd just be a few less I gotta deal with." Deagan dropped back into his chair, stuck Fennel's card into a drawer, and reached for the sandwich.

When we got outside, Fennel handed me the notepad. "You okay, sweetie?"

"Don't even."

Fennel laughed, nudging me with his elbow. "At least he cooperated. Check out the name toward the bottom."

Anthony Lovretta applied for a job at Speedy Delivery four months ago. "Say all the bad things you want about Speedy Delivery, but at least they're smart enough not to hire a thief as a deliveryman. You ran their records and performed backgrounds on everyone at the company. Did you come across anyone fitting our unsub's description?" I asked.

"Possibly, but no one had a record." Fennel reached for his phone. "I'm guessing if our killer delivered the packages, like we originally thought, then he's an off-the-books, fill-in driver." After checking to see what kind of progress had been made on narrowing down the potentials from the assistant app, Fennel sighed. "The techs don't have anything yet. Like I said before, there are so many users. We're not going to find him this way."

"We could have some officers go down to Speedy and flash around Lovretta's photo and see if they remember him talking to anyone," I suggested.

"They barely cooperated with me. I'm guessing the only person who would even admit to remembering Lovretta would be the guy who interviewed him for the job."

"So what do you want to do?" I asked.

But before Fennel could share his brilliant strategy, my phone rang. I glanced down at the display and swallowed. It was Kincaid.

"Detective, how many times have I warned you to stay out of my business?" Axel asked, anger seething just beneath his otherwise calm tone. "I don't appreciate your meddling. And I'm only saying this once. Stay away from Marilyn Archibald."

"Mr. Kincaid," I said, catching Fennel's attention, "what exactly is the problem?"

"Don't start that Mr. Kincaid bullshit with me, Liv. I don't enjoy your attempts to handle me. If you want to handle me, I expect you to use your actual hands." He exhaled, regaining his composure. "Marilyn Archibald called and wanted to know what I said about her. How dare you? God, every time I turn around, you shove another knife in my back. Is this fun for you? Is this how you get your kicks? Is this how you repay me for my help?"

"I didn't say a thing about our meeting yesterday." Which was true enough. "And I will not defend my actions to you. I'm doing my job, Mr. Kincaid. I'm trying to stop a murderer. You should understand that. You claim to be a friend to law enforcement," the saccharine dripping from my words, "so help me out here."

He grumbled but didn't rescind his previous claim. "Why are you pestering Marilyn? What do you want now? Didn't I tell you to contact my attorney with the rest of your questions? I'm sure she told you the same."

I put the phone on mute. "Marilyn called Kincaid about us."

Fennel clucked his tongue at me and shook his head in mock disapproval. I unmute the conversation, but Axel still hadn't said anything.

"Yes, I'm very clear on your stance and Ms. Archibald's. However, whether you believe it or not, I am trying to stop a killer. And the only way to do that is by asking questions. Speaking of which, a few more have popped into my head." I waited, expecting Axel to tell me to fuck off or contact his attorney. Instead, he remained silent, so I soldiered on. "After you accepted delivery of the chandelier and candlesticks, did anyone from Ms. Archibald's company follow up to make sure the items were delivered?"

"They're candelabras," he corrected. But this time, it was my turn to wait him out. "Yes, someone called a few days later to make sure the items arrived undamaged."

"Do you remember anything about the caller? Did he or she identify himself?"

"He," Axel said. "I didn't get a name, and if I did, I don't remember it."

"Can we have a look at your phone records?"

Axel barked out a laugh. "Sure, just as soon as you get a court order, which you and I both know will never happen because you don't have cause. If you did, you wouldn't be asking. You'd be telling."

"You're right, which is why I need your help. I'm desperate." I knew ingratiating myself to him would make him more compliant, even if it was just giving him additional ammunition to fire against me. "This is a matter of life and death."

"It always is with you. Is that part of the cop training? I'd say it's something you picked up working homicide, a little poetic embellishment, but you haven't been a murder cop that long."

Ignoring his rant, I asked, "Have you seen Marilyn Archibald since her mother's passing?"

"I probably have. I don't recall. Explain to me your obsession with this topic. With her."

A part of me hoped Brad would take the phone and just ask if the two of them were sleeping together. After all, he's the one who wanted to know. I just wanted to know what the connection was and how any of this tracked back to a killer. I just wasn't sure how to explain that to Kincaid without jeopardizing our case.

"She might be in danger."

"I asked you that point blank last night," Axel said. "If this is another one of your manipulations, so help me."

"It's not. We don't know enough yet, but we have reason to believe it's a strong possibility. Your safety may also be in jeopardy."

"Yes, I do remember you mentioning that last night."

"I'm serious," I said.

Axel hesitated for a moment. "I have some things to check into. Should I need anything, Detective, I have your number. And I urge you to stay the hell away from Marilyn Archibald if you know what's good for you." He hung up before I could say another word.

"Arrgh." I shoved the phone back into my pocket, frustrated and infuriated.

"I told you she's sleeping with him," Fennel said, having decided this based on my side of the conversation and what little he could hear from Axel's end. "No man is ever that concerned about a woman's safety unless he's already staked his claim."

"Wow," I stared at my partner, "you and Deagan have more things in common than I thought."

"Liv, c'mon, I'm not being sexist. I'm telling you how Neanderthal men like Axel Kincaid think and behave."

I glared at him but kept my mouth shut. Speaking to Axel always made me itchy for a fight. Brad knew this. He'd been my handler during the undercover operation and had dealt with the brunt of my rage, but he stuck by me anyway.

"I also think Axel's threat and behavior work in our favor," Fennel said.

"How?"

"Kincaid fears for her safety, which means he might have some idea who poses a threat. Maybe with some cajoling and plenty of libations, you could get him to share his suspicions with us." Fennel waggled his eyebrows. "Or are you afraid to go back into the lion's den?"

"I'm not afraid. But Axel gave me whatever he's willing to disclose last night. I don't think he knows anything else. And if he does, he won't share." But what he said before he ended the call resonated within my bones. "Maybe he knows the killer-thief is working for her and is afraid we'll figure it out. His overprotectiveness might not be about her safety. It could be about her freedom."

"I don't know." Fennel thought for a moment. "If that's the case, wouldn't Axel call the mayor or someone and have us back off? He has those connections, and logic dictates Marilyn Archibald does too."

"I guess we'll see what happens. But Axel has some suspicions. He said he's going to check on some things. That can't be good. Assign some units to keep an eye on him. We might not be able to do much, but if we put him under surveillance, he might lead us to something valuable."

"Assuming of course he doesn't make the surveillance team." Fennel keyed the radio and placed the request. "And from past experience, Kincaid always makes the surveillance team, eventually."

"It's still worth a shot," I argued.

"Yeah, it is." Fennel scratched his head. "In the meantime, we need to get back to the office, run down this new intel, reinterview the previous victims, and see where this gets us."

"Was that what you were going to say before Axel called?" I asked.

"That and I want to take another stab at Lovretta. It's time we make him sweat."

TWENTY-ONE

"This is ridiculous." Fennel pushed away from his desk. "We're so close, I can taste it. Yet, it doesn't bring us any closer to identifying the killer."

Since returning to the precinct, we'd reinterviewed all the surviving victims, confronted Mr. Zedula about his deception to the point we even threw around words like obstruction of justice, but it didn't get us any closer to nailing the killer. After a lot of cajoling and threatening, Zedula finally gave up his mystery buyer – a dot com billionaire who wanted the tiara for his wife. That torpedoed our theory that the mystery buyer could be behind the theft. He lived too far away and had far too much money to risk it by doing something this stupid.

However, putting in hours of legwork hadn't been a total waste. We narrowed our killer's pattern. Each of the victims had been contacted about their purchases after the items were delivered, with one exception – Dieter Arnold. The musket had been delivered to his father's house, not his. Though, by the time it arrived, his father had already passed, so the delivery was redirected to Arnold's address. He received a call from Speedy Delivery about verifying the new address, and when a second call came in a week later, it had gone to his deceased father's cell phone. But by then, Arnold had the device and had been fielding whatever calls his father received, most of which had to do with lingering business. But it verified one of our theories. The killer didn't have access to the same information Speedy Delivery did. So our killer probably wasn't one of their regular employees. But he had more than likely delivered the musket to Arnold's house and later made the call based on the estate sale records. Only two copies of those records existed prior to our investigation. One belonged to the auction house, and the other went to Marilyn Archibald.

"Our killer has to be someone Marilyn Archibald employs," I said. "At this point, that's the only thing that makes any sense."

"I already placed a call in to a judge, but what we have is flimsy. Luckily, we have access to our victims' phone records. We just have to hope something pops. As soon as we can connect the calls to someone on Marilyn's payroll, we'll get what we need," Fennel said.

"Are we cross-referencing them with the calls Anthony Lovretta received?"

"Yep. The techs are on it. This is their top priority. I got us bumped up the list. But it's still going to take time," Fennel said. "Patrols are keeping watch over the six potential targets we've identified."

"Did they have anything useful to add?"

"Not really. When I reached out, only two of them even took this seriously. The rest thought it was a scam."

"Two's better than none," I said. "Is Kincaid one of them?"

Fennel snorted. "He didn't even answer the phone when we called."

"Have you checked with the surveillance team to see what he's up to?"

"As far as they know, he's at Spark. Whether that's true is probably another story."

"Like you said, Kincaid can take care of himself." And though a part of me would have loved to build an airtight case against Axel for drugs, grand theft auto, or prostitution, I still didn't want to see the man murdered.

Frankly, I didn't have time to deal with another homicide. And in his own twisted, demented way, he'd actually stuck his neck out for me twice. "Damn you, Axel," I mumbled.

"Huh?" Fennel asked.

I shook my head. "Nothing.

Brad pulled on his jacket. "I'll update Lt. Winston and meet you at the car."

"Okay." I massaged my temples and hoped Mr. Gildan would not be present while we spoke to Anthony Lovretta. I didn't want to deal with the sleazy attorney again.

Since the department stashed Lovretta at a motel with a few unis sitting on him, I figured he might be more relaxed and willing to cooperate without his lawyer present. After all, we held up our end of the bargain, even though every fiber in my body told me Lovretta hadn't held up his. But that didn't matter. The more convinced Lovretta was that we bought his cock and bull story, the easier it'd be to get him to slip up and give us something that was actually worth a damn. At least, that's what we were hoping.

Unlocking the car, I slid into the driver's seat and checked my messages while I waited. Emma had sent a text. She picked up an extra shift and thought she might crash at the hospital. Obviously, she didn't plan on coming home tonight.

Are you okay? I texted.

I watched the three dancing dots, indicating she was typing a reply, and then they vanished. A few seconds later, her response appeared. *I'm fine. Stop worrying. Just think, in a few more days, we won't have to coordinate our schedules or worry about overnight guests. No more awkward encounters in the kitchen because you won't be here.* And to make the words come off less bitchy, she followed them with a string of celebratory emojis, party hats, dancing women, noisemakers, and popping champagne bottles. If I wasn't a hardened cop, my feelings might have been hurt.

"Ready?" Fennel asked, sliding into the passenger seat.

I sent back a few party emojis of my own and tucked my phone into the cupholder. "Yeah." A few seconds later, my phone beeped with an incoming text. "Can you grab that for me?"

Brad picked up my phone. "Emma says your dad dropped off more boxes and she put them in your room. They ought to be enough to pack up the rest of your stuff."

"Tell her thanks and put my phone on silent."

Fennel typed out the message, hit send, and stared at the screen for a few seconds before turning off the sound. "Damn, even though she's trying to hide it, I don't think I've ever seen Emma this upset, and I can think of at least two instances where my balls retracted in fear because she had turned that anger on me."

"I can't believe she's still pissed at me about what happened with the pervey guy in our kitchen."

"It's not about that, Liv. I know you don't want to hear this, but Emma doesn't want you to move out."

"Yes, she does. She's overjoyed. Did you see the emojis?"

"That's bullshit, and you know it."

"Emma doesn't need a roommate. After college, I asked her if she wanted to get a place together and she said no. She wanted to stand on her own two feet. She has a good job and works hard. She never wanted a roommate. She ended up stuck with me due to circumstances, and now that I'm trying to rectify the situation, she's," I held up my hands in exasperation, "doing whatever it is she's doing."

"Just because she doesn't need a roommate that doesn't mean she doesn't want one. And we're not talking about just any roommate. We're talking about you, Liv. You're her family. How old was she when she came to live with you and your parents?"

"Sixteen." I blew out a breath and resisted the urge to honk at the row of cars standing still in front of us. "I don't remember whose idea it was for her to come live with us. I just know that it was the first time Emma and I both had someone to watch our backs."

"And you've been like sisters ever since," Fennel said, making my life sound like a Lifetime movie.

"Please," I rolled my eyes, "you know Emma. She's not made of sugar and spice."

"For the record, DeMarco, neither are you."

I stuck my tongue out at him. "The point is she wants me out of her apartment. She only let me move in when I worked long-term undercover because I was never around. Now I'm around all the time, interfering with her kinky one night stands. But she wants me to feel terrible about everything. Leaving. Not leaving. I don't know what she wants."

"She's acting out because people she's loved have always left her. Her mom died, and her dad was killed while trying to score. She doesn't want someone else to leave her."

"I've always stuck by her. She should realize I'm not abandoning her. My parents haven't abandoned her. Hell, you've been to enough of my family dinners to have witnessed firsthand how much my mom fawns over her. If my mom could magically make Emma her biological daughter, she'd do it in a heartbeat."

"Now who's bitching?" Fennel teased.

"I'm not. I just wish she'd tell me what she's feeling instead of acting like a rebellious teenager. I am not her mother or, for that matter, my mother." I cringed. "God, isn't that a scary thought? Promise me, if I turn into my mother, you'll put one in my head."

"I thought we weren't putting things like that out into the universe," Fennel reminded me before sliding down in the seat, pressing his fingertips together, and murmuring, "I see you don't want to be like your mother. And you don't want Emma to think that you're her mother," using his best Sigmund Freud impression. "So what I'm hearing is you're afraid Emma's going to do something reckless and get hurt. And you don't want to be responsible for it. So you're pulling back and giving her space to do what she wants in the hopes that she'll make better choices, decisions you approve of, just like a mother." He stifled a snicker and stuck with the German accent. "But the more space you give her, the more rebellious she's acting. Just like any child with her mother."

"I hate you."

Fennel laughed and straightened in the seat and picked up my phone. He tapped on the screen a few times.

"What are you doing?" I asked, distracted by the snail's

pace at which we were now moving along the freeway.

"I'm telling Emma you love her and you'll get your crap out of her place this weekend, but that doesn't mean you're leaving her."

"Not a Lifetime movie, Fennel."

But he sent it anyway. A moment later, the screen lit up, and Brad laughed. "She told me to give you back your phone and to stop sticking my nose where it doesn't belong or she'd remove it and reattach it somewhere else. She also said I better clear my schedule this weekend because someone has to do the heavy lifting and it sure as hell won't be either of you."

I smiled. "Thanks."

"For what?" Brad asked. "I never agreed to move your stuff."

"But you will," I said. "And you gave Emma and me a common enemy."

"Well, if there's one thing I've learned from my time on this planet, women live by a code. Chicks before dicks."

"I thought it was hos before bros."

"Yeah, but you carry a gun. I'd be insane to call you a ho."

"Smart man." I winked at him. "Maybe you should consider taking your own advice."

"How's that?"

"If you leave homicide, I won't take it personally. I know you're not abandoning me. Transferring was my idea, and when I put in for it, I told you I wasn't leaving you. That didn't mean you had to come with me."

"Damn, you're still trying to get rid of me. That's not happening. You ought to realize by now you're stuck with me, DeMarco."

"But you hate homicide."

"I hate murders. I hate the gruesome scenes and seeing the victims. I hate making notifications. God, I really hate that. But guess what, we're cops. We've always had to deal with this. You can't deny that."

"I guess not, but..."

"You worry about me. I get it. And I know I've given you a few reasons to worry, but I'm okay, Liv. And when I'm not, you'll be the first to know." He smiled. "Honestly, I'm worried about you. The way we cope with the shit we see is to get drunk or laid, most of the time both. How are you coping? Do you and Jake have something going on?"

"No."

"You sure? Matching coffee cups could give a guy the wrong idea."

"Jake picked up breakfast. He's got this food obsession I don't quite understand, but he said he wanted to try that new farm-to-table joint. I guess he figured he'd be nice and get me something too."

"No wonder you're hoping I'll gracefully bow out. You think Voletek supplies better snacks than I do."

I laughed. "Yes, that's exactly it." Finally, I spotted the motel sign and put on my turn signal. At least we made it in under a half hour, though I had no idea how, given the traffic. "By the way, how come you never mentioned softball? Since when do we keep secrets from one another?"

"It's not a secret. I just don't want you at the games."

"Why not?"

"No, Liv. Just no." He shook his head several times emphatically.

"Fine," I grumbled, parking two spots away from the other unmarked cruiser. The place was practically deserted. I climbed out of the car and looked around. "Did Winston have this place shut down?"

"I don't know, but at least Lovretta can't complain about the noise." Fennel took off his sunglasses and hung them from his collar. "He should be in suite 304. Winston said we have guys on standby across the hall in 303."

"Looks like we're pulling out all the stops for this lying sack of shit." We took the stairs up, and I peered over the railing as we passed the second floor and headed to the top level. "We better get something useful out of him today."

On the third floor, Fennel suddenly stopped. He held up his closed fist, and I halted, taking one step back and to the side while I unholstered my weapon. He already had his gun in hand. Something was wrong. I just didn't know what it was. He signaled, and I put a hand on his shoulder.

We moved slowly, halfway down the hall. I kept my eyes peeled for anyone on the right. Fennel focused on the left. In the middle of the hallway, we stopped. Doors 304 and 303 were both slightly ajar and directly across from one another. That's what Brad had noticed.

He pointed down at a red smear. The doorframe to 304 was splintered. Did the protection detail bust in? I tapped Brad on the shoulder, and we split up. I went into 303. He went into 304.

TWENTY-TWO

My heart stopped. Every part of me wanted to immediately run to the downed officers and check on them, but that wasn't smart. I had to be smart. I kicked open the bathroom door, spinning and pointing my Glock behind the door before approaching the shower and shoving the curtain aside. Bathroom's clear.

Moving on, I peered into the bedroom but didn't waste time checking it. It looked clear enough, and the men bleeding didn't have time for me to be thorough. Continuing into the living room, I kept my head on a swivel and crouched down beside Officer Jenkins and felt for a pulse. Nothing. Wait. It might just be weak. I crouched down closer, feeling shallow gasps against my cheek. Grabbing the radio off the table, I pressed the button.

"Officer needs assistance. Request immediate backup to this location. We have two officers down. I repeat two officers down."

"Units are on the way."

"Be informed, two plainclothes detectives are on scene. Possible active shooter still in the area." I checked the other officer's wounds. Like Jenkins, Kearney had been shot twice in the chest. But he coughed and sputtered as he started to come to. "Hey," I said, grabbing the stack of paper napkins off the table and pressing them into his hand before pushing his hand against the blood soaking through his shirt, "wake up, Kearney."

He blinked, gasping and moaning. "Shit."

"I know it hurts."

He looked at Jenkins. "Ron?" He tried to move, but I held him still.

"I don't know. But you'll be okay. Help is on the way. Keep pressure on this. You got your gun?"

Kearney managed to pull it free from his holster while keeping pressure on the bullet wound. At least he and Jenkins had vests, but it didn't appear they'd done much good. "I didn't see him coming. It was just one guy, but he moved so fast. Black clothes. Face mask."

"That's okay. Backup's a few minutes out. Ambulances are rolling. We'll get you two out of here." I put the radio down beside him. "Tell dispatch what's going on. And if an unfriendly comes through that door, blow a hole through him. Got it?"

"Yes, ma'am."

Dashing across the hallway, I pressed my back against the wall, took a deep breath, and spun with my Glock leveled in front of me. This suite was the mirror image of the one I just left. A quick glance into the bathroom assured me Fennel had already cleared the bathroom, so I kept moving down the narrow opening until the suite branched into the bedroom and living room.

On one side stood the doorway that led into the bedroom. From here, I could make out the bed, unmade and messy. But most of the room was blocked from view. I took a step closer, but movement in the living room caught my eye before I could explore the bedroom.

I could barely comprehend the gruesome scene before me. From what I could tell, Anthony Lovretta had been shot. His body slumped forward while blood dripped down the sides of the table and onto the floor. My partner stood beside him at an odd angle. Not fully standing, but in an odd crouch, like he was stuck.

I burst into the living room to assist. Suspects weren't supposed to die in police custody, particularly from a gunshot wound. Fennel looked up, his expression sending chills through me.

"Liv, get out of here. Go," Fennel ordered urgently. He tried to straighten, and that's when I realized my partner had his fingers pressed into the bullet wound, literally applying pressure to Lovretta's severed artery. If he moved, Lovretta would die.

Before I could react, a bullet flew past us, and Fennel ducked. The muffled sound nothing more than a soft pop. I turned, aiming, but it was too late. A man, covered head-to-toe in dark clothing stood just feet away from my partner. He wore a solid white mask over his face.

He leveled his gun at Brad's head. From this distance, he wouldn't miss.

"Drop the gun," I said.

"No." The killer kept his unwavering aim on Fennel. "I thought you told me your partner was waiting outside. You shouldn't lie to me, Detective Fennel. That's one of the rules. Didn't I make that clear?" The mask muffled his voice into an unrecognizable growl.

"Liv, get out of here," Brad begged.

But I didn't budge. I kept my gun trained on the killer. "What are the rules?" I asked, stepping closer. Even though one of Brad's hands was occupied, I didn't understand why he didn't have his gun aimed with the other, and that's when I realized my partner was handcuffed to the table. I didn't understand how that happened or even what was happening.

My phone beeped an alert, probably as a result of the imminent police response. Officers and paramedics were on the way. Until they arrived, we were on our own. So I just had to buy time.

"Toss your gun away. Your phone too. Then we'll talk," the masked man said. Even if he didn't have a gun pointed at my partner's head, I'd recognize that build and outfit anywhere. This was our killer-thief.

"Shoot him," Brad hissed.

"She won't," the killer said. "She knows if she pulls that trigger, she'll kill you. Just look at her face. She doesn't want that. Do you, sweetheart?" He held the silenced weapon steady, his finger poised on the trigger. "Toss your gun or this conversation becomes moot. I'm a lot faster than you are. Your partner can attest to that."

So I tossed my gun and kicked it toward him. "What do you want?" I placed my phone on the edge of the table and held up my palms.

"A lot of things. But right now, I want to know what's waiting on the other side of that door. By now, you must have called for backup. That's the notification you just received, isn't it? How many units did you request?"

"Just ambulances for the officers you shot," I said.

"What did I say about lying?" He took a step closer to Brad, but I moved into his path.

"Liv, don't." Fennel jerked against the table, making the handcuff rattle and causing Lovretta to let out a pained shriek.

"I'm not lying. But an officer down call usually results in additional units. So tell me what you need to escape. Tell me what you want," I repeated, staring into the killer's eyes. No matter what, I wouldn't let him kill Brad. Right now, that's all that mattered.

"What I want?" The killer laughed. "I want everything."

"The only way you get everything is to get out of this fucking room. I can get you out of here, but only if you let us live."

"How?"

"I'm magic," I said. "I'll walk you out of here. You get to the exit and vanish, just like that. We won't follow you. You have my word." I stepped directly in front of his gun. "But you have to put down the weapon."

"How stupid do you think I am?" the killer asked. "I don't have shit for brains like this one." He jerked his chin at Fennel. "You clear the room first before you help the victim. That's how that works. Didn't you learn anything, Fennel? And you definitely don't let some asshole get the drop on you. You're lucky I thought I needed you, or else I would have shot you in the head. But apparently, I was wrong. I don't need you since Liv's going to escort me out."

"You touch him and the deal's off," I said.

"Oh, I'm not gonna touch him. I'm gonna shoot him."

"That'll be the last thing you ever do," I warned.

"Liv," Fennel grunted, "end this." Based on Lovretta's wound, Fennel didn't have time to properly clear the room. The killer had left him with an impossible choice. Had Brad checked every nook and cranny, Lovretta would have exsanguinated. And the longer this standoff took, the more likely that was to happen and the more likely it'd be that our killer would realize there was no reason not to add another two victims to his growing list and waltz out the front door before help arrived.

"They're outside. But I can walk you past them," I lied. "If we encounter problems, you can use me as a hostage. But we need to go now."

"No, take me," Fennel said. "I'm taller. Broader. I'd be a better human shield. Leave her. She's useless."

"I'm easier to control," I said. "I'm less likely to overpower you."

Fennel cursed at me, but I ignored it. If I'd gone left instead of right, I'd be the one cuffed to the table instead of him.

Thudding footsteps made the floor vibrate. Backup had arrived. We were out of time.

"It's now or never," I said. "If you want out, I'll get you out."

"Do what I say." The killer took a step closer, grabbed my arm, and twisted it behind my back before pressing his gun into my ribs. "We're gonna walk to the door, nice and slow. You call out, you'll be dead before you hit the ground. And I'll turn and shoot your partner in the head. You know I'm a good shot. You've already seen my handiwork. Now move."

For a good shot, I wondered why he made such a mess of Lovretta and the two officers across the hallway. And then I realized he left the mess on purpose. He staged it like that, just so we'd see it. But he didn't expect us to show up in the middle of his killing spree. And since the motel only had one way in and out, he was stuck. We finally caught the bastard, except we were unprepared.

"Just relax. Stay calm. No one else needs to die right now," I said.

As we approached the open door, we heard radio calls and heavy footsteps on the stairs. The cavalry arrived, but I no longer felt relief. Instead, all I felt was dread.

"Tell them to stay back," he ordered as officers emerged at the top of the steps, and he ducked back behind the splintered doorframe.

"Stay back," I bellowed, noticing Officer Kearney across the hall. He hadn't lowered the weapon, and I wondered if he had a bead on our suspect. "This is Detective DeMarco. We have a situation here."

"I can see that, DeMarco," the senior officer replied. He halted his men, but the unit held their position.

Across the hallway, Kearney keyed the radio and switched channels to update them. I held my breath, praying the killer didn't notice he'd left the officers across the hall alive. But the killer was too busy assessing the rest of the floor to notice. He searched for another way out, but the hallway came to an abrupt dead end. There was no escape. Idly, I wondered if that's how they coined the term dead end.

"Either you hold up your end of the deal, or I'll kill your partner. You decide." The killer pressed against the wall, protected from the armed officers in the hallway. Even though my colleagues were only a few feet away, I was alone. It was just the shooter and me.

"I have to speak to them. Out there." I waited for him to let go of my arm before I took a step forward.

But he pressed the gun to the back of my head, and I bit my lip. I didn't want to die. The fear and adrenaline coursed through my veins, and I tried to recall my training. Fennel was only feet away. I needed to control the situation. We'd find a way out of this. We had to.

I took a small step forward and then another. The killer didn't follow, but I could still feel the bull's eye on the back of my head. Stepping into the hallway with my hands slightly raised, I pivoted until I faced the tactical team. They had their weapons aimed at me, but I could hear the request for non-lethal force. They had a plan. That was good. Plans were good.

"I need you to pull your men back." I blinked, hoping to

communicate with my eyes. "Officers need your help, but you gotta let me get this guy out of here first."

"DeMarco, we can't do that," the sergeant said.

"You have to. Three men are bleeding out. We don't have time. We don't have any other options, gentlemen." I moved another step further down the hall, away from the door, hoping to get the killer to step out.

"Get back here," the killer growled. When I didn't move fast enough, he fired a shot into the suite.

"Okay." I raised my hands a little higher. "Brad, you okay?" I called.

"Yeah," came back my partner's anguished response.

"We're cool, see," I said to the tactical team as I moved back into the room.

"Don't try that shit again," the killer warned. He pressed the muzzle of the gun into my neck, and I winced as the hot metal burned my skin. "They have five seconds to back down or I start shooting. Five. Four."

"Commander, I need those stairs cleared now," I shouted, unsure if they would listen. But we were out of time.

TWENTY-THREE

Hand-to-hand combat training was mandatory, but I'd watched enough security footage to have a general idea of how this guy moved. Close quarters fighting, particularly when he had a silenced weapon trained on me, wouldn't end well. I'd need to get him to drop the gun and hope the responding units spent their downtime at the range. Needless to say, I didn't care for those odds.

"We're coming out. Hold your fire. I repeat. Hold your fire." I stepped into the hallway again. The killer yanked on my belt with his free hand to hold me flush against him. He knew I wouldn't try to overpower him. I didn't have the time. Officers Jenkins and Kearney needed emergency medical interventions now. Any attempt to subdue the offender would delay the necessary help they needed. Plus, Lovretta would be dead in minutes, if he wasn't already.

My thoughts went to Brad. I didn't know how this asshole got the jump on my partner, but there'd be time to deal with that later, I hoped.

"Don't try anything, or I'll kill her," the masked man said. He urged me forward, even though the officers hadn't moved. "Get against the far wall, single file."

"Do it," I said, watching the team leader hesitate. "Two

officers need assistance in 303 and my partner needs help in 304. They do not have time for games. The sooner we clear out, the sooner paramedics move in. You got me?"

"Yes, ma'am." He signaled, and his men took up a position against the right side of the hallway.

The killer hugged the left, keeping me between him and the other cops, whose guns remained trained on us. We moved at a crawl. The killer expected them to open fire at any moment. But it wasn't a regular tactical unit. Based on their uniforms and weapons, they had to be patrol. Their gear had probably come from their trunks. They weren't prepared for this. They simply responded to my radio call. ESU would have taken the shot. But these were street cops.

A bullet whizzed past and struck the wall just above the killer's head. The discharge in the enclosed space echoed and boomed, causing the four officers against the wall to tense. The shot didn't come from any of them. It came from Kearney.

"Hold your fire," I breathed, feeling the killer's muscles tense as he released the grip on my belt and wrapped his arm around my neck, holding me in front of him as he crouched behind me. "Kearney, hold your fire."

I didn't get a response. I tried to glance back, but I couldn't see into the room. Something told me that shot hadn't been intentional. Kearney might have blacked out or convulsed.

"Get me out of here," the killer snarled. "Now."

"Take it easy," I said. "Everyone keep cool." More sirens sounded in the distance. This was taking too long. I focused on the cops across the hall. "Our guys need your help. Give it to them."

The lead officer nodded, making a show of placing his finger back on the trigger guard. The other three followed suit.

"Nobody move," the masked man said. "Not until we're clear."

"Let them help the officers you shot," I said. "They'll get out of our way, and we'll get out of theirs."

The killer didn't move while he thought about my suggestion. "Fine. Get into room 303 and close the door. If

I see any of you, she's dead."

The lead officer met my eyes. "You're gonna be okay, DeMarco."

"I'm not worried about me. I'm worried about them. Now go."

Slowly, they edged along the wall, toward the door. As soon as it closed, the killer dragged me at nearly a sprint down the stairs. We rounded the corner, and he shoved me in front of him, slamming my side into a doorknob as we turned. I hissed in pain, and for a second, I thought I caught movement above us. But I didn't dare slow or look. I knew procedure. Cops didn't let killers walk, regardless of potential hostage situations. They'd be on our heels in seconds. We had to keep moving until I could find a way to take control of the situation. The less potential casualties in sight, the better my chances of overtaking and subduing this asshole.

We made it to the ground floor just as another squad car turned into the parking lot. "Just keep cool," I said. "You have plenty of time to get out of this. No one else needs to get hurt."

He laughed. "You actually think I'm going to let any of you live?"

"What does that mean?"

But he didn't answer. Instead, he shoved me down the narrow walkway that led from the parking lot to the other side of the motel, what the booking websites referred to as the courtyard rooms. We kept moving, him pushing or dragging me along the way. But the one thing he didn't do was run.

"Why aren't you in more of a hurry?" I asked when he suddenly stopped beneath the staircase at the other end of the courtyard. We were hidden here, and I wondered if he planned on shooting my fellow officers when they pursued.

"You'll see soon enough." I tried to turn, and he fired a shot so close to my temple, that despite the silencer I went deaf in one ear. "Cuff yourself to the railing. Make them tight."

"Is this what you did to Fennel?"

He must have realized I intended to try something, so

he spun me to face him, held the muzzle of the gun against my forehead, and stared into my eyes. "Don't test my patience."

Slowly, I slipped the handcuffs off my belt and tightened one around my wrist. The tension was thick. He wanted to kill me. I could see it in his eyes. It was just like Lovretta described, which made me think maybe the jerk had actually told us the truth. "How'd you hook up with Lovretta?"

He didn't answer. Even at this distance, I could hear the squawks of radio calls being made. Emergency Services must be on the way. I couldn't see if ambulances had arrived or if the rooms had been cleared. But they'd fan out and start searching.

"You're a skilled thief. Why kill?" I asked.

He forced me against the open slats at the underside of the steps, grabbing the dangling bracelet and hooking it around the post. He tugged to make sure it was secure and tightened the one on my wrist to a point of pain. The clicking of the handcuffs made my stomach clench.

"How'd you know to do that? Did you used to be a cop or something?"

He hit me hard. I didn't even see it coming, but I found myself on my knees, stars exploding in front of my eyes. I tried to get to my feet, but he kicked me with enough force to spin me around and knock my cheek against one of the metal rungs. The only thing keeping me from collapsing onto the ground was my chained wrist.

"Now for the grand finale." He reached into his pocket and pulled out another burner phone. "Hey," he kicked me, "pay attention. You don't want to miss the fireworks."

"What?"

He pressed send, grabbed my head, and forced me to look across the courtyard. The only thing I could see from here was the reflection of the flashing lights in the walkway. Then he jerked my head to the side, and I thought he was going to snap my neck. It'd be a different MO to add to the murder board. Hopefully, Fennel would find that piece of information useful. But suddenly the killer's hands were gone, and then the third floor exploded in a ball of flame.

"Brad," I screamed, watching in horror as the blown out panes of glass showered down on the sidewalk and the flames leapt out the window, followed by dark billowy smoke. "No."

The rage gave me the strength to turn and rise, but the masked man was gone. "I'm going to kill you, you fucking asshole. Do you hear me? You're dead. You're fucking dead."

Scrambling, I searched my pockets for my handcuff key. Finding it, I hurried to unlock the cuffs, my hands trembling. I couldn't stop the shakes. Oh god, Brad.

More sirens sounded. Ambulances and fire trucks. It was too soon for them to have gotten the call about the explosion. They must have been responding to the original call. How many were dead? Kearney? Jenkins? The four responding officers? Lovretta? My partner?

Finally forcing the key into the lock, I turned it and pulled my wrist free just as an actual tactical team with shields moved in formation through the opening and into the courtyard. I tried to stand, but my legs were weak. Tugging on the rungs of the steps, I pulled myself up, catching a glimpse of someone skittering around the edge, ignoring the warnings and orders of the tactical unit.

"DeMarco?" Fennel's voice cut through the radio squawks and barked orders. "DeMarco?" he yelled.

"Here." I slid out from beneath the staircase, emerging into the light. Every gun pointed at me. I held up my hands. "I don't know where he went, but he couldn't have gone far. He was just here. Sweep the area. He's still armed and extremely dangerous." I gulped, looking up at the burning building. "I don't know what other surprises he might have in store."

"Fan out. Check everywhere. Move in teams. Be mindful of tripwires." ESU broke into three teams of two and moved around the building, knocking on doors and checking rooms as they went.

Fennel ran toward me. Blood soaked his white dress shirt and covered his hands and arms up to his elbows. "What were you thinking?"

"Did they make it out?" I asked, fighting to hold back the sudden emotional onslaught. "Kearney, Jenkins, the responding officers, were they..." I gasped. "Did they make it out?" I was on the verge of hyperventilating, but the adrenaline and anger made me want to run in all directions at once to chase down the asshole responsible. How could I let him get away again? "Lovretta?"

"Patrol got Kearney and Jenkins out in time. EMTs were with Lovretta when it blew." And that's when I noticed the burns on the back of Fennel's arm and neck. "What the fuck's wrong with you?" he suddenly snapped. "Don't you ever do anything that stupid again. Do you hear me?" His eyes were wet, and he spun in a circle, putting his hands on top of his head. "Why didn't you shoot him? I told you to shoot him."

"He would have killed you. He would have jerked and pulled the trigger, and you'd be dead."

"You don't know that."

"I fucking do," I said, shaking so hard I had to grab the rail for support. "And so do you." I turned and stared off to the side. The building had been cleared. ESU was now scouring the other side of the parking lot, but the killer was gone. He disappeared the moment he let go of my head. We wouldn't find him, but I knew he wasn't finished. This wasn't the grand finale. It was the beginning of the end. "He's gone. But he'll be back. He should have snapped my neck. I don't know why he didn't. I don't know why he didn't kill me. He planned to kill you. All of you. We showed up too soon. He didn't expect that. It's the only reason any of us are alive."

Brad grabbed me in his arms, burying his face in my hair and squeezing hard. We trembled, damp, sweaty, exhausted, and too hyped up to remain still.

"Liv, look at me," Brad begged. "I'm sorry. This isn't your fault. We'll get him. I promise we're gonna get him." He gulped down some air, pressing his forehead to mine before letting go.

"Area's clear," someone from tactical said. "Offender's in the wind."

"Yeah." The words caused physical pain, and I winced.

So did Brad.

My partner pointed to the gash on my cheek from where the asshole hit me. "Are you okay?" His focus kept shifting between what was happening in the periphery and our conversation. Obviously, I wasn't the only one hyped up on adrenaline. He grasped my face in his hands, quickly assessing my head and neck for any injuries. I had a nice welt forming on the back of my head and the gash on my cheek. But those were inconsequential. No matter how hard I tried, I couldn't stop trembling. It was the adrenaline surge and the shock of what just happened.

"We need a casualty report," I said, pushing away. "We need to find out if anyone else was on the third floor." I blinked. "Do you have any idea where the bomb was?"

"Beneath Lovretta's chair," Fennel said.

"You knew?" I stared at him.

"That's why I let him get the jump on me. I needed to buy time to try to defuse it."

"Are you out of your mind?"

"Glass houses, Liv."

"Don't." I stared across the courtyard, watching the flames decrease as the firefighters continued to battle the blaze. "We need a casualty report." I marched toward the opening, turning when Brad didn't follow. Another member of ESU had stopped him, and I shuddered, seeing the blood and burns on him. *He could have died*, the voice in my head said, *and you could have too.*

A strong wave of nausea bubbled inside of me, and I ran to the edge of the property and wretched until my body couldn't take it anymore. Fennel crouched next to me, a little green, but managed not to heave. He stroked my back and made sure my hair didn't fall in front of my face. He didn't say anything for a long time. Finally, he spoke.

"Thank you."

I wiped my mouth, watching as more and more units arrived. "For what?"

"Saving my life. I'd be dead without you."

"But you said..."

"I know what I said." He stared out at the mess before us. "You put yourself in his crosshairs to save me. And it absolutely terrified me. But thank you."

I noticed his hand was shaking and reached for it. "We're okay."

"Yeah. Come on, let's get cleaned up. We got a shitstorm to deal with."

TWENTY-FOUR

I sat atop one of the tables in the briefing room, my feet in the seat in front of me. My leg hadn't stopped jittering, but I sipped my coffee slowly, hoping no one would notice. Fennel rested his hips against the table beside me, one hand drumming a beat while he repeatedly flexed his fingers on the other.

Unlike the rest of the department, I knew the tremor was a remnant of his time in Afghanistan. A little something he brought home from the war. But today he'd been thrust onto another battlefield. We'd gotten lucky with only one fatality so far – Anthony Lovretta. The EMTs who'd been working on him heard the bomb beep when it went live, and Brad had almost gotten them clear by the time things went boom. They'd sustained some nasty burns but nothing life-threatening. The same couldn't be said for Officers Jenkins and Kearney.

"Any news?" I asked, holding the cup between my knees when another member of our growing task force entered the room.

"Last I heard, Kearney and Jenkins are still in surgery. The docs have to remove the bullets and clean out the damage," Lisco, another female homicide detective, said.

"Their chances would have been worse if you and Fennel hadn't arrived when you did."

"I wish we'd gotten there sooner," Fennel said.

"Any idea where the rest of Lovretta's protection detail were when this went down?" I asked.

"From what I heard, they went on a dinner run. Supposedly, Kearney and Jenkins told them it was okay to take off and stretch their legs, but until the brass verifies their story, it's anyone's guess what actually happened. But no one wanted to sit around watching over that two-bit thief." She let out a sarcastic huff. "Now they won't be able to sit for a week with the ass-chewing they received."

"They both didn't need to get dinner. One of them should have stayed in the suite," Fennel said, "but I can see why someone would need a break from Lovretta." Fennel stared at the floor. "Despite that, the dude didn't need to die."

I pushed my thigh harder against his in support. "It might have been worse if they stayed. We might have three cops in surgery."

"Yeah. Who knows?" Lisco said. "All I know is a lot more people would have been hurt if it wasn't for the two of you. And in case no one's said it yet, I'm glad you guys are part of this unit." She studied the burns on Fennel's exposed skin and the bandaged gash on my cheek. "Did you have medical check you out? Winston's a stickler about stuff like that."

"We're fine," Fennel said before I could answer.

"Hell of a thing," she said, taking a seat at a table near the front.

I'd written my statement and recounted the event a dozen times, but we didn't know much. Motel cameras caught the killer on the courtyard side of the motel. He disappeared down the narrow walkway and reemerged on the parking lot side. The parking lot camera spotted him briefly climbing the drainpipe that ran parallel to the stairs. He never appeared on the cameras the protection detail monitored until he swung in, feet first, through the opening, landing in a crouch in the third floor hallway. From there, he hugged the walls, moving beneath the cameras and remaining out of sight. By the time Kearney and Jenkins realized what was happening, it was too late.

"Why did he climb the drainpipe?" I asked, tapping on the rim of my cup.

"I don't know." Fennel sounded tired.

We'd barely said two words to one another since we left the scene. He didn't want to talk about it, and neither did I. But we didn't have a choice. A building exploded. A cooperating witness was killed in protective custody, and we knew of six more potential targets. This wasn't over yet.

Lt. Winston entered the briefing room, followed by a few stragglers. He pointed at Fennel. "All right. We're all here. Tell us how this happened. What do we need to know moving forward?"

Everyone turned around to stare at us. I hunkered down, resting my forearms on my thighs, finding the contents of my nearly empty cup fascinating. Fennel blew out a breath.

"Our killer, alias Wild Bill, arrived at the motel at approximately 18:15. Minutes after team one went to get dinner. Sticking with his MO, he found the most complicated method of gaining access," Fennel said.

Winston picked up a remote from the podium and clicked the button. Surveillance footage caught the masked man for a few fleeting seconds before disappearing. Winston rewound the footage and paused it on a still of the killer poised in a crouch. The solid white mask standing out in stark contrast to his dark clothes.

"Preliminary reports from both the bomb squad and fire department indicate several bricks of military grade explosive. He didn't fashion it from items he found at the scene. He brought it with him." Fennel pointed to a bulge beneath the killer's jacket. "It doesn't look like much, but it blew out a six room block. Three on both sides of the hall." Fennel tucked his trembling hand into his pocket. "I got a glimpse of the device. He taped it beneath Anthony Lovretta's chair. It appears Wild Bill intended to booby-trap the body by setting a bomb with a pressure plate detonator."

"So we find Lovretta. We move him off the chair, and

everyone goes boom." Winston licked the outer corner of his bottom lip. "Sadistic piece of shit."

"Yeah," Fennel said, "except DeMarco and I showed up unannounced and interrupted his staging."

Winston rubbed his forehead and glared at me. "And you let him escape again."

I kept my eyes on the cup in my hands, even though the angry and incredulous looks burned into the top of my head.

"Upon arriving, we found the doors to both rooms ajar. I told DeMarco to check on the backup team. I went into 304. The first thing I saw was Anthony Lovretta bleeding out at the table. After performing a brief sweep, I didn't spot anyone else in the room. I don't know where the killer was hiding, but he got the jump on me while I attempted to provide aid to Lovretta."

"Is that when you spotted the bomb?" Lisco asked. She'd been taking notes from her spot near the front. Lifting my eyes just enough to see her, I couldn't help but think she'd missed her calling to be a news reporter.

"Yes." Fennel sucked in a shaky breath. "The problem I'm having is how Wild Bill knew when and where to strike. No one was supposed to know where we stashed Lovretta. So how did he find that out?"

The lieutenant studied each of the faces in the room as he said, "Maybe we have a leak. Anyone get drunk last night? Run their mouths at a bar? Go home and tell their wife or husband what they did at work yesterday? Come on, let's hear it, people. Who blabbed?"

No one made a peep.

Winston strode down the aisle toward the back of the room. Toward us. "I know I didn't say anything about hiding a witness." He stopped diagonally in front of Brad. "Did you say something, Fennel?"

"No, sir."

"How 'bout you, DeMarco?"

"No, lieutenant." We didn't even know where Lovretta had been placed until we decided to pay him a visit today.

"Detective Lisco," he barked, "I'll need you to make a list of everyone who knew where we were keeping Anthony

Lovretta. And I mean everybody. Judges, lawyers, the pizza delivery guy."

"On it," she said, furiously scribbling a note on her pad.

"You spent the most time with this guy, DeMarco. What can you tell us?" Winston asked.

"Not much. He stays covered. Gloves. Hoods. Aside from his build, the only physical characteristics we have to go on is the description Lovretta gave us."

"And you didn't get anything else besides that?" Winston asked. "You stood toe-to-toe with this guy and negotiated a hostage exchange, you for your partner, and you can't tell me anything else?"

"He has dead eyes. Empty. Like his soul."

Winston chuckled. "Does he also like long walks on the beach and cuddling by a fire? This isn't a dating app, DeMarco."

Looking up from the dregs of coffee in my cup, I twisted my neck to the side to look at the lieutenant, wincing at the sudden sharp pain. "He's a good shot. He doesn't waste lead. He took the time to clean up his brass after shooting Kearney and Jenkins, so he wasn't afraid of running out of time or getting caught. He has an ego. He knows he's good and pointed out every mistake we made along the way." I drained the rest of the coffee, ignoring the bitterness of the leftover grounds. "I think he used to be a cop."

"Is that why you let him escape twice?" Winston asked.

I wasn't accustomed to being raked over the coals in front of my entire unit, but I held my tongue. Even if I deserved it, Winston had no right to do that. But now wasn't the time to argue with a superior.

"She didn't let him escape," Fennel said, his voice a low growl.

Winston returned to the podium at the front of the room. "All right, listen up. We still don't know who this guy is or what he looks like. Until we have proof to the contrary, we should assume Anthony Lovretta's statement is rock solid. It's probably why the killer permanently silenced him. We'll run that description on the eleven o'clock news. The hotline will be manned twenty-four seven. No one shoots two cops and gets away with it. In the meantime, let's find this leak and get it patched. This is our priority now. Whatever other cases you're working on, they take a backseat to this. Got it?" Winston waited for the affirmative grunts before he said. "Now get your asses back to work."

Fennel pushed his hips away from the table. His gaze on the frozen image of Wild Bill. I hopped down from the table and grabbed my cup.

"Not you two," Winston said.

In the last month, I'd grown to hate my commanding officer. On my first day in homicide, he'd taken a standoffish approach, allowing me to sink or swim. But as the days went by, I couldn't help but feel he had chained my feet to an anchor. Or maybe I was projecting my guilt over allowing Wild Bill to continue his killing spree.

Winston waited for the door to swing closed before he said, "Do you seriously believe the killer is a cop?"

"It's the only thing that makes sense," I said.

"What do you think, Fennel?" Winston asked.

"Liv's right. He's been trained, probably works private security now."

"For Marilyn Archibald?" Winston asked.

"Yeah." Brad and I said simultaneously.

"But Liv's right. He said things and knows things a civilian wouldn't. He had to have held a badge at some point." Brad glanced out the glass doors, but no one in the bullpen paid us any attention. "Area surveillance doesn't show any vehicles staking out the motel, and no one's been loitering since Lovretta was placed yesterday. Correct me if I'm wrong, Lieutenant, but the department tends to use a select few safe houses. Anyone with prior knowledge could have cycled through until they found the right one. And Kearney's unmarked was parked outside. To a civilian, it looks like a regular car, but someone on the job would recognize it for what it was."

Winston rubbed his mouth. "Okay, I'm picking up what you're laying down. How does this fit in with your prior theory?"

Fennel looked at me, hoping I'd speak up.

"We assume someone on Marilyn Archibald's payroll is

responsible for the theft and murders. We hoped to narrow it down by finding a connection between the unsub and Anthony Lovretta," I said.

"Like I said, we think the killer is a member of her security team. We have copies of the employee records she voluntarily turned over when we made the initial request, but we have no way of knowing if she gave us everything." Fennel waited, hoping to avoid spelling it out, but the LT was a stubborn bastard. "We have no way of knowing if she might be behind the thefts and purposefully left out the killer's information."

"Stealing back family heirlooms, that's definitely not a first." Winston jerked his chin at me. "Let's say I buy all this. You think a judge will too? You got friends in high places, DeMarco. What do you think?"

"It's worth a shot." But if Marilyn Archibald was as connected as Axel Kincaid, she'd have the judge's order rescinded before we ever saw a single piece of paper.

"We do this, and it'll be a frontal assault. Officers will have to raid her offices and confiscate the data. We're homicide cops, not the SEC. I want a guarantee of what we're getting before I put my ass in hot water for two new hotshot detectives I barely know." He tapped on the table. "As soon as you get something concrete, we go in, metaphoric guns blazing. Until then, I'll keep surveillance teams all over Ms. Archibald's skinny ass. Anyone even remotely close to resembling that sketch shows up, I'll take 'em."

"Thank you," Fennel said.

"Yeah, thanks," I added.

Winston looked at us again. "Either of you get an EMT to check you out on scene?"

"We're fine," Fennel said.

"Until medical clears you and the paperwork's in my hand, you aren't doing a damn thing around here, cop killer or not."

"But, Lieutenant," I protested.

"No, DeMarco. No. I read your report. What you don't seem to realize is the reason you got that twinge is because the bastard intended to snap your neck, but for some reason stopped at the last second. Maybe he got spooked. Maybe he changed his mind. It doesn't matter. What matters is you're alive, and it's my job to make sure you stay that way. I know who your father is, and he'll have half of headquarters crawling up my ass if I don't." Winston looked at Fennel. "And son, you don't mess around with burns. They get infected easy. You get a bad enough infection, and the next thing you know, they're amputating limbs. It happened to someone in records. So I need that clearance." He waved us toward the door. "Get going. This isn't a vacation."

TWENTY-FIVE

The waiting room looked like a police convention. Jenkins came out of surgery twenty minutes ago. I watched officers bombard his wife with their well-wishes and sympathy. She kept her arms wrapped around her middle, nodding and offering tight smiles.

"Excuse me, Mrs. Jenkins," I approached, causing the uniform speaking to her to step aside, pat her on the arm, and rejoin the rest of the men parading around, "you looked like you needed a break."

"Was it that obvious? I didn't want to be rude."

I shook my head. "Men are oblivious. Don't worry about it. You already have enough on your plate. My friend works here. If you'd like some peace and quiet, I can get someone to take you back to the nurse's lounge while you wait for them to move your husband into his room."

"That's okay. But thank you, anyway." She studied me. "I'm sorry. I didn't get your name."

"Liv."

"I was told a Liv DeMarco found my husband and radioed for help. Are you that Liv?"

"Yes, ma'am."

She threw her arms around me and hugged me. "You

saved his life."

"I didn't. The officers and paramedics who pulled him out of that room saved him. I just made a call. I wish I could have done more."

She let go, keeping her hands on my elbows. "Thank you."

"I'm just glad he's going to be okay." I laughed. "Now I sound like the rest of them." I turned to look at the chair I abandoned. "I'll leave you alone." I almost asked if I could get her a cup of coffee or a snack, but I knew every other cop in the waiting room had already done it.

On my way back to my seat, I stopped by the desk. "Any word on Officer Kearney?"

The nurse recognized me. "He's still in surgery." She reached for one of the charts that had been dropped off. "Has the doctor spoken to you yet about your tests?"

"No." I leaned over the counter, hoping to get a glimpse at the paperwork. "Should I be concerned? I feel fine."

She gave me that professional, reassuring smile that I'd seen Emma practice in the mirror when she first became an RN. At the time, Emma had asked if I practiced my facial expressions in the mirror for when I had to give upsetting news. I thought she was crazy. But since it had become such a common occurrence lately, it probably would have been easier to slip behind a façade. But years undercover taught me how to hide behind a mask. I snorted, just like Wild Bill.

"Did I miss something?" the nurse asked.

"A voice in my head said something sarcastic." I watched her, wondering if she'd phone the doctor for another consult or talk to one of the nearby cops about keeping me on a fifty-one fifty.

"The ones in my head say some funny things too." She grinned. "While you wait, you want me to see if Emma's busy?"

"No, I'm just waiting on my partner. We have to get back to work once our forms are signed."

"Suit yourself." She turned her attention to the computer, and I wandered back to my seat. A few minutes later, a doctor came out, spoke to Mrs. Jenkins, and escorted her through the double doors to her husband's room.

"Hey," Fennel nudged me, and I turned, "you okay?"

"Yeah. I thought you'd come out that way." I looked at his partially unbuttoned shirt, which poorly concealed the thick dressing on his neck and shoulder. "Tell me Winston was wrong. You get to keep the arm, right?"

"I have to. It's my pitching arm."

"You pitch? Now you know I have to come to one of your games."

"We'll see."

He brushed my braid to the other side. "What'd the doctors say? Do they need to perform a decapitation?"

"Hardy har." I ran a hand over the back of my head, feeling the welt I hadn't noticed until the PA pointed it out. "I'm fine, but they made me get a CT scan. I'm waiting for someone to give me the results and sign my sheet."

Fennel dropped into the chair beside me and pulled the folded paperwork out of his pocket. "It helps if you flirt with the doctor."

"I'll remember that next time."

"Why don't you ask Em to expedite things?"

"I don't want to bother her."

"Whatever you say, Liv." He watched our colleagues mill about the waiting room. "Any news?"

"Jenkins is out of surgery. Doctors are hopeful he'll make a full recovery. No word yet on Kearney."

"He'll be okay." And Fennel said it with such confidence, I believed him. We fell into an awkward silence, which rarely happened. We talked all day, every day, about everything. But this was different. "Y'know, I don't think I like Winston much."

"Join the club," I said.

"Can I be president?"

"Jake's president."

"Lucky bastard," Fennel said. "Vice president?"

"Sure, take my title."

"Why can't you be secretary? You have better penmanship."

"But you're better at paying attention and taking notes."

I sighed. "We can't keep doing this. We have to talk about what happened."

"This isn't the time or place." He nodded at the officers sitting a few feet away from us. "The department might have a leak. You heard Winston. We have to be careful."

But I knew my partner, and he wasn't ready to talk about what happened. However, we had a killer to catch. This conversation couldn't wait forever.

"Detective DeMarco?" a gray-haired man in a lab coat called.

I stood. Fennel, too. We crossed the waiting room. "That'd be me."

He looked at Brad, confused.

"This is my partner. You can speak freely in front of him," I said.

"Your scans are clean. But that's a nasty bump. Given your history, I'm sure someone went over concussion protocol with you the last time. Have you experienced any symptoms?"

"No."

"She got sick at the scene," Brad said.

"That would count as a symptom," the doctor said.

"No, it wasn't. That was trauma, not to mention the drama this one caused." I nudged Brad hard, annoyed that he sold me out.

The doctor ran a flashlight in front of my eyes for the third time since I stepped foot in the hospital. He asked about blurry vision and problems concentrating, and when I pointed out that I already went over this with the person who initially performed the exam, he apologized.

"Still, I'd like you to take it easy for the rest of the day. Do you think you can do that?" the doctor asked.

"Sure." I held out the form. "Now if you wouldn't mind signing this."

As we headed out the exit, Brad said, "Hey, there's Emma." He pointed to a bench near the loading and unloading area. "Do you want to say hi?" I followed his gaze. Emma wore dark blue scrubs and unsuccessfully attempted to fix her hair. "What is she doing? Taking a break?"

Suddenly, Emma smiled, and I wondered if she'd seen us. Brad raised his hand to wave, but I caught sight of a man approaching with a white paper bag and a pathetic bouquet of wild flowers, Emma's favorite. Grabbing Brad's hand, I pushed it down by his side. "She's not smiling at us." I jerked my chin at the guy. "That's the perv from the other night. Eric Whatshisface. No wonder she said she wasn't coming home tonight."

We watched as Emma stood up, kissing him hard enough to knock him back a few inches before admiring the flowers and taking a seat on the bench. Eric opened the bag, pulled out a plastic tray of salad, and handed it to her. Brad sized him up while I did my best to hide behind my partner and a support pillar.

"I didn't know pervs brought people dinner. Guess they have to eat too," Brad said.

"Look at the cocky way he moves. That's a definite sign of trouble."

"I don't know. Emma seems to like it."

"Come on, we have work to do." I turned and headed for the car, unsure which bothered me more, Emma lying about her plans or Emma dating the guy who propositioned me for a threesome. It'd be best to focus on work and not which of Emma's coworkers might be joining them tonight.

"You don't judge perps this harshly. Stop worrying, Liv. Emma can take care of herself. Hell, Emma could hold her own against an angry momma bear. She can handle that clown."

"I just don't want her to get hurt." And something told me Eric would hurt her.

"You're a good friend, but she has to make her own mistakes." He waited until we turned the corner before adding, "And no matter where the pieces fall, it's not your fault. You didn't push her into this guy's arms."

I snickered. "Stop reading my mind."

He held up his palms. "Unfortunate side effect of working so closely together. So where do we go from here?"

"I've been thinking a lot about Wild Bill being a cop. We assume he's on Marilyn's payroll, probably part of her security team, but who else do we know who worked security?"

"Ezra Sambari," Brad said. "You think they knew each other?"

I fished out my phone and scrolled through my contacts for Penny Sambari's phone number. It was a little after eight. She should be home. "Hi, Mrs. Sambari, this is Detective DeMarco from homicide. Would you mind if my partner and I drop by to speak to you? It won't take long." I waited for her to agree and hung up.

"Are we taking a detour?" Brad asked.

"Yep."

TWENTY-SIX

Penny sat beside me on the couch, a box of tissues on the coffee table and a photo album spread open on her lap. "Ezra always looked so handsome in uniform." She pointed to a few photos. "That's when he worked with the armored truck company."

"Did he ever work for the Archibalds?" I asked.

"Not that I recall. But he moonlighted a lot. Hang on." She put the album on the table and disappeared down the hall. She returned a moment later. "This might help."

"What is it?" Fennel asked.

"His resume," she said. "Ezra always kept one on hand in case an opportunity presented itself."

"He didn't like his job?" Fennel asked.

"He did," Penny said, "but with these security gigs, it's just a matter of time. Leo travels internationally a lot. Most of his buyers are in Europe. We know he plans to permanently relocate."

"What was going to happen to your husband's job?" I asked.

"You'd have to ask Leo, but Ezra and I are happy here. We have no desire to relocate. We have enough saved. I have a good job and benefits. Money isn't a problem." She stopped, the words grinding her brain to a halt. A strangled gasp escaped, and she covered her mouth. Swallowing, she apologized.

"No need, ma'am," Fennel said. "We are so sorry for your loss. If you need anything, please call." He put his card on the table and jerked his chin at the door. "Come on, Liv. We've taken up enough of Mrs. Sambari's time."

Once we were back in the car, Fennel took the resume and carefully read it line by line. "No mention of Marilyn Archibald or any of her holdings. But see this?" He pointed to the list of events Sambari had included, along with his duties. "A lot of private security shows up at these functions. Ezra could have crossed paths with our killer at any one of them. We'll have to cross-reference it to events Marilyn and her mother attended."

"Should we be worried Penny's statement makes it look like the theft might have been an inside job?" I asked.

Fennel shook his head. "They don't have money problems. And based on this list of temporary security gigs, Sambari probably wouldn't have had trouble finding work. Nothing tracks back. I don't think the killer used Sambari the same way he used Lovretta."

"Don't you find it odd Sambari worked so many jobs? Why didn't any of them stick?"

"Do you have any idea how many cops moonlight as security on the side? Most security jobs are just temporary. Clubs and hotels only need bumped up security for big events. When VIPs roll into town, they bring their own protection, but it's never enough. So they hire fill-ins. When you know the right people and hit it just right, you stand to make a lot of money in a short amount of time. And if you do a good job, the next time something big is going on in town, you get a call. Based on this, Sambari would probably be better off doing these random gigs than staying at his steady job. I don't think he was in this for the money. He probably just liked having a nine to five. But I bet he knew our killer or at least recognized him as a friendly face from one of these other gigs. When Marilyn showed up to check out Leopold's inventory, Sambari probably didn't even give her security detail a second glance."

"And the killer thanked him by shooting Sambari in the back of the head."

"It's easier than staring into the eyes of someone you know when you pull the trigger," Fennel said.

"That assumes our killer is capable of feeling human emotion."

We returned to the precinct. Before long, we matched eight events on Sambari's resume to the Archibalds. Since Marilyn and Agnes attended most of the same events and shared an employee pool, it was possible Agnes originally employed our killer, and when he learned his years of hard work and dedication hadn't been rewarded, he lashed out by going on a killing spree.

"We'll need access to Agnes Archibald's records too." I reached for the phone.

"Do you think we have enough?" Fennel asked. "It's circumstantial."

"Yes, but Agnes is dead, and the killings link to her estate sale. That should be more than enough. If we do this quietly and get the information from tax records, Marilyn won't find out. And if she does, by then, it'll be too late to stop us."

"Sneaky," Fennel smiled, "I like it."

By the time I got off the phone, someone had turned on the eleven o'clock news. Most of the department stopped what they were doing to watch. Lt. Winston came out of his office. Before the broadcast even finished, the phones started ringing.

"Now we sift through the crank calls, kooks, and crazies," Winston said. Pointing at Detective Lisco, he summoned her into his office.

"I'm gonna check with Jake," Fennel said. "His guy might know something about private security since he works at a security firm."

"You mean Renner?"

Fennel nodded.

"Worth a shot." I went back to figuring out a way to identify our killer. Deciding to check and see if any of these venues had security footage stored from the events in question, I made more calls. Most of the venues turned me down. A few said to check back during normal business hours. A couple even accused me of being a paparazzo.

Tabloids never interested me, but the photos and video footage they bought might contain some candids of Marilyn Archibald or her mother, Agnes, and their security teams. Since Winston ordered us to work around Marilyn Archibald, we had to do things the hard way.

How could a police lieutenant worry more about politics and his own career over the lives of his officers? It made me sick. This was why I didn't like Winston.

"Hey," I said to a cop I recognized from the hospital waiting room, "any word on Kearney?"

"They encountered some complications during surgery, but everyone's trying to be optimistic. We're collecting to help him and his wife out. Not much else we can do now, except pray."

"Yeah." I noticed the two large empty coffee cans with labels. I'd drop some money into them before leaving tonight.

After that bit of bad news, I found myself even more determined to ID the killer. I mapped out potential connections. Lovretta hooked up with the killer at Speedy Delivery. Ezra Sambari made nice with him at these functions. This case was one big Venn diagram. I just had to find the overlap.

"Shift's over," Fennel said. "We have to knock off."

"Yeah." I hung my spiderweb sketch on the board. "We both know this asshole works for the Archibalds. We should be storming the gates and arresting every single current and former male member of their staff."

"And if Marilyn Archibald wasn't so connected, we would. Unfortunately, law and order doesn't apply fairly. And we know it."

"I don't like it."

"Neither do I." Fennel turned off his computer and grabbed his jacket, watching as several officers manned the hotline. Calls hadn't stopped coming in. "But patrol is all over Marilyn, her office building, and her holding companies. If anyone fitting the description walks out of one of those buildings, we'll bring him in."

"Is that why Winston put it on the news?" I asked.

"That'd be my guess."

"Wonders never cease." I sorted the stacks of papers, wondering how much I could accomplish at home. At least there'd be nothing holding me back from scouring internet gossip sites and tabloid news stories.

"Want to get drunk?" Fennel asked.

I pointed to my head. "Possible concussion, remember?"

"Right. Let's hope tomorrow brings with it some good news."

We emptied our wallets into the coffee cans and went our separate ways. I watched Brad drive off, a growing unease spreading throughout my body.

On the way home, I listened to my messages.

"Hey, honey, it's your dad. I saw the news. Just wanted to make sure you're okay. Did Emma tell you I dropped off some boxes? That should be the last of them. Mom wants to give your new place a good scrubbing before you move in. She said she's going over tomorrow with the spare key you gave us. I told you giving her a key was a bad idea. Anyway, if you don't want her to do it, call me back and I'll come up with something to distract her. Actually, call me back either way. I'm not going to bed until I hear from you."

Hitting speed dial, I put the phone on speaker and tucked it into the cupholder. Two rings later, my dad answered. "Hey, Olive. You okay?"

"I'm fine, Dad. Thanks for the boxes."

"Yep." He paused, waiting for me to fill in the blanks. When I didn't, he said, "I saw the news. Not much of a sketch. Looks like every other Tom, Dick, and Harry."

"I know."

"Did the witness provide the sketch before or after he looked through the mug books? If it was after, he might have just reiterated some of the common features he noticed," Dad said. "Maybe you should take another pass at him."

I reached for my water bottle, suddenly parched. "We can't."

"Did he disappear?" My dad swore. "Someone should

have been keeping an eye on him."

"He didn't disappear. He was killed at the safe house. His detail was shot."

"Shit. Who? Do you know them?"

"Kearney and Jenkins." I thought about Jenkins humming in the hallway. "It's bad."

"Who found them?"

"Brad and me." I turned into the parking lot, muttering answers as Dad hammered me with questions. "Look, I gotta get some sleep. We got a long day ahead of us. We have to find a way to nail this bastard."

"Yeah, no problem. Just be careful. I love you, Liv."

"Love you too. I'll see you Sunday."

Trudging up the steps, I cautiously unlocked the door, half-expecting to find an orgy going on in the middle of the living room. But no one was home. I even checked Emma's room and the bathroom, afraid that after the day I had, I might shoot the next person who snuck up on me.

Convinced I was alone, I filled the tea kettle with water, turned the burner to low, and went to shower. By the time I got out, the kettle had just started to whistle. I took my mug of chamomile into the bathroom, dried my hair, painted my toenails, and tried to turn my brain off. When I was done pampering myself and my toes were dry, I crawled into bed. It was a little before one.

I rolled over, beat my pillow into a preferable shape, and twisted and turned, hoping to find a position that didn't annoy the twinge in my neck. Finally, I found a comfortable position, but every time I closed my eyes, I'd see one of two things, Kearney and Jenkins or the windows exploding outward. And no matter how hard I tried, I couldn't make it stop.

An hour later, I turned the lights back on and reached for my tablet. But the tabloids and gossip sites didn't particularly care about Marilyn or Agnes Archibald. They might be wealthy, but scandal didn't follow the family. The Archibalds were old money. They didn't have twitter accounts or celebrity feuds. I checked. So I'd have to scour the photo collections from each individual event to see if our killer made it into any of the shots, which would be damn near impossible to determine since we still weren't sure what he looked like. I just hoped Lovretta got it right.

Instead of giving myself eyestrain, I texted Brad and asked him to get a team together to explore this angle in the morning. We'd have to look for everyone and anyone who might be involved or connected in some manner to our killer. Then I stared at my phone for five minutes, but my partner didn't reply. Hopefully, he was asleep or with Carrie and not passed out somewhere. "God, Brad." I shook off the fear and grief that swept through me the moment I saw the explosion.

Deciding I needed to do something more productive with my time since sleep was out of the question and I was too fried to concentrate on work, I grabbed the tape and packing supplies and opened the top drawer of my nightstand. I'd just finished packing the left side of my room when I heard a noise in the hallway.

Reaching for my Glock, I checked the time. Who the hell was banging on my door at this hour? I dragged myself off the floor and headed to the door. After a quick peek through the peephole, I opened it.

"Hey, I got your text," Brad said, leaning against the doorjamb. "I called in some favors and got the techs to get started scouring the internet for sightings, but I think the sketch Lovretta gave us is bogus. I just don't know why he had to die over bad intel, y'know?" Brad reeked of tequila, but he didn't appear drunk.

"Are you okay?" I stepped away from the door so he could come inside.

"Didn't I say I'd let you know when I'm not?" He rested his forearm against the doorjamb and squeezed his eyes shut. "I'm sorry I yelled at you before. I haven't been able to stop thinking about that, which is kind of stupid."

"Brad, come inside." As soon as he entered the apartment, I closed and locked the door. "How much have you had to drink? Did you drive here?"

"I haven't had a drop." He pulled his shirt away from him and sniffed it. "I broke up a bar fight. After that, I didn't feel much like hanging around there. And since I knew you were still up, I thought I'd stop by." He looked at my oversized t-shirt and pajama shorts. "Shit, Liv, did I drag you out of bed? Jeez, I'm sorry. I should go."

"I can't sleep either. I tried, but that didn't work. So I've been packing. Wanna stay? You can help."

He glanced around, remembering Emma wasn't home and wouldn't be coming home anytime soon. "Yeah, but first, let me wring my shirt out into a glass. There's probably enough liquor here to get me buzzed."

"Take off your shirt. I have a few of my dad's old t-shirts that should fit you. And Emma has hard cider in the fridge. Help yourself. I won't tell her."

"Cool, thanks."

While Brad cracked open a bottle, I pulled the tape off the box I just sealed and grabbed a shirt off the top. "When's the last time you changed your bandage?" I asked.

"You sound like Winston. It's not that bad. Just a few second degree burns. I've done worse barbecuing." But he put down the bottle, took the clean shirt, and went into the bathroom. He'd been here often enough to know where everything was. He came out a few moments later. "I rinsed my shirt and left it hanging in the bathroom. Is that okay? I don't want Emma to have a conniption."

"It's fine," I said, holding out the bottle. His hand still had a slight tremor. I stared at it, which always made him self-conscious.

"Drinking makes it worse. And not drinking obviously doesn't have much of an effect, so what's the point?" He knocked back a gulp and slumped onto one of the island stools. "Y'know, maybe I'm not okay."

"What can I do? Do you want to talk?"

He shook his head and drank his cider. He finished the bottle, rinsed it, and put it in the recycling bin. "All right, let's get you packed up. Lord knows, we're not going to have any time between now and moving day."

We went into my bedroom, unloaded my bookshelf, emptied my dresser drawers, and transferred my hangers into the large wardrobe box I thought was a rip-off but my dad splurged on anyway. By the time we finished, it was almost four. The only things left were the clothes I left out to get me through the next few days and my toiletries.

"Let's just hope Emma doesn't decide to redo these boxes," I said as I held the box closed while Brad taped it shut.

"I wouldn't worry. She's probably too busy with her new boytoy and whatever third they picked up tonight."

"Ugh. Imagery, Fennel. Imagery."

Brad laughed. "Payback's a bitch, isn't it?"

"Speaking of, I thought you would be at Carrie's tonight."

Brad bit his lip and gave a little headshake. "She has a rule about how often we get together. It's to avoid either of us getting too attached."

"How's that working for you?"

He snorted. "It's probably for the best. I haven't been able to stop thinking about you all night."

"Brad?"

"No, not like that." He flexed his hand. "When you stepped between me and Wild Bill, I thought he was going to splatter your brains all over me."

"You were afraid I was going to mess up your nice shirt," I teased.

"Yeah."

"Yeah." But I watched as Brad tried to bury the growing panic. He'd lost most of his unit in Afghanistan, and today served as a major trigger. He couldn't lose me. And he thought he did, just like I thought I'd lost him. "It's almost four. I don't know about you, but I'm still wired. Want to watch one of those terrible TV movies Emma always DVRs?"

"The ones we mock mercilessly?" Brad asked.

"Yeah."

"Sure."

He popped another hard cider and settled into his normal spot on one end of the couch. I sunk into a spot in the middle, wincing when I twisted the wrong way. Brad's eagle eyes didn't miss a trick.

"Hey, come here." He patted the spot beside him, fluffing a pillow next to his good shoulder for me to lean against. "We're quite the pair, aren't we?"

"I'm not complaining." As far as I was concerned, the only cops who had any right to complain were Kearney and

G.K. Parks

Jenkins.

"Me neither. I'm just stating a fact." He took another sip from the bottle.

About halfway through the movie, my eyes started to close. It was easy to fall asleep when the plot was entirely predictable. I knew the ending within the first twenty minutes, but that was the nature of almost all rom-coms. After all, who didn't like a happy ending?

At some point, Brad covered us with a throw, stretching his legs out on the sofa beside mine.

TWENTY-SEVEN

The sound of Emma giggling woke me. I blinked and stared at the front door. Brad hadn't moved, but we somehow ended up in a tangle with the blanket and throw pillows. A deeper, muffled voice spoke, but I couldn't make out the words. Emma giggled again.

"No, you can't come in," Emma said. "My roommate's here."

Another muffled response.

"It's not that she doesn't like you, Eric. She just doesn't know you." Pause. Delighted squeal. "You're so bad." Laughter. More giggling. "No, we never experimented in college. Liv's my family. Don't be gross. But you know, she's moving out this weekend. You could come over Sunday and help me rechristen the place."

Ugh, someone shoot me now. Emma's voice grew softer, so I could no longer make out the words. At least the universe had put me out of my misery. I closed my eyes, hoping this was a bad dream, a result of the crappy movie I watched before going to sleep. Out in the hall, Emma and Eric were reenacting their own rom-com. This was all just a figment of my imagination. A concussion dream.

But then the front door opened and closed, and Emma

took a seat on the edge of the coffee table, her knees brushing against the side of the sofa. "Liv," she whispered, "what's Brad doing here?"

"Sleeping," I mumbled.

"I can see that. Is this what happens when I'm not around. How long has this been going on? We have a rule about common areas."

Some rule. I opened an eye and stared at her. "What?"

"You and Brad," she leaned closer, practically resting her chin on the other side of his chest, "are you two a thing?"

"No."

"Then why are you asleep like a pile of puppies?"

"A pile of puppies?" I blinked. Until now, I hadn't actually believed I sustained a concussion. But that made no sense.

"You know, they sleep on top of each other in all kinds of weird positions that never look comfortable. I should tell Maria to bring Gunnie with her today. I bet the furball would feel right at home cuddling up on top of this mess."

"My mom's coming over?"

Emma gave me a duh look. "Well, yeah. I told her I'd help get your new place ready, and then we're supposed to go to lunch."

"Aww, Em." Slowly, I sat up, peeling my cheek away from the pillow that had been resting atop Brad's arm.

"Liv, what happened?" She pointed to the bandage. "Are you okay?" She looked down at Brad, noticing the dressing poking up from beneath his collar. "What happened to the two of you? Is this why he's here?"

"I nearly got blown up and Liv got pistol-whipped," Brad said, even though he had yet to open his eyes. "Now can you please be quiet? I'm trying to sleep."

"Fine, don't tell me what happened," Emma said, plucking the empty cider bottle off the table and glaring at my partner.

"That is what happened." I disentangled myself from the mess and took Emma's offered hand for balance as I climbed over Brad to get off the couch. Glancing at the clock, I nudged my partner. "Hey, sleeping beauty, it's after seven. We need to get going."

Grumbling, Brad sat up, rubbing his hands down his face. I didn't know if he slept at all or had just stayed put so I could sleep, but he wasn't happy about the announcement. We normally didn't pull doubles, but Wild Bill changed all the rules. Until we stopped this guy, we'd have plenty more late nights and early mornings.

Emma slid into the empty spot beside him and lifted the short sleeve away from his bicep, revealing some of the less severe burns. "Come on, tough guy, let a professional take a look."

"I'll start the coffee. Do you want breakfast?" I asked.

"You gonna call Jake and ask him to bring us some?" Brad retorted.

"Maybe." I went into the kitchen to fill the pot while Emma dragged Brad into the bathroom to patch him up. Once the coffeemaker was set, I went into my room, changed clothes, glad to have showered the night before, and took a moment to breathe. *No more days like yesterday*, I vowed.

"Your turn," Emma announced, pointing at me from the bathroom door while Brad filled a mug with coffee and rummaged in the fridge.

"Em, I'm fine." But she dragged me into the bathroom anyway. I took off the bandage, washed my face, and brushed my teeth. While Emma dabbed at the bruised gash, I pulled my hair into a ponytail. "How was your night?"

"Fun."

"Are you being safe?"

She rolled her eyes. "Yes, Mom."

"Em, I just don't know anything about this guy. But after almost shooting him, he asked me if I wanted to jump in bed with you two. That doesn't speak well to his character."

"I'm a nurse, Liv. I'm not an idiot. I can take care of myself." She poked the cotton swab harder against my cheek for emphasis. "The two cops who came into the ER with GSWs, is that connected to this?"

"Yeah. Brad and I found them."

"Shit. Why didn't you call me?"

I looked at her. "You know why."

She put down the cotton swab, affixed another oversized band-aid to my face, and gave me a hug. "We fight. We bitch. We get over it. You need me, I'm there. Just like I know if I need you, you'll be there." She looked at the half-empty bathroom, my towels already packed away. "I forgot how much bigger this place looks without your crap cluttering it up."

"I knew you couldn't wait to get rid of me."

She smiled sadly. "Neither of us is doing a great job of handling this. I thought living together would be the hard part, but it's the conscious uncoupling that's giving us a problem."

I cringed. "After what I overheard you and Eric talking about in the hallway, don't use words like that."

She laughed. "So who's Jake? And why did he bring you breakfast? Maybe we could double sometime."

"Just because you're hooking up with someone, it doesn't mean the rest of us have to pair off. This isn't Noah's Ark." Ignoring the petulant look Emma gave me, complete with her hand on her hip, I checked my reflection in the mirror. "I gotta go. But we'll talk about Jake another day. Just be careful. There's a killer on the loose."

"Only one?"

"I wish."

My travel mug sat on the counter next to a baggie of orange slices and grapes. "Call Jake," Brad said, "or we might starve to death." He caught Emma's eye. "After your lunch with Liv's mom, you might want to buy some groceries. Oh, and I added hard cider to your list. You're out."

"Don't you have food and drinks at your place?" Emma asked. "And a bed?"

"Company's better here, except when I'm trying to sleep." He grabbed his shirt, dangling from Emma's finger, gave her a peck on the cheek, and headed for the door. He held it for me while I made sure I had everything.

"See ya, Em. Thanks for the patch job," I called, pulling it closed behind me.

Brad and I split up, and I detoured to pick up breakfast while Brad went home to shower and change. We met back at our desks forty-five minutes later. Last night's time and effort had yielded little results. The tabloids and entertainment sites had been contacted and IT had scoured the internet for photos and videos, but with hundreds of thousands to go through, it would be easier to find a needle in a haystack.

"Fennel," Lt. Winston said, "Agnes Archibald's employee records just got turned over to us. I'll have the boxes moved into the conference room when they arrive. Voletek, you wanted something to do, so you and Fennel get started on that. You too, Lisco. We want this done quickly and quietly. Run them through for potential physical descriptor matches. Any match you get, write down the name. Let's get through as much as we can as quickly as we can. No time to be wishy-washy. Once Archibald's attorneys find a way to shut this down, they will."

"Wonder why?" I mumbled sarcastically, pushing away from my chair.

"Not you, DeMarco. I need you for something else." Winston turned on his heel and went into his office. Fennel and I exchanged a look. This couldn't be good. "I don't have all day, DeMarco," Winston bellowed.

Hurrying into the lieutenant's office, I shut the door. "What's up?"

"What's up is I got a call this morning from city hall. For the record, I don't enjoy starting my day like that. It makes my asshole clench. Now I got this pucker situation to deal with which makes it even harder to remove the stick that you detectives shoved up there but love to bitch about." He snorted, waiting for me to realize I was supposed to reply.

"Um...sorry?"

"Yeah, anyway, you've been tasked with a special assignment. Apparently, one of the potential targets you contacted has decided he's in need of protection. You told him his life is in danger, and he wants us to ensure his safety. No motel this time. He's calling the shots, and he wants you on his detail. No other cops," Winston said. "I told city hall that detectives only handle these types of assignments under special circumstances, but I was told this is a special circumstance. Any idea what makes you so special?"

"Who asked for protection?" I asked, even though I knew the answer.

"Axel Kincaid."

"He doesn't want my protection. He wants to torture me."

"In that case, bring a taser and pack some beanbag rounds. Either way, you keep him alive, DeMarco. You understand? No more screw-ups like yesterday. I already got two cops in the hospital. It's a damn miracle they're not in the morgue. And you be careful out there." He studied me for a moment. "Guess you and Fennel aren't a total waste of space." And then Winston did something I rarely ever witnessed; he smiled. "That's why I offered you a position here in homicide. When you and Fennel caught this case, I'll admit, I had doubts. Now I'm rethinking those doubts. Don't make me regret my decision." He jerked his chin at the door. "Dismissed."

"Hey, Brad, do you have a minute?" I asked from the doorway of the conference room where he, Voletek, and Lisco had rearranged the furniture and prepped the area for the expected files.

Stepping out of the conference room, Brad looked around. "What's going on? Did you get reassigned to a different case?"

"No, Kincaid requested a babysitter."

"You? Shit. I don't like this. Did you disclose your history to Winston? Axel has an ax to grind. And given Kincaid's association with Marilyn Archibald, it could be a setup. He might be handing you off to the killer. You're the one who needs backup and protection, not Kincaid."

"He won't hurt me," I said, even though I was never really sure when it came to the eccentric club owner.

"But Marilyn might. And his relationship with her trumps whatever weird infatuation he has with you."

"Listen, Kincaid provided security footage from his nightclub, but we weren't able to ID the driver from the footage. Unless he has something more concrete, I don't see why he would need our protection. I'm hoping this means he wants to talk. The last time we spoke he said he had to check into a few things. I don't know what those things were, but now it sounds like he's terrified. And Kincaid doesn't get scared. He gets even."

"You can't flip him for info," Fennel said. "He's not a snitch. I think he has that stitched on a pillow somewhere."

"I gotta try."

I turned to leave, but Fennel grabbed my arm. "You check in with me every hour on the hour. If I don't hear from you, I'll send in a hostage rescue team to get you out."

"Okay."

"If I find anything solid, I'll let you know. You do the same."

I nodded. Today was just getting better and better.

TWENTY-EIGHT

"Detective DeMarco," George greeted me at the door, "Mr. Kincaid is waiting for you upstairs. I believe you know the way."

"Anyone else inside?" I asked.

George didn't answer, which left a sinking feeling in my stomach. He hit the button, and the door buzzed open. Removing my sunglasses, I took a deep breath, checked the time, and stepped inside.

Normally at this early hour, the cleaning crew would be hard at work, and Kincaid would be asleep, either upstairs or at home, possibly with a guest or two. So when I emerged at the top of the staircase, I was surprised to find the man awake, fully dressed, and in the midst of a meeting with his general manager, Fox.

"Ah, Detective, lovely of you to join us." Kincaid stood. "Fox, you remember Liv."

Fox turned around. Even the fancy title wasn't enough to take the street out of the ex-con. "Yeah," he said, a dead-eyed look of pure hatred burning into me, "the last time we spoke, you accused me of killing a lady of the night."

"I misjudged you, Fox. I didn't realize you were that poetic," I said.

Fox swallowed, his gaze falling on Kincaid. "You sure about this, boss?"

Kincaid nodded. "Let me know what you find. Liv will have questions for you when you return."

Fox stood and brushed past me.

"Where are you going, Fox?" I asked. But he didn't answer. He went to the door, twisted the lock, and pulled it closed behind him. By now, I was annoyed by the lack of responses Kincaid's staff had given me. "Where's he going, Axel? What game are you playing now?"

"No game, Detective. You asked for my assistance, and I provided it. Now you're here to return the favor." He blew out a tired breath and got up from the table. "May I get you something to drink?"

"It's not even ten a.m."

"That's never stopped me before, but I meant coffee or tea. You look like you could use the caffeine. Aren't public servants allowed to sleep?"

"Maybe you should speak to someone at city hall about that."

He went into the kitchenette and fiddled with the espresso machine. "That'll be my next call." He looked at me over his shoulder. "Would you like some coffee?"

"Yes, thank you."

"Cream? Almond milk?"

"No."

The machine whistled and beeped, steam rising as the dark liquid poured into the cup. Axel seamlessly switched the full mug with the empty one, waited for the coffee to finish pouring, and turned off the machine. "It's Italian roast, but I don't see that as any reason not to embrace Irish tradition. But I'd hate to offend your heritage, Liv. What do you prefer in your coffee? Grappa? Sambuca? A nice brandy?"

"Coffee," I said.

"You know, it wouldn't kill you to have a bit more fun."

"I wouldn't be too sure." I took the offered mug, watching as Axel topped his off with a heavy dose of whiskey. "And once again, I feel the need to remind you that I'm on duty."

He took a sip, deflating against the kitchen counter that doubled as a bar. "What happened to your face?"

"I got too close to a crazy guy with a gun."

Kincaid must have seen something in my eyes because he lost all interest in his drink. "Who?"

I stared at the window with its impenetrable blackout shade. "The same man who probably wants you dead, so why don't you start by telling me what's changed since the last time we spoke? From what I recall, you didn't want police protection, but maybe I'm not thinking clearly. After all, I did get hit in the head."

"So you've seen him. You know who he is. Have you made an arrest yet?" Axel asked.

"No." But I laid my cards on the table. Axel ate up damsel in distress stories. "It was a chance encounter, but he wore a mask, a solid white one, along with a hooded jacket and gloves."

"I saw the news. I don't believe your sketch is accurate."

"Why not?" I asked.

"Because I don't recognize him. And Fox doesn't recognize him."

"And the two of you know every psycho in this city?" Which wouldn't surprise me.

"Only the wealthy ones. But no, that's not the reason I say that. The reason I say that is because of what you told me. You said the killer must have been at the auction. I wasn't in attendance, but Fox was. And he's good with faces. It's how I kept undercovers out of Spark for years, at least until you stepped up to the plate. You were still fresh blood. You hadn't been a cop long enough to have gotten on Fox's radar, so he didn't recognize you. He's still angry about that."

"Maybe I just do a damn good job blending in."

Kincaid picked up his mug and took another sip. "That's because at Spark you were just a beautiful young woman in a sea of other beautiful young women." He eyed the bandage, the bruising barely noticeable around the monstrous band-aid Emma stuck to my face. "Do you think it'll scar? I know several men who work in plastics. I could convince one of them to see you for a consultation."

"I'm good."

Axel drank a bit more coffee and topped off the cup with more whiskey. "You said he wore a solid white mask?"

"Yes."

"Porcelain?"

"I don't know." I hadn't thought about it. "I figured it was probably one of those cheap plastic Halloween masks."

"The hood wasn't attached to it, though?"

"No."

Getting up, Axel went to the bookcase and pulled out what I thought had been an oddly shaped bookend. But when he flipped it around to face me, I realized what it was. "Did it look like this?"

"Where did you get that?" Just seeing the thing made my blood run cold. I broke out in a flop sweat, my right hand automatically coming to rest atop my holstered weapon.

"Easy, Detective. It's just a mask. It can't hurt you."

"Where did you get it?" I repeated, wondering if there was even the slightest chance Axel had been behind the attack. But he was too tall, and Fennel and I would have recognized his voice after spending months listening to his conversations. Axel Kincaid didn't kill Anthony Lovretta or shoot Officers Kearney and Jenkins, so how did he get the killer's mask? "Answer the question."

Gently, Axel set the mask down on the coffee table, holding his palms up as he backed away and took a seat on the couch. "Please, relax. You need to calm down. No one else is here. You're safe."

"Where did you get it?" For a moment, I was back at the motel, handcuffed beneath the stairs, my head in the killer's hands, seconds away from a dirt nap, and then the third floor exploded. And for those few horrible seconds, my world came crashing to an end. "Answer me."

Axel sighed, realizing it wasn't a switch I could flip on and off. "I'd prefer not to say."

"I don't give a fuck what you prefer."

"Liv," Axel's eyes traveled from my face to my hands and back again, "you're shaking."

I held my position. I was a cop first. And Axel had the

killer's mask sitting on his bookshelf. Fennel might be right. This felt like a trap. And suddenly, the claustrophobia set in. I blinked hard, forcing the encroaching walls to remain where they were. I clawed at the top button on my shirt with my free hand until I got it undone, my skin burning. "How'd you get that mask? Who left it here?"

"Those were handed out at a masquerade ball last winter."

"Whose? Marilyn's?"

"Yes, Detective. It was Marilyn Archibald's masquerade ball."

"Handed out?" I forced my hand away from my gun. "To whom?"

"To the guests, servants, caterers."

"What is this? Some *Eyes Wide Shut* shit?"

Axel laughed. "No, it was a masquerade ball to raise money for a foundation. The masks were just to make it fun. Again, I understand why that concept might elude you." He nodded at the mask, so I picked it up. "All the men had one. The caterers, servants, guests. The women were given delicate beaded masks that fastened with lace."

I picked up the mask, finding it lighter than I thought it would be. "Did you wear this?"

A grin spread across his face. "Why would I hide one of my better features? But it makes a nice party favor."

Printed inside the mask was a personal thank you message, along with the charity's name, date, and donation amount. "This is your receipt?"

"We wouldn't want to waste paper and kill trees, now would we?"

I held it out to him. "Put it on."

He cocked an eyebrow at me. "I always suspected you must have kinks."

"Axel, just do it."

He reached out and took the mask. "Do you promise not to freak out and shoot me?"

"I'll try to refrain."

He pulled the thick strap over the back of his head. "Happy?" he asked.

"Say something else."

"What do you want me to say? That I feel ridiculous?"

"It doesn't move."

He lifted the mask off his face. "It's porcelain, Liv. Of course it doesn't move. It's not some thin plastic mask." He studied me. "His didn't move either, did it?"

"No, it did not." I dropped onto a chair, my notepad and pen already in hand. "It's time you tell me what's going on."

TWENTY-NINE

"What I'm about to say cannot leave this room? Do you understand that, Detective?"

"I can't promise anything."

Kincaid stared at me with his cold blue eyes. As usual, he didn't like what I had to say. He ran a hand through his hair, hoping to keep his cool. "I'm gonna need a hell of a lot more than whiskey," he mumbled. But instead, he took another sip of his coffee. "Fine, have it your way." He picked up the mask. "The killer you're pursuing must have attended the masquerade last winter. That means he could be any of the guests, the hired help, or a bodyguard." He waved his hand at me. "Shouldn't you run along, now that you have some answers?"

It took every ounce of self-restraint not to say the first thing that came to mind. "Tell me about Marilyn Archibald. Is she capable of murder?"

Kincaid's expression went completely neutral. It's why he always won at poker. He knew I couldn't read him. "Marilyn's capable of anything, but you're barking up the wrong tree. This isn't her doing. She wouldn't put a hit out on me."

"Are you sure about that?"

Something flicked just behind Axel's eyes, but I couldn't tell what it was. "You wanted to do this the hard way, so we're doing it the hard way."

The only thing I wanted to do was wring Axel Kincaid's neck. "What can you tell me about the masks?"

"They were special ordered for the party. I believe the final count was 250. Though, I had better things to do than count them."

"You said they were handed out to guests."

"Yes."

"Okay. And the staff?"

"Didn't we just go over this?" Kincaid reached for his cup, bored with the conversation.

"Did Marilyn's guests bring their own security and bodyguards?" I asked.

"I'm sure a few did, but I wouldn't know. I don't travel with an entourage."

"Did Fox go with you? What about Emilio?"

Kincaid smiled, but his nose kept crinkling to the point it was almost a twitch. Obviously, I'd broken his poker face. "No, I didn't bring that conniving, back-stabbing piece of shit to the masquerade. Emilio didn't belong in a place like that. Perhaps I should thank you for finally putting him where he does belong."

"I take it you haven't seen him since the trial."

Kincaid got up from the couch. "We're not talking about that."

"Good because I rather talk about Marilyn Archibald."

"Leave her the fuck alone," Kincaid barked with such ferocity I feared what he might do next. "She isn't behind this, but someone close to her must be." He pointed at the mask. "You need to find out who and stop him before he hurts someone else. Before he hurts her."

"That is what I'm trying to do, but I can't do that when your friend," I put air quotes around the word, "shut us out. Her attorneys claim our case isn't strong enough, and because she's Marilyn Archibald, heir to the Archibald fortune, we've had a hell of time getting anything out of her."

"She won't give you her records?" Kincaid asked, a mix

of surprise and pride in his voice.

"She gave us some. Not all. We don't know what we're missing. You obviously care a great deal about this woman. Why won't you help us help her?" And then a sick thought went through my mind. "Where's Fox?"

"Checking into a few matters. When he returns, he'll answer any questions you may have."

"What have you done?" I asked, wondering if Kincaid wanted me here to keep me distracted or to ensure he had an airtight alibi.

"Nothing." He refilled his mug and made another cup of coffee for me. "So, how do you propose I help Marilyn?"

"First, I need that mask." I pointed to the table. "Can I have someone pick it up?"

"Fine, but if you turn around and try to arrest me for murder, you'll regret it."

"You need therapy. Not everyone is out to get you."

"Not everyone, Liv. Just you."

I couldn't necessarily disagree, so I kept my mouth shut, phoned Fennel, and told him what I learned. Now that we had evidence to link the killer to Marilyn Archibald, a judge couldn't deny our requests any longer. We'd finally get access to her records. But there was more to the story that Axel hadn't said. I wouldn't give up until he told me everything.

"What else can you tell me about the masquerade ball? Did anything happen?"

"The few things I remember about the masquerade ball have little to do with Marilyn or the charity."

"Were you Marilyn's date?"

A funny look came over Axel. "No."

"Is she seeing anyone romantically?"

"Not that I'm aware, but I'm sure she has many suitors."

"Are any of them jealous?" Maybe that's how the killer picked his victims.

"Since I don't know who they are, how would I know if they're jealous?"

"Good point." I turned to reach for a pen and winced. Rubbing my neck, I wrote down the previous victims' names. "Okay, do you remember if any of these people attended the masquerade ball?"

Axel looked at the names. "I don't know who any of these people are."

"Hang on," I pulled up their ID photos on my phone, "do they look familiar?"

"What part of masquerade ball don't you understand?" Axel pointed at the mask. "Everyone looked the same. Men with white masks. Women with beads and lace."

"So everyone wore a mask the entire night?"

"No."

I stared at him. "Just look at the damn pictures."

"Didn't we already do this?"

I was frustrated, torn between wanting to cry and causing Axel physical pain. The bastard always knew how to push my buttons. "I'm just double-checking."

"No. I don't think they were at the masquerade. I doubt Marilyn had much use for this guy." Kincaid flipped to the image of Kevin Maser.

"I wouldn't be too sure. Maser was a top computer programmer."

"Did he work for her?" Kincaid asked, and I shook my head. "Where did he work? Or did he have his own startup?" Deciding it'd be easier than to ask why Kincaid wanted to know, I told him. He nodded and asked about the occupations of the other four victims. At least today he expressed more of an interest than he did the other night. He stared at the photo of Ezra Sambari for a long time. "I believe I've seen him downstairs on occasion. He wasn't a member, but you know how that goes. A lot of my members travel with a bodyguard or two, especially when entering a situation that might get heated."

"I thought nothing illegal goes on inside Spark."

Kincaid winked. "Of course not."

"Do you remember who Sambari might have been guarding?"

"No."

"Do you think you could find out?"

"That would take time and quite a bit of effort on my part. Once again, I'd be happy to oblige if you can present a judge with probable cause."

"Bite me."

"I would rather enjoy that."

Ignoring him, I asked, "Does Marilyn have any enemies? Maybe a few disgruntled employees? A woman in her position must have tons. What do you know about them? Has she mentioned anything to you about receiving threats or getting into arguments with anyone recently?"

"Marilyn doesn't speak to me about her business."

"What do you talk about?"

"Everything else."

I put my head in my hands and stared at the countertop. Asking about Marilyn Archibald wouldn't get me anywhere. The harder I questioned Kincaid, the more he bucked my efforts. Since Axel told me about the mask because I'd given him information, I'd have to do this a different way. Perhaps if I wasn't so sleep-deprived, I would have realized this sooner and saved my blood pressure from going through the roof.

"Any idea how one would go about unloading some hot merchandise?"

"Like what?" Axel asked. "A musket? Or some emeralds and diamonds?" Those details hadn't been disclosed to the public. And I never mentioned them when we previously spoke. "You shouldn't be surprised. Word gets around, especially when A.K. Limited owns half the pawn shops you and your partner canvassed."

"So you bought the musket from Anthony Lovretta?" And Kincaid wondered why I was determined to connect him to a crime.

"I didn't buy it, Detective. I don't micromanage. Those shops are investments. I have business managers and accountants who handle those things and competent staff working in each of the shops. I only take a hands-on approach here at Spark."

"Do you know Anthony Lovretta?"

"What if I do?"

"Well, for starters, I hate to be the bearer of bad news, but Lovretta was killed last night. He was the latest victim in the killer's spree."

The words hung in the air like a thick fog. Kincaid didn't

say anything. He didn't move. He barely blinked. Based on his lack of reaction, I couldn't be certain he'd heard what I said. But I knew Kincaid. The news surprised him, and now he had to come up with a new strategy.

"As far as I know, Lovretta wasn't flush with cash, so I'm not sure where you two might have crossed paths," I said, growing impatient.

"I never said we did."

"And yet, that isn't exactly a denial either."

He looked at the time. "Excuse me, I have some business I forgot about. Feel free to make yourself comfortable. I should only be a few minutes."

"I can't let you leave," I said. "You requested police protection."

"I'm just going in the bedroom." He pointed to the upper level of the loft. "You can keep an eye on me from here." Without waiting, he went up the steps, dialing along the way.

Keeping one eye on Axel, I looked around the lower level of the loft. But I didn't find any high-end laptops, jewels, expensive watches, or chess sets on the bookcase. If Kincaid or one of his pawn shops had bought the stolen merchandise from the killer, he wasn't keeping it in his apartment. The mask connected him to Marilyn Archibald and the killer, but Axel didn't realize it until I told him what happened yesterday. More than likely, he didn't know who our killer was either. If he did, the man would probably be dead by now.

"Would you like a tour?" Axel asked, coming down the steps. "Or would you prefer to secretly search on your own? I can go back upstairs and wait until you're done, but, spoiler alert, you won't find any contraband."

"Axel, please."

"Please what?" He moved closer, brushing a strand of hair that had fallen free away from my face. I flinched, backing away. "Men shouldn't hit women," he muttered.

"You're wasting time. Right now, he's out there, plotting another break-in or planning a murder. Help me stop him. Please."

"I don't know anything else, Liv. And since you refuse to

agree to my terms, I've told you what I can."

"Anthony Lovretta." I stared up at him, giving him my best doe eyes. "C'mon, he's dead. He agreed to cooperate. We put him somewhere safe, but the bastard still found him. Whatever you say we can attribute to Lovretta. No one has to know it came from you."

"I'll know," Kincaid said.

"Then why did you request my protection?" I asked. "We both know you're more than capable of taking care of yourself."

"Apparently not. Come with me. I want to show you something."

THIRTY

"When did this happen?" I asked.

"The day after you came to see me." Kincaid faced away from the TV, more intrigued by my expression than what was happening on the screen.

"The same day I paid Marilyn a visit?"

"Yes."

That would explain his hostility on the phone. I watched the footage again. "Why didn't you report this? You should have told me what happened."

"I wasn't sure it was connected. Occasionally, I have disagreements with friends. It might have been a misunderstanding. An egregious misunderstanding."

"Was anyone hurt?"

"No."

"You could have been killed." I watched the video again. Axel pressing the unlock on his remote and being blown backward as his orange Maserati turned into a fireball. "Where's the car now?"

"At one of my garages. I hired experts to check it out. The detonator was wired to the unlock mechanism. Apparently, I blew up my own car." By now, any evidence that might have existed had been destroyed or compromised.

"What about this video? How'd you get it?"

"Anonymous sender." Axel held up a hand. "It can't be traced. I had people check. Based on the quality, it was recorded with a cell phone. The bastard had to be close. We've scoured my security feeds, but he's not on them."

"You must have cameras around back where you keep your car," I said. "What did they show?"

"Nothing."

"The department has experts. We can—"

"No." And the look in his eyes warned me not to argue. "I'm not reporting this. I just wanted you to realize that I am taking this seriously. And so should you."

"Then tell me what I want to know."

Axel pulled the USB drive out of the TV and locked it in his wall safe, probably afraid I might pocket it. He should have realized I was a cop, not a thief. But I let it go. The footage made me nauseous, and I fought to keep thoughts of last night out of my head. The back of my leg collided with his bed, and I dropped onto it.

"You don't look so good, Liv." Axel said. "Do you want to lie down?"

"No." My head pounded. "Aren't you tired of keeping secrets? Anthony Lovretta," I tried again, "has he worked for you?" And then I figured it out. "You're the guy who can get anyone anything they want. At least that's what I heard when I worked downstairs. Lovretta said when he used to steal, it was easier to move product when there was a demand for his supply. He funneled rare items to you via the pawn shops."

"You can't prove that. And I wouldn't exactly call them rare, just difficult to procure through legal means."

So it was true. "How'd you contact him with your requests?" I asked. "It can't be like ordering off the internet, can it?"

"Liv, if I ever dealt with Anthony Lovretta, and I'm not saying I did, it would have been through a third party sometime before he got pinched the last time. I would never force someone to turn to a life of crime once they go straight. Hell, look at me."

"Oh yeah, you're a model citizen."

"Be that as it may, Lovretta visited that pawn shop to

unload the musket because he'd done business there in the past and was considered a preferred seller. He received cash with no questions asked."

"That's it?"

Axel nodded.

"The killer contacted Lovretta as soon as he stepped out of the pawn shop. Did you know that?" I asked.

Axel's features hardened, making him unreadable. "I did not."

"Does this third party have a name? He could be our killer."

"He is not."

"How can you be sure?" I asked.

"I just am."

"Fine." No amount of begging or threatening would convince Axel to give up a name. "You said you recognized Ezra Sambari from your club. What about the others? Have you had any dealings with anyone else the killer targeted?" I stared into Axel's eyes, searching for the truth, but he didn't want me to see it. I just didn't know why. "What about Kevin Maser? You singled him out. Said Marilyn wouldn't have had any use for him, at least until I told you what he does for a living. Did you use him for anything? Maybe you felt like hacking the Pentagon."

"Flattering, but you give me more credit than I deserve." For a moment, the wheels turned while Axel debated if he should say anything else. Finally, he said, "I'm choosing to trust you by telling you the company where Maser worked wrote the program that operates my security systems, Spark's security system. The cameras, doors, windows, sprinklers, everything. But I don't think I've ever had any interactions with Mr. Maser."

"What about Arnold or Starmon? Anything on them?"

"I don't know."

"How about art? The woman he killed had a private collection, but she worked as an art dealer."

"I've bought several pieces, but I don't remember from whom. Fox usually handles things like that, unless I'm buying for myself."

"Do you have any art here?"

G.K. Parks

"Whatever I have, you've seen."

I turned, finding only provocative photos of the female form on display. "Not the same kind of art."

Axel shrugged, but I didn't know what his house looked like. For all I knew, he could have Rembrandts hanging in the bathrooms. And that's when I realized it.

"You're the common denominator."

"I've been called worse."

"You link everything together, but you're not the killer."

"For once, we're in agreement."

"Which means if Marilyn Archibald isn't his primary target, you are."

Axel nodded. He already figured it out, which is why he asked for police protection. My protection. "Bravo, Detective."

"Why didn't you just say this in the first place?" Three of the pieces didn't fit, but since Kincaid was cagey, they could connect and he just wouldn't tell me how.

"I thought I might be wrong. I needed an expert, such as yourself, to reach the same conclusion."

"You're an idiot."

THIRTY-ONE

"How are you holding up?" Fennel asked.

"Kincaid's driving me crazy." I glanced back at Axel who sat at the same large round booth where I'd found him the other night, this time without a supermodel glued to his hip. "He won't talk about Marilyn. He won't tell me if he knows our other vics."

"Do you think he accidentally let it slip about Kevin Maser and the masquerade ball?" Fennel kept an eye on Kincaid.

"No, he wanted us to know. There's more he wants me to know. But for some reason, he won't come out and say it."

"Any idea what it is?"

I shook my head. "He wanted it off the record, and I told him no. So he's been playing games ever since."

"Like he wants you to guess?" Fennel shifted the mask around, reading the note written inside. "If we didn't go toe-to-toe with the psycho bastard last night, I might think Kincaid's our guy. Everything points to him."

"He isn't."

"I'll take a crack at him and see what he has to say. We'll compare notes, and then I gotta head back. In the meantime, take a break." He shoved a brown paper bag into my hands and crossed the empty dance floor to speak to Axel.

Taking a seat at the bar, I opened the bag to find a few bottles of water, some fresh fruit, and a couple of the organic chocolate bars I liked. This was our ritual before I went undercover, so I didn't know exactly why Brad brought me chocolate now, but I wasn't complaining.

After taking a bite, I checked my messages and called Mac. I'd given her so many assignments these last few weeks, I was sure I was the last person she wanted to talk to. But as usual, Mac remained her upbeat, bubbly self, despite the bad news. Facial rec didn't return any hits on the sketch Lovretta provided. And the IT department continued to search the internet for photos and videos from the various events Sambari listed on his resume.

"Shift gears," I said. "We now have reason to believe the killer attended Marilyn Archibald's masquerade ball." I gave Mac the date and location. "Fennel already put in for the warrant, so we'll have her guest list and records soon, but you might as well get started looking for this guy." I glanced back at the men to make sure Axel remained occupied. "We're now working under the assumption Axel Kincaid is his next target. My gut says the killer is someone close to Marilyn Archibald, probably part of her security team, but he could be a jealous lover. I don't know if Marilyn's pulling the strings or not, so find whatever press coverage and social media footage you can, and see if you find any shots of Kincaid and Ms. Archibald. My guess is she got tired of Axel, or someone else got tired of dealing with the competition."

"This is more twisted than a daytime soap," Mac said. "Maybe Marilyn's a black widow."

"She's never been married."

"Maybe she has them killed before they get too close," Mac suggested.

"Stop watching true crime dramas on TV."

"You're no fun," Mac whined. "But be careful, Liv. I heard what happened yesterday. The whole precinct heard what happened."

I lowered my voice. "Lisco's supposed to be investigating the department for a possible leak. Have you heard anything?"

"No, was I supposed to?"

"Just figured since you flit between departments, maybe the boys over in IAD had mentioned something." From Mac's silence, I feared I overstepped. "Never mind," I said, trying to put a joking tone into my voice, "I'm probably just paranoid after last night. Nearly getting blown up can do that to a person."

"No sweat. I'll let you know if I uncover your masked man."

Turning, I watched Fennel close his notepad. That was my cue. Taking another bite of chocolate, I braced myself and crossed the room.

"All right, that's everything I need." Fennel held out his hand, and I was surprised when Kincaid shook it. "I have to get back. As soon as I know anything, we'll let you know. Until then, listen to Liv. Do whatever she says. She'll keep you safe, but if anything happens to her, I'll hunt you down. Got it?"

"Thank you, Detective Fennel," Axel said, causing me to draw my sanity into question. Perhaps I should go back to the hospital for another round of brain scans.

Fennel turned. "DeMarco, walk me out."

I followed Brad out of the club, nodding at George, even though he pretended to be busy and ignored us from the booth near the door. Once we were outside and across the street, clear of Spark's surveillance cameras, which may or may not record sound, Fennel glanced around.

"Wild Bill blew up Kincaid's car. Considering who's involved, I guess we should have been prepared for a Vegas-style show, complete with pyrotechnics," Fennel said. "Every time I think we're close to IDing this killer, thief, magician, demolition expert, whatever he is, he does something to throw another wrench in our plans." Fennel slid his sunglasses down his nose and nodded down the block. "Surveillance van is staying put. Patrols are beefed up around all our victims, but I'll get a unit to remain on standby a block from here. Kincaid won't let us position a tactical team in his club, but he should."

"Kincaid probably has his own tactical team on standby," I said.

"If that were true, why'd he ask for a bodyguard? Something else is going on, Liv. I don't like leaving you alone with him. It feels like a setup."

"I'm not alone. You have half the force patrolling three square blocks around the club. I'll be fine. I can take care of myself."

"Lovretta had four armed cops watching his back, and we all know how that turned out." Fennel sighed. "Lisco hasn't identified any leaks in the department, so we still don't know how our killer found Lovretta. But I'm working on a new profile based on our latest intel."

"Let me guess, former cop turned private security who works for Marilyn Archibald. White male. Twenty-five to fifty. Approximately 5'9. 160-180 lbs."

"Disgruntled, skilled in evasion technics and bombmaking," Fennel added.

"You're thinking former military?" I asked.

"I'm thinking former something. Maybe he worked in one of the PD's special units or at least trained. Perhaps he got passed over or couldn't pass his psych evals, so he quit. You've picked up skills working UC. So have I. I'd bet we're not the only ones. I just don't know which of our special units crack safes, bypass security, and plant bombs."

"At least you know where to start with Marilyn Archibald's employee records."

Fennel snorted. "Oh yeah, we got her employee records. All three thousand of them."

"What?"

"She's not making this easy. At least Kincaid offered up the mask. That's one connection we would have never made. I thought it was some Michael Myers shit. I didn't realize it was significant."

"Me neither." I lowered my voice to a whisper. "Did you ask Axel if he's sleeping with Marilyn?"

"He denied it. Why?"

"He insists she wouldn't take a hit out on him, but he won't tell me anything about them or their relationship," just that they don't talk about business. I don't know what their connection is, but according to Axel, she has several suitors. And since at least three of the previous victims could be stepping stones to get to Axel, I'm thinking if Marilyn isn't behind this, then our killer is another lover or one of her protectors, who wants Axel out of the picture."

"Misplaced affection can make men do crazy things," Fennel agreed. "All right, I'll see what turns up. In the meantime, you get twitchy, call it in. Better safe than sorry." He opened the car door, glancing back at the club a final time. "For someone in fear of his life, it's weird we're the only cops Kincaid will talk to."

"He has trust issues when it comes to law enforcement."

"Then why does he trust us? We tried to bury him."

"It's because we owe him, so he's collecting," I said.

"I never agreed to a quid pro quo," Fennel said, but he saw it in my eyes, "but you did."

"Women were getting kidnapped off the streets, Brad. What choice did I have?"

"I know, but I don't have to like it." He gave my hand a quick squeeze, and then he got behind the wheel and drove away. When I went back inside, I found Axel examining the contents of the brown paper bag.

"Checking for hidden recording devices?" I asked.

"I can't be too careful," Axel teased, sliding the bag toward me. "Is that what cops eat on a stakeout? You should be careful, Liv. Chocolate's a gateway drug, and from what I remember from my misspent youth, fast food's a big seller with the police. Anything that doesn't take time to order that can be scarfed down in between answering calls is a big pleaser."

"Spent a lot of your time in the back of a squad car, did you?"

"I'm not that guy anymore. I've been telling you this since the moment we met."

"How'd you get out of the life?" I asked. "Most people aren't lucky enough or smart enough to escape. And you," I spun, again tweaking my neck in the process, "have achieved things even the most hardworking and brilliant people have not. Do you want to explain that to me?" I rubbed my neck, wishing Fennel had tossed a few heat wraps in the bag.

"Marilyn."

"Go on."

"Only if it stays between us."

"I can't agree to that. What if it's material to the investigation?"

"It isn't." He stared at me, desperate to tell this secret, though I had no idea why. "I want to tell you, Liv. But this could hurt people I care about."

"Like Marilyn?"

"Yes, Marilyn. And me." He inhaled deeply. "It'll focus your investigation and save time, but you can't disclose this detail to anyone. Your partner's focused on the wrong things. I think you are too. That's why you need to know, but you can't speak a word of it. Not ever."

This must have been why he'd made our earlier interaction so painful because he wanted me to agree to his terms, but I didn't circle back around. Instead, I launched questions in every other direction, hoping to get to the heart of the matter, but Kincaid held me at bay. He wanted me to know whatever this was, but he only wanted me to know once I agreed to his terms. I didn't understand how he thought I could shift the investigation without providing an explanation or evidence, but it had to be important. He wouldn't have gone to this much trouble or risked sharing his secret otherwise.

"Okay," I relented.

But a part of him didn't believe me. He exhaled. "I'm choosing to trust you. Do not stab me in the back again."

"Okay." I stared at him, unsure what to expect but automatically assumed the worst.

He swallowed, moved in close until his lips were against my ear, indicating even George didn't know this secret. "Marilyn Archibald is my mother."

THIRTY-TWO

"What?" I choked.

Kincaid glared at me. "Let's go upstairs. We could use the privacy." He practically dragged me up the steps, slamming the door behind us. "I'm serious, Detective DeMarco, not a word to anyone. Got it?"

"Yeah." But none of that made sense with what I knew about Axel Kincaid, and I knew a hell of a lot about Axel Kincaid. "How?"

His brow furrowed, confused by the question. "I know you have an aversion to fun, but at some point, someone must have had the birds and bees talk with you." He cocked an eyebrow. "If not, I'd be happy to demonstrate."

"She can't be your mother."

Axel Kincaid bounced around foster care, practically growing up on the streets after his mother died of an overdose and his father had been arrested for assault and attempted rape. So Axel had fallen through the cracks. He had a rough beginning and the anger issues to match. His juvie record, though sealed, read like that of any violent criminal before he turned to carjacking and eventually GTAs. Before Kincaid allegedly went straight, he'd figured out how to boost six-figure cars, something even the most skilled car thieves often struggled with. The police assumed that's how Axel had gotten his seed money to start Spark, and things just blossomed from there. Once he had enough capital, the rest of his problems disappeared, probably due to the clientele to which he catered and the high-priced attorneys and fixers he had waiting in the wings.

"Surprised me too," he said, taking a seat.

Quickly, I did the math in my head. "She would have been nineteen or twenty when she had you."

"Uh-huh." He picked up his empty coffee cup from earlier, but he'd already had enough to drink. "Turns out 'taking a semester abroad' actually means keeping the fact that you got knocked up at a frat party a secret from the entire world. No one has any idea, not even her family. They would have disowned her, or cut her off, or something. I don't know. Anyway, as soon as she delivered, she thought about dumping the baby," Axel snorted, "me, off at a fire station. Y'know, no questions asked. But let's be real. Questions are always asked, so supposedly she found a woman in desperate financial need and paid her to say she had a kid. Even had a birth certificate drawn up with my parents' names on it, claiming I was a home birth. Since crack whores with infants aren't that uncommon, no one asks any questions, except for child protective services, if they're having a slow day, and they never have a slow day."

"How'd you find out the truth?" I asked. "Did your mother tell you?"

"Liv, my mother ODed when I was four years old. She didn't tell me shit. My dad, her dealer, took care of me for a while, but they hadn't always been in touch. He didn't know who I belonged to, but I was a paycheck. And he was okay with that until he got arrested, and I got placed. After that, I never saw him again."

"Axel," I began.

"Save it. I don't want pity. I'm just another fucking statistic, like you. Our paths were determined for us early on. You were always gonna be a cop, and I was always going to be a criminal. Right now, I'd probably be locked up for the next few decades or dead. But when I was sixteen, facing some pretty serious charges and being told I could be tried as an adult, this lawyer comes to defend me. He said he was doing it pro bono. I don't know what he did, but the next thing I know, I got a slap on the wrist and community service. But it didn't stop there. At that point, the lawyer began the process of having my records sealed."

"Marilyn Archibald did that."

Axel nodded. "A few weeks later, I have my eyes on a classic Porsche. It sits in this garage, day in and day out. The video cameras are a joke, and no one's around. I make my move. Disengage the lowjack, get her started, and take her to this guy I always used who ran a chop-shop and could move exotics. The pay was decent. Except when I pull up, several armored SUVs are waiting. They box me in. I figured I'm done. The Feds got me."

"It was Marilyn."

Kincaid smirked. "Gold star, Detective. Anyway, it turns out she set a trap. The car was hers. She gave me two options, get locked up for the rest of my life or go to work for her. But there were conditions. I had to finish school and intern at one of her companies. At the time, they were running a rehabilitation program for juvenile delinquents, so I blended right in. No one thought anything of another punk learning the ropes on how to climb the ladder of corporate America. But the program fizzled. Getting into the right schools to have the kind of job Marilyn trained me for wasn't happening. And honestly, working some dead end job didn't hold much appeal after figuring out how to make a quarter of a million dollars in a matter of minutes."

"So that's when she told you?"

"No. Not at first. She set up a blind trust that didn't link to her or any of her companies, said it was because I showed promise. At that point, it was more money than I'd seen in my entire life. But there's no free lunch. And I wouldn't accept her offer. This woman had me dead to rights but gave me a second chance, and now she wanted to give me even more. I wasn't buying it. She wanted something in return."

"That must have been a hard decision."

Axel shrugged. "After a particularly bad night, I came

close to staring down a murder charge. Luckily, the guy pulled through. The same lawyer came around again, got me released on bail, and that's when Marilyn told me the truth. Even though no one knew what she'd done, she'd been keeping tabs on me my entire life. She said when she saw the way things were going, she had to intervene."

"That's how you got Spark."

He looked around the loft. "We didn't speak for five or six years after that. She paid me and left me alone to make my own decisions. After all, she's the one who fucked up and fucked me in the process." He took an unsteady breath. "Eventually, I got myself together, mostly, and we ended up bumping into one another at various functions. The circles we travel are small. I don't know. We've grown closer. I'd say we're friends."

"She's your mother."

"Yeah, and I'm her dirty little secret."

"You think the killer discovered your connection?"

"I'm not sure, but I don't see how anyone could possibly know. Marilyn's careful."

"With her mother passing, maybe Marilyn's feelings toward you have changed," I said, hating to imply the woman might now want him dead.

"Let me put it this way, if Marilyn wanted me dead, she wouldn't have bailed me out fifteen years ago. She wouldn't have given me enough money to buy this club and get the place off the ground. And she wouldn't invite me to her functions. She's not behind this."

"You're probably right. But you could make a claim to a piece of Agnes Archibald's fortune."

"No. I have no interest in those people or that world. Like I said, Marilyn's never told anyone about me. No one in her family knows I exist. This isn't some family drama over wealth and riches."

"But you could make a claim, right? You could offer up some DNA and challenge Agnes Archibald's will. As far as I know, the only heirs are her three daughters. That would make you the only grandson. Unless one of them suddenly decides to adopt, you eventually stand to inherit everything."

"I don't want it, Liv. Those people didn't want me. And I don't want anything else from them. Marilyn made it right. She might have destroyed my childhood, but she bought back my place in this world. I don't need their wealth. I have my own. And I've made that quite clear to Marilyn. She isn't behind the threat."

"I never knew Axel Kincaid was so noble."

"Not noble, just self-actualized." He stared at me. "You can't speak a word of this to anyone. You promised. Doing so would destroy them and me, and I don't want that. I've worked too damn hard to become the man I am. Good or bad. This is it. End of story."

"So why'd you tell me?"

"It seemed necessary, and since you owe me, this is me collecting. When your partner asked if I was sleeping with Marilyn, I knew you didn't understand the dynamics at play. Now you do."

Axel was right. This changed everything. Someone discovered Marilyn's dirty little secret and decided to nip it in the bud before it was too late. Every break-in, theft, and murder linked to Kincaid. I just didn't know how. But I was about to find out.

THIRTY-THREE

"I don't remember agreeing to let you turn my loft into police central," Kincaid said as I moved another board into position.

"Shut up and help me."

"Why, Detective, I never knew you could be so bossy." He lined up the final board just as Fox entered the loft.

Immediately, I drew on the intruder, earning a glare from Fox. Shoving the gun back into my holster, I mumbled, "Sorry."

"Yeah, right." Fox gave the redecorated loft one look and turned to Axel. "I didn't realize she was moving in."

"She's not." Kincaid wiped his palms on a towel. "How'd it go?"

Fox gave me another uncertain look. "Are you sure about this, Axel?"

"Yes." Kincaid waited, but Fox didn't speak. "Well, go on. Tell me what you found."

"Nothing. The surveillance is clean, boss. This asshole knows where we have eyes, even the hidden cameras. We have nothing on him. The guy moves like a ghost."

"And the tiara?" Axel asked.

"No word."

"Who did you contact?"

"Everyone. The word's out on the street. The guy he robbed reported it to the police and hired Cross Security to find it. But the killer has to be sitting on it. The only piece from the Archibald collection that he's moved so far is the musket, thanks to Tony Lo."

"Anthony Lovretta?" I asked.

Fox blinked, annoyed that I was still in the room. "You for real?"

"Tony Lo, that's what you call Anthony Lovretta?" I asked again.

"Yes, Detective DeMarco." Fox turned back to Axel, hoping I'd stop asking questions. "According to whispers, the cops arrested Tony Lo with some watches taken from another scene. It's like this asshole wanted Tony to go down for the murders, but the putz couldn't even do that right."

"Liv's already told me about that," Kincaid said. "No one else has tried to pawn anything from the estate sale?"

"No, sir," Fox said. "We'd have heard about it."

Axel jerked his chin at me. "Liv wants to ask you about the victims. Tell her whatever you know."

"Boss, I don't like this," Fox warned.

"Do I look like I care?" Kincaid asked. "We have bigger problems right now."

Grabbing a marker, I moved to stand beside the blown-up photographs of Francis Starmon, the dead dogwalker, the stolen watch collection, and the pocket watch purchased at the Archibald estate auction. "Do you recognize anyone or anything?"

Fox crossed his arms over his chest, his biceps bulging, as he stared down his nose at me. No one could deny Fox was a scary son of a bitch, but Kincaid kept him on a tight leash. I wasn't scared, though I probably should have been. After what felt like an eternity, he uncrossed his arms. "Yeah, we know him. That's Frankie." He looked back at Axel. "You remember, Frankie, right? He's the architect who came up with the new floor plan when you renovated downstairs and soundproofed up here."

Axel shrugged.

"When was this?" I asked.

Fox blew out a breath. "I'd have to check our records, but it was before you came to work here. I don't know. Last year, maybe."

"Okay," I scribbled a few notes down and stuck it on the board beside Starmon's photo. "What about him?" I pointed to the dogwalker.

"I've never seen him before," Fox said.

"All right." I bit my lip as thoughts percolated to the surface. Architects often signed their work and filed the plans. A record of the new blueprints would be filed with the building inspector and kept on file. Building layouts and schematics were part of the public record. "Do you know if Starmon kept any notes or photos of the renovations he did on Spark?"

"Most architects have portfolios," Axel said, mirroring my inner dialogue.

"Yeah, that's how we chose him. He showed us his book with images of former jobs and provided the best mockup," Fox said. "Plus, he gave us a good price."

"Okay." I shot a text to Fennel and told him to contact Starmon and ask about Spark. Something told me the killer-thief had taken more than just the man's watch collection. "What about her?"

"Rosalee." Fox's face fell, and he focused on me. "Is she okay?"

"She's dead."

"Shit," Fox cursed, "I liked her. That fucking bastard. You figure out who he is, and I'm gonna kill him."

"I'll pretend I didn't hear that. When's the last time you saw her?"

"Last month, maybe six weeks." Fox approached the board and ran his fingers over her face. "How'd she die?"

"Stabbed with a kitchen knife."

"Was it quick?"

"Probably not," I admitted.

Fox turned, storming across the room. Even Kincaid got out of his way. "That ain't right. She didn't do nothing to no one." He turned, his eyes wild. "This can't stand."

"How do you know her? How does she connect to Axel?"

I asked.

Fox rubbed his eyes, dropping onto one of the stools at the counter. "I took her to Axel's place to get a feel for his taste. She took some photos, figuring if she found an artist with a piece that fit, she'd let us know."

"So she was your personal art dealer?" I asked Kincaid.

"Yeah," Fox replied, but I had a feeling that was just an excuse for Fox to get together with Rosalee from time to time, though I didn't ask. Fox was too volatile and emotional at the moment for me to ask, even with Kincaid just feet away.

"And she has photographs of the inside of Axel's house?" I asked, making sure I had the details correct.

"So do half the sluts in the city who insist on taking selfies," Fox muttered.

I looked to Axel, but he didn't deny it.

"Save your breath, Liv," Fox said, pouring himself a shot and knocking it back, "Dieter Arnold's the last guy in your lineup there. He works at an accounting firm and conducted a private audit. He's never been to Spark and never met Axel. He just looked over our books to help us cut the fat." Fox downed another shot. "Anything else?"

Kincaid met my eyes, but when I didn't immediately open my mouth with a question, he dismissed Fox. The door slammed, and I jumped, still a little hypervigilant after yesterday. Reaching for my phone, I planned to call Fennel, but Axel grabbed my wrist. "You promised you wouldn't say a word."

"I won't." I stared into his eyes. "You can trust me." I tugged, but Axel held tight. "Let go, or I'll put you on your ass."

He released his grip, holding up his palms as he took a step back.

"Hey, Brad," I said when my partner answered, "some new details have come to light. I know why our killer targeted those victims. We have a new angle to consider, but I'm afraid it's already too late."

After I filled in Fennel with as many details as I could, he said, "So the killer's collecting intel on Kincaid. I'm guessing Frankie, Rosalee, and Dieter had the files saved on their computers. The killer might have accessed them when he broke in. The thefts and murders might have been to cover his tracks. We were too focused on the obvious to bother to check to see if computers or files had been accessed."

"Yeah."

"So the killer's researching a way to get to Axel. It's probably how he managed to set the explosive on Axel's car without being seen. Maybe that was plan B."

"What was plan A?"

"The killer hoped to use Anthony Lovretta, aka Tony Lo, to get a face-to-face with Axel, since Axel used him in the past to get some hard-to-find items. And since Axel's so close to Marilyn and we know Marilyn wanted to get the tiara back, maybe the killer figured Axel would take the bait and buy the tiara for his beloved. And Anthony Lovretta could arrange the exchange and deliver Axel to the killer, except Axel didn't bite when Lovretta brought in the musket. We did."

"Yeah."

"So the killer had to do in Lovretta before the reformed convict squealed," Fennel said. "This is great, and it'll make our case a slam dunk, if it ever goes to trial. There's just one problem."

"It doesn't bring us any closer to identifying the killer," I said.

"Just a minor detail," Fennel said. "But it does firm up our theory that the killer is someone close to Marilyn Archibald, probably one of the people who accompanied her to Zedula's, except the person who could identify the killer is also dead."

"Sambari."

"Yep." Fennel blew out a lengthy breath. "I'll keep on it. Marilyn won't take our calls. She's refusing to cooperate. We're thinking about bringing her in for interfering with a police investigation, but with the friends she has, we'll all be knocked back to traffic. If Axel or anyone else remembers anything, let me know. I'll update Winston. We'll probably send some detectives over to question the other potential targets and see how they connect to Axel

Kincaid or Spark. Maybe if we figure out the kinds of information they possess, we might figure out what the killer is planning next. After all, the car bomb was an epic fail."

"But that was his first try. He's learned since then. That's how he took out the entire third floor."

"Don't remind me." Fennel lowered his voice, and a door slammed shut. "Be careful, Liv. We might be cops, but we're not the Secret Service. If it comes down to you or Axel, I won't mind going to his funeral. Yours, I wouldn't survive."

I hung up, fear and dread wrestling for a prime position in the pit of my stomach.

THIRTY-FOUR

Since the killer had to be a member of Marilyn Archibald's security team, Axel phoned Marilyn and convinced her to shortlist the names she'd already given us. Like her son, she had a distrust for the police, so when she handed us her employee records, she didn't mess around. That's what was taking so long, and while we sifted through every man on her payroll who potentially fit the description, Axel's life hung in the balance.

Axel held out the list of ten names. Eight were the members of Marilyn's personal security detail. The other two were her assistants. "Those are the regular members of Marilyn's team. They go everywhere she does."

"Thanks." I texted the list of names to Fennel and let out a breath. But waiting was one of my least favorite parts of police work. "Can I use your computer?"

Axel recognized all the people on the list from the various social gatherings and visits he had with Marilyn. But none of them had ever demonstrated any outward hostility toward Axel. Four of them were too tall, muscle-bound, or female to be our acrobatic killer. That left us with six possibilities.

Axel scooted closer on the couch, throwing his hand

over the backrest as he leaned in. "Do you think whoever wants me dead discovered Marilyn's secret?"

"Either that, or he doesn't like her infatuation with you."

"It's not an infatuation, Detective. You know better."

"But he might not." I turned to Axel. "Since he wore the mask yesterday, I'm guessing whatever set him off links back to the masquerade ball. Do you remember anything strange happening that night?"

"I don't."

"Did you and Marilyn argue about anything?"

"We usually argue. Marilyn thinks Spark's a liability. She thinks it's an unnecessary risk. She doesn't understand that risk is exactly what I need. It's what a lot of people need. It's like I told you after you arrested me," he snorted, currently finding that amusing rather than irritating, "we have the same job, Liv. We do what we can to keep people from going crazy and hurting others. People need an outlet. I need an outlet. So I let them explore their thrill-seeking side in a safe, controlled environment."

"Sure."

"I know you don't see it, but that's what this is. How many overdoses have happened at Spark? None. No other club in this city can say that. Do you know how many date rapes have been reported where the victim had met her attacker at Spark? Zero. Spark is the safest club in this city."

"Or you find other ways to make sure your problems go away."

Kincaid didn't dignify my retort with a response. "Marilyn's visited on occasion, but she's afraid just being here might sully her reputation, even though we have a no camera policy, which you're aware of. Honestly, with the elected officials and A-listers who slip in and out of this place, we have to enforce those rules or we'd all have a lot to lose."

"So you argued about the club?" I asked.

"Probably."

"I thought you said you didn't talk about business."

"Marilyn doesn't talk about her business, but since one could argue she's an investor in mine, she thinks she can talk about my business."

"Why haven't you paid her back?" I asked.

"I tried. She won't take the money." Suddenly, Axel stood up. "Hang on."

He jogged up the steps, returning a moment later with a ledger. He flipped back several pages. "I offered her a blank check that night." Axel showed me the carbon copy.

"What did she do with it?"

"I'm guessing she ripped it up. The money never left my account." He glanced at the door, but we were alone. "She likes having something tangible connecting us. And since she has no control of Spark, I usually don't think too much about it."

"And no one knows about her connection to your club? Not even Fox?"

"No. Only you, Detective."

"And probably the killer." No matter how much I thought about it, I couldn't shake the glaringly obvious fact that the killer had intimate knowledge of our investigation and police procedure, though we might have misread some of the facts. The musket might not have been delivered to Lovretta and pawned to attract our attention; it was sold at that pawn shop to get Axel's attention. "He's a cop or used to be," I said.

"I'm not surprised. Marilyn only hires ex-law enforcement and ex-military for security."

"That doesn't make this any easier." And without access to the databases, personnel files, or evidence, there wasn't much I could do from inside Axel's loft. I'd just have to hold tight and wait for Fennel to come through. I'd gotten as much information as I could and passed it along. Now I just had to hurry up and wait.

A few hours later, Brad called to tell me he was on his way. Shift was technically over, but OT had been approved for everyone until we caught the man who shot two cops and killed six people. Detective Voletek had even taken photos of Marilyn's security team to the hospital and showed them to Kearney and Jenkins, both of whom were conscious and facing a long, hard road ahead of them. But since the killer wore a mask, they couldn't make a positive identification either.

Kincaid's intercom beeped, and George told him Detective Fennel was here. "Send him up," Kincaid said.

A moment later, Fennel knocked and I opened the door. "Shift's over," he said, looking at the work I'd done inside the loft. He turned, finding Kincaid watching us from the couch. With the way Axel stared, you'd think we were his favorite television program. "Units will keep an eye out. If they spot any suspicious activity in the area, they will check it out. I'd be happy to have officers assigned to keep watch inside, but that's up to you, Mr. Kincaid. I noticed you have your manager stationed downstairs managing your empty club with a nine mill in his waistband."

"Fox is behind on paperwork. And I'm sure he has a carry permit or you're mistaken." Kincaid turned the full intensity of his gaze on me. "Aren't you bunking down for the night? You said you'd stay."

"Liv, no," Brad mumbled beside me. "The doorman has a shotgun. Kincaid has enough protection."

"He needs our help, Brad. You said it yourself. Lovretta had four armed cops watching his back, and the killer still got past them. I can't go anywhere. Not until we get this guy. We only had six names to check. How much longer can this take? We have to be scraping the bottom of the barrel by now."

"Yeah, about that," Fennel scratched the stubble on his cheek, "we should speak in private." Kincaid didn't move, so Fennel and I crossed to the kitchen and huddled beside the refrigerator. "It turns out three of Marilyn's regular guys called in sick the day she visited Zedula. We verified their stories. They ate some bad wings at a bar the night before and ended up with food poisoning. Two fill-ins came from her pool, but the third was just a temp. Voletek and Lisco are speaking to the other members of Marilyn's security team in order to get a description since she doesn't keep photo IDs on file for the temps, but we have a name, Billy Dreyfuss. According to her records, he's former special ops, worked specifically with one of the teams. She hires him regularly to fill in or work big events, but he's a floater. He had difficulty rejoining civilian life but found his calling working private security."

"Wild Bill," I said.

"Sounds like it. There's just one catch. And you're not going to like it."

"What is it?"

"His place has been cleared out. His landlord and neighbors haven't seen him in a month. And the way they described him isn't much more helpful than the way Lovretta described him. We tracked his credit card and financial activity. He withdrew everything around the same time he dropped off the grid. We don't know where he's living or what he's doing now. But he planned this out very carefully. He has no intention of getting caught. We have his driver's license photo and a BOLO out on him and his car." Brad held out a printout, and I looked at the image. "Dreyfuss updated his license six weeks ago and had a new photo taken. DMV overwrites the old ones, so it doesn't give us much to work with."

Billy Dreyfuss wore a bandana around his head, thick glasses that provided an awful glare, and had a dark beard that would make Santa Claus jealous. Facial rec wouldn't be able to give us much. I doubted even a Vegas casino would have better luck making heads or tails out of this mess. Unfortunately, this wasn't a banned gambler, this was a cold and calculating killer.

"Not exactly what I expected," Fennel said.

"He did this intentionally."

"Yeah, which means he's been planning this since the estate auction. Maybe before."

"What about police personnel records?" I asked.

"Four William Dreyfusses have been on the force at some point. One cadet who washed out a few years ago appears to be our Wild Bill. He enrolled in the police academy but only lasted a few months before being thrown out for injuring three other cadets during training. Winston has officers running down the other possibilities, just in case. And our computer techs have come up with variations of the ID photo, so we're passing those out to patrol. We'll bring in anyone remotely fitting the description. Marilyn Archibald's been told about the lead, and her security teams are monitoring her buildings and businesses to make sure he doesn't show up there. The problem is we really don't know what he looks like. This guy knows how to become a ghost. He can blend in or disappear without anyone batting an eye. For all we know, he could be in the wind."

"He isn't. He wants Axel."

THIRTY-FIVE

He checked his gear for the fourth time. Weapons. Ammunition. Kevlar. Climbing gear. Det cord. Charges. He had the club layout memorized, along with various escape routes. He left his car on the street several blocks away, ready for extraction. It wasn't supposed to come down to a frontal assault. But Axel Kincaid didn't cooperate. The police interfered. They intercepted the bait and captured Anthony Lovretta.

So he recalculated and moved on to plan B, but the police interfered again. The two officers he shot might have been saved when the other half of the security detail returned from dinner. Of course, that would have been up to them. If they saved their brothers instead of focusing on the dead snitch, the third floor would have been cleared when he detonated the bomb. And if the police chose wrong, then they'd all die when Lovretta was moved off the pressure plate.

It was simple, but those two detectives fucked it up. According to the news, the only casualty was Lovretta, but it could have easily been more. A part of him wanted it to be more. He held DeMarco's life in his hands, quite literally. But he stopped at the last second. She was a soldier, like him. Just doing her job, like him. But she messed up, just not as badly as her partner. The police academy taught basic procedures. Those things had been drilled into him. He memorized them, repeated them, learned them. But these so-called detectives made foolish mistakes. He could have killed them. Instead, he gave them one last chance. Hopefully, they'd back off and let him complete his mission. But something about DeMarco and the way she screamed at him and defied him made him certain she'd be trouble. They'd be trouble.

He could always move on to another plan. He had plenty of contingencies and a lot more ways to gain intel on Axel. But he wanted this over. War required sacrifice. He wouldn't lose sight of his mission. He'd save Ms. Marilyn from this bastard no matter what it took, no matter the cost. And tonight he was prepared to kill anyone who got in his way.

*   *   *

"Is that it?" the clerk asked.

"Hang on." I grabbed a few fruit bars, beef strips, and a bag of organic nuts and placed them on the counter with the bottles of water, heat wraps, and bandages. "Do you have any instant cold packs?"

"Did you check aisle nine?"

"Those you have to freeze."

"I thought I saw some around here. Let me see if I can find them." He stepped around the counter of the twenty-four-hour pharmacy and found them tossed into the bucket with the travel-sized tissues. "How many do you want?"

"Two."

The clerk pulled them out of the bin and rang them up along with the rest of my items. "That'll be $42.31."

Brad hadn't complained or asked for anything, but since he agreed to camp out at Kincaid's with me, I wanted him to be comfortable. Frankly, I was just happy to have a few minutes to run down the street and pick up some things from the drugstore, so I splurged and picked up the snacks I knew Brad liked. Luckily, we were both cops, or someone might have thought this was a bribe. A bribe might have been cheaper.

But supplies were expensive, and my neck had been killing me all day. More than anything, I needed a break from the loft. Axel had mostly behaved, but being trapped inside the lion's den kept me tense and on edge. Wild Bill posed the biggest threat, but a small part of me feared Fox and George and maybe even Axel. But I would do this job to the best of my ability.

While I tucked my change away, a man approached the counter. I grabbed my bags as the clerk went through his routine. I was almost out the door when the man behind the counter called out, "You forgot something, miss."

I turned, reaching for the smaller bag with the snack food. "Thanks."

"Liv?" the customer asked.

I looked up, half-expecting to run into someone from my UC days when I'd been Olivia Bell. Instead, I blinked as recognition dawned on me. "Eric?"

He had his hair down tonight in a moppy, brown mess of stringy strands. "You remembered."

"You left an impression."

He cringed. "That doesn't sound good."

I glanced down at the box of condoms and lube. "Big plans tonight?"

"You caught me. I'm on my way to Emma's. She said you'd probably be working late. But we can behave ourselves while you're home, unless you rather not miss the fireworks. Offer still stands."

I glared at him.

"Lighten up, I'm just kidding. I didn't mean to ruffle your feathers." He paid for his items and moved to the side so the next customer could check out.

"No ruffling here."

"I'm glad." He peered out the window. "I was going to take Emma out to dinner. You should join us. She talks about you all the time, so we ought to get to know each other better."

"Really?" Emma hadn't said much to me about Eric. But we hadn't really talked since the incident in the apartment.

"Yeah, you're some fancy homicide detective, right? Have you ever worked undercover, like on TV? I bet you have some crazy stories. I'd love to hear them."

"Not really."

"Can I offer you a ride?" he asked. "We're going to the same place, right?"

"Actually, no."

"Oh," he peered out the door, probably looking for a squad car or crime scene tape, "are you working right now? I hope that's not dinner." He jerked his chin at the bag.

"Just snacks."

"Well, I'll let you go. Have a good night. Maybe I'll see you later." He went out the door, and I followed.

"Hold up." I kept my head on a swivel. From here, I watched a patrol car lazily drive up the block. The surveillance unit was down at the other end, keeping an eye on Spark. Fennel could hold down the fort for a few more minutes. "I want to ask you something."

Eric laughed a bit nervously. "Should I be worried?"

"How'd you and Emma meet?"

"At the hospital."

"Do you work there?"

"Sort of. I'm an ambulance driver."

"What company?"

He brushed his hair behind his ear and grinned. "You know, after the other night, a guy might think this is foreplay. If you break out the cuffs, I'm gonna get really excited. Do you want to strip search me after you interrogate me, Detective?"

"What's your last name?"

"Seriously?" He gave me an incredulous look, realizing I wasn't joking.

"Humor me," I said.

"Reynolds. Do you want my date of birth and social security number too?"

"Only if you're offering," I said.

"Unbelievable. I was trying to be nice. But you got a problem. You need to work on that." He stormed away, and I watched him go.

"Asshole," I muttered, shaking it off and heading back to

Spark. But Eric had gotten under my skin. The way he walked, the way he talked, the smug look in his eyes, I didn't like any of it, especially that stupid haircut. What did Emma see in this guy?

Entering Spark, I nodded at George who had buzzed me in the moment he spotted me on the security camera. Fox barely looked up when I walked in. Fennel was right; they were both packing. I just wondered whose side they'd be on once we removed our mutual enemy. It'd probably be best not to stick around and find out.

When I went up the steps, I knocked. Fennel answered, and I handed him one of the bags. He poked his head inside. "You didn't have to get me anything. We can order in."

I looked around the loft, realizing we were missing someone. "Where's Axel?"

"Shower," Fennel said. "Don't worry, I made sure he couldn't give us the slip. No windows."

"Good to know." I dropped onto one of the stools and opened the box of heat wraps. "Do you want me to take first watch?"

"You look used up, Liv. And for some reason, I've found my second wind. I'd prefer to go first because in four hours, I'll be crashing hard."

"Okay." I peeled off the backing and stuck the wrap to my neck. Sighing, I opened a bottle of water and took a sip.

"What's wrong?"

"You'll never guess who I just ran into." I took my water to the couch and cozied up in the corner. It wouldn't be hard to fall asleep right here. The hard part would be staying awake. "Eric Reynolds."

"Who?"

"Pervey guy." I shifted around until my head was supported by the bend in the arm. "Do you want to know what he was buying in the drugstore?"

"Please don't tell me condoms."

"And lube."

Fennel grimaced. "At least they're being safe. Tell me you didn't shoot him."

"I didn't shoot him."

"But you thought about it."

"I really did." I let my eyes close. "There is just something about him. He gives me bad vibes."

"What'd you say his last name is?"

"Reynolds." I opened an eye to see Brad dialing. "What are you doing? You can't run a background check on Emma's boytoy."

"Correction, *you* can't run a background check on Emma's boytoy, but I can do whatever the fuck I want. She's not my best friend."

"It's a breach. Abuse of power. You could get in trouble."

Brad waved off my protest. "Hi, yeah, this is Detective Fennel, can you do me a favor? No rush, but if you get a chance, dig up whatever you can on an Eric Reynolds. He's in his late twenties. Thanks. I appreciate it." He hung up. "See, problem solved. Now get some sleep. In four hours, I'm kicking you off that couch."

But I didn't sleep. I sent a message to Emma, apologizing for pissing off Eric. Then I rolled onto my back and stared up at the skylight. Movement in the bedroom caught my attention, and I watched Axel run a towel over his hair. Considering Axel Kincaid was nocturnal bordering on vampire, he must be exhausted from being awake during normal daylight hours. He left his door open, aware I was watching. He smiled down at me before turning off his light and getting into bed.

My mind wandered, but I found myself obsessing over Eric. *This is stupid,* I thought. Maybe I was jealous, but Emma dated frequently. And none of them bothered me, except for the ones who broke Emma's heart, stole her stereo and bluray player, or that one guy who emptied her wallet and tried to do the same to her bank account. Okay, so I had plenty of reasons not to like the guys Emma dated, but I normally gave them the benefit of the doubt. But Eric bothered me from the first moment I laid eyes on him. It had to have been the creepy way I found him lingering in our kitchen. What was he looking for? Emma was a health nut. We didn't have whipped cream, chocolate syrup, or caramel in the house. Maybe he wanted coconut oil, but Emma knew not to pair that with latex.

No matter how hard I tried to push thoughts of Eric and our two brief encounters out of my head, I couldn't. At least it was better than thinking about Wild Bill. My head hurt just thinking about how hard he hit me. *You don't want to miss the fireworks*, that's what the smug bastard said.

Actually, that's what two smug bastards said in the span of twenty-four hours. My heart rate shot up, and I reached for my phone. The sudden movement caught Brad's attention.

"Liv, you okay?" he asked.

I dialed Emma, waiting for her to answer. "Dammit, Em, pick up the phone." It went to voicemail, and I checked the time. "Where'd Emma say she was going today?"

"She and your mom were going to clean your place and then out to lunch. I told her she should go to the grocery store. Why? What's wrong?"

"Lunch. But she didn't have today off, so she's working the night shift." I hung up and called the hospital. Emma sometimes left her phone in her locker or turned it off while making rounds. As soon as someone answered, I told them who I was and implied that I had to speak to Emma about an urgent police matter.

A minute later, Emma came to the phone. "Liv, what's wrong?"

"You're at work?"

"Yeah."

"Have you seen Eric?"

"Not today. I told him maybe we'd get together Sunday. Why?"

"Have you told him about me? What I do? My current cases?"

"He knows you're a cop. You almost shot him."

"Does he know I work homicide?"

"Um..." Emma hesitated. "Maybe."

"What else, Em?"

"I don't know what we've talked about. We don't do a lot of talking, but after you scared the crap out of him, he had questions. I can't remember what I said. Is there a problem?"

"Em, listen to me, I need you to stay at the hospital, okay? Tell security to keep an eye out. If you see Eric, do not go anywhere with him alone. Do you understand? Call security. Call the police. Don't go home until you hear from me."

"Liv, you're scaring me. What's going on? What do you think Eric did?"

"I will tell you everything later, but right now, please just trust me and do what I say."

"Okay."

"One last thing," I swallowed, hoping I was wrong about everything, "do you have any photos of Eric?"

"I took one when he was sleeping. He doesn't know about it. He was weird about letting me take selfies with him. He said he didn't want it to get around because he could get in trouble at work."

"Send it to me." I hung up.

Fennel watched me. "You gotta be shitting me. Why on god's green earth do you think Emma's boytoy is Wild Bill?"

"Something he said." I tapped my fingers against my phone. "But think about it, Brad. You saw the way he moved yesterday in the parking lot. You even said it looked cocky. And isn't that exactly how you said our killer-thief moves."

"A lot of guys walk around like that." He jerked his chin skyward. "Case in point."

"No, this is different. He was inside my apartment. He was looking for something. Intel. Information. Something."

Brad paled. "You connect to Kincaid. You could have valuable intel on him, on Spark. Hell, you worked in the club."

"See?"

Fennel scratched his jaw. "Okay, let's not jump to any conclusions yet." But even before my phone buzzed with Emma's snapshot, Fennel phoned Voletek and had him go to the hospital to keep an eye on Emma. Deep down, Brad knew I was right. And we both hated ourselves for not realizing it sooner.

THIRTY-SIX

"Didn't you say his name is Billy Dreyfuss?" Axel asked, clearly tired and annoyed. "Now you're telling me it's Derek something."

"Eric Reynolds," I corrected, holding out my phone while Axel rubbed his bleary eyes. "It's an alias. Look at the photo. Do you recognize him?"

"I just told you I don't know." He reached for his phone.

"What about Marilyn?" I asked.

"She hasn't responded since the last time you asked me a whole two seconds ago." Kincaid tugged on the silk tie holding his robe closed. "Why don't you go downstairs and pester Fox with this?"

Fennel nodded and headed for the door.

I dropped my head into my hand and rubbed my neck, but my leg jittered up and down. Kincaid took a deep breath, went to the espresso machine, and brewed a cup. He took a sip and chuckled.

"What's so funny?" I asked.

"This adds an entirely new dimension to women keeping me up."

"Sorry."

"I know. You're just doing your job." He put the cup

down. "What's wrong with your neck? You've been rubbing it all day."

"Wild Bill."

"I don't follow," Axel said.

"He likes to play rough." I worked my jaw and looked away. "For some reason, he decided at the last minute not to kill me."

Axel stepped behind me and pulled my sloppy ponytail free from the elastic band. Then he brushed my hair to the side and gently eased his thumbs into my pulled muscles and strained tendons. I'd almost forgotten how good his hands were. I dropped my forehead to the counter as he removed the heat wrap and worked the remaining tension out with his fingers.

"I overheard you talking to Detective Fennel," Axel said, "you think someone you care about is in danger because of me."

"No, because of me."

"Because you connect to me," he said.

"Or it's because Brad and I caught this case." I reached back and put my hand over Axel's so he'd stop before I turned into a puddle on top of his counter. The man might be a lot of terrible things, but he had a gift.

"Offer still stands. Quit your job and come back to Spark. You can waitress. I'll even keep you out of the cages."

"Do you offer a pension and benefits?" I asked.

He slid around until his hips rested against the counter beside me. "We could work out an entire benefits package."

"Does that line usually work for you?"

Before he could reply, the lights went out. I stood, my gun already in hand. I looked out the open doorway and down the dark steps. No light came from downstairs either.

"The backup generators should have kicked in by now," Axel said. He moved in front of me, the only light coming in from the skylight, which cast eerie shadows around the room. Axel hit the hidden switch, revealing the hidden security panel. "What the hell?"

"What is it?" I asked, sliding along the couch until I found my way across the room, keeping my back to Axel while I swept the tiny beam of my flashlight from left to right.

"The power's out, so the security system went into lockdown mode."

"What does that mean?" I asked.

"Liv?" Fennel called, heading up the steps with the flashlight held beneath his gun. "Did you guys trigger a lockdown?"

"No," Axel said. "The power went out. Security system must have automatically engaged. The doors are sealed shut. We're trapped inside until the power comes back." Axel tapped on the keyboard, but nothing happened.

Fennel went to the window, lifted the shade, and peered out. "Half the block's out," he said. "Could just be an outage." But he keyed the radio, only to meet static.

"And we're jammed?" I asked, my eyes darting around the dark room. "He's coming." And if I hadn't been so stupid, I would have realized it the moment I laid eyes on Eric. He didn't follow me back here, but he knew where I was and what I was doing. He was playing with me.

"The doors are locked," Axel said. "He won't be able to get in."

"He stole Kevin Maser's work computer. He's taken control of your security system," I said, realizing this just a little too late. "By staying here, you've made yourself a sitting duck."

Fennel peered down at the street. "Units are right outside. They must know something's up. I'll try my cell."

But before my partner could dial, a shadow moved in front of the skylight. I ran at Axel, shoving him away as the glass rained down on top of us. I didn't even have time to call out to Fennel before a man in full tactical gear rappelled down, spraying the room with gunfire. Grabbing Axel by the collar, I dragged him into cover behind the counter. Fennel slid across the floor, meeting us on the other side. We both popped up, firing at the man in the middle of the loft.

"He's wearing Kevlar," Fennel said, ducking down, "and probably has night vision or thermals." Another spray of automatic fire pummeled into Kincaid's Italian marble counter.

"Let's hope for night vision." I aimed my flashlight at the attacker's face while Fennel fired a few shots, low and from the side, but our bullets weren't even making a dent.

"Bitch," came the now familiar voice. He tossed something at us.

"Grenade," Fennel shouted, but it only released smoke. "Move. I'll cover you."

I shoved Axel in front of me, and we ran for the only exit, using Wild Bill's smoke grenade against him. Fox was on the stairs, heading toward us with George at his heels. They reversed course, and we ran down the steps. Fennel slammed the top door and raced down after us. Once we were out, Fox shut the bottom door and locked it. George and I grabbed a table, turning it on its side and barricading the door.

"Everyone okay?" I asked.

Fennel looked at me. "That won't hold him. Dreyfuss worked special ops and is a demolitions expert. He locked us in here for a reason. We need a way out."

"George, get to work on the front door," Axel ordered. He looked at Fox. "I'll try to reset the security system." Fox handed Axel a gun, and even though he was the person Fennel and I were supposed to protect, we let him go to his office alone. Fox took up a position between the hallway and the barricaded door, putting himself between Axel and the killer.

Fennel and I moved a few tables, flipping them on their sides to create blockades. "Last time I volunteer to take first watch," Fennel mumbled.

"Last time I repay a favor," I said. With my gun aimed at the barricaded door, I pulled out my phone, surprised to get a signal. "He's only jamming radio communications. Our phones work." So I called for backup and put the call on speaker. Dispatch redirected me to the units already outside, and I updated them on the situation.

"We'll break down the doors," the sergeant said.

"Can't," Fox said, "they're reinforced steel. The frames too. With the locks engaged, they can't be broken into. Top of the line security."

"Great," I mumbled.

"All right," the sergeant said, "we'll have to breach through a wall. It'll take some time. We have to get a team down here with charges. Can you hang on until then?"

"Do we have a choice?" Fennel asked.

"Work on getting the security system reset. The sooner we get you out, the sooner we can come in and get this asshole," the sergeant said.

"Liv," Fennel said, but we all heard the explosion and then movement overhead, "he's in the ceiling."

"Is that even possible?" I asked Fox.

"He must have breached a wall or compromised the airducts." Fox aimed at the ceiling, following the sounds. "We have catwalks and support beams up there. That's what the entire upper level looked like until Axel carved out his loft apartment. The bastard could come down anywhere."

"DeMarco, get to Axel," Fennel said.

I moved from my cover position behind the table, past Fox, and down the hall. Axel's office stood at the end. He had the door open and was cursing. Another rumble sounded overhead. Wild Bill knew the layout. He knew about the renovations. He knew where Axel's office was.

"It's no use," Axel hissed. "Without power, I can't turn on the system. We need to get the backup generators online first."

"Leave it," I said, pressing myself against the doorframe. "He's in the ceiling. He must know this is where you'd hide."

"I'm not hiding." Axel gripped the gun in one hand while he strode out of the office. No, he certainly wasn't hiding. He looked like he was about to kill. He entered the main room, his eyes searching the ceiling. George continued to work on the door and security system from his control booth, and Fox and Fennel kept their eyes trained skyward, guns aimed at the ceiling, tracking the sounds.

"Dead center, over the dance floor," Fox said to Axel.

"We drilled holes for the chandelier and wiring," Axel said. "You think he's using them."

"What?" I asked.

"Fiber optic cables," Fennel said. The room was too dark for us to see anything, but Fox and Axel were speculating on ways Wild Bill might have eyes inside.

Without warning, Axel fired in a pattern above the chandelier. For someone who supposedly didn't own a gun or use guns, he had precision aim, especially in the pitch black. I didn't hear a single bulb or piece of glass shatter. We all waited, listening, straining to hear movement.

And then something exploded above, temporarily illuminating the club in orange and reds before the flames fizzled out and dry wall and ceiling tiles crashed down around us. Wild Bill swung down from his perch, nylon cord preventing him from falling from the ceiling. He landed in front of Axel, coming up from a crouch.

"Drop your weapon," Fennel shouted, though at this point, everything sounded muted, even my partner's voice.

Wild Bill spun, firing at Fennel, who dove out of the way in the nick of time. Wild Bill turned. I fired. Fox fired, as did Axel, but after a few shots, Axel's gun clicked empty, and despite the lead hitting him, Wild Bill brought his gun up, aiming.

There wasn't time. I dove onto Axel, knocking him to the floor as another barrage erupted where Axel had stood. At least in the dark, I couldn't tell how close he'd come to hitting us. Thankfully, I had a vest, but Axel didn't.

Suddenly, a bright light illuminated the middle of the dance floor, and George opened up with the shotgun. The force knocked Wild Bill to the ground, and with the sudden blinding light, Fox exchanged the magazine in his gun for another in his pocket.

"Drop your gun," Fennel shouted, but even on his back, Wild Bill wouldn't give up. He reached for his weapon, and Brad moved to kick it out of his hand, but Fox fired.

The first shot went into Wild Bill's shoulder, blood blossoming as the killer let out a surprised scream. Fennel kicked Wild Bill's gun away, but Fox fired again, this time into Wild Bill's opposite knee.

"That's enough," I said. "Hold your fire." I climbed off Axel. "We got him." I offered my hand to the club owner, but Axel ignored it. Fennel moved to flip Wild Bill around to cuff him, but Fox hadn't lowered his gun. And Brad didn't move. He didn't trust Fox either.

"Fox, put down the gun," I said, raising mine to mid-thigh.

"Nope."

"I said put down the gun. We got him." I aimed at Fox, which caused George to aim at me, and Brad to aim at George. "I didn't realize we were going to Mexico." I glanced at Axel, who stood there staring down at the killer.

"Why?" Axel asked. "Why me? What the fuck did I do to you?"

Wild Bill sneered, huffing and trying to edge backward, but even with our Mexican standoff, he was boxed in, no weapons in sight, and with two joints taken out, he wasn't in any condition to fight or escape. "Why you?" he gasped. "That's what I want to know. Why you?" Spittle sailed from his mouth. "Marilyn's leaving you everything. I saw the paperwork on her desk. You, some piece of shit club owner. She works hard to make this world better, safer, and you destroy that. But she wants to leave you everything when she dies. Like you'd ever carry on her legacy. What makes you so fucking special? I saved her life. Me. I did. And she told me that she'd take care of me. That she'd make a special place for me. That I'd be repaid. That I mattered."

Axel snorted. "You saved her? How?"

Wild Bill looked up, defiance in his pinprick eyes. "She was almost abducted last year after leaving a party. Some assholes wanted her car and money. Asshole car thieves like you. I was in the follow car. I pulled them off of her, shot them, saved her."

"I didn't send them after her," Axel said. "I'm not a carjacker."

"Maybe not now, but you used to be. That's who you are."

Axel walked over to Fox, placing his palm on top of the gun. "No more." Fox gave him the gun, and I lowered my weapon. George did the same, and Fennel blew out a breath.

"Billy Dreyfuss, or should I say Eric Reynolds, you're

under arrest." Fennel flipped Wild Bill over, despite the pained gasps, yanked his arms behind his back, smiling a little when twisting the destroyed shoulder joint to get the killer's hands into the cuffs. Then he patted him down and flipped him back over. "You might want to tell us how to get the power back if you want the paramedics to get here before you bleed out."

But Wild Bill didn't answer. I looked down at him. "Why Emma?" I asked.

"She was a means to you, Liv." He grinned, his eyes darting to Axel. "And she was a means to you, just like all the rest."

Axel fired once, dropped the gun, and raised his hands before Fennel and I could draw on him.

"Son of a bitch," Fennel said while I aimed at Axel. "What'd you do that for?"

"It's over, Detectives." Axel nodded to George, who kicked the shotgun away. "We mean you no harm."

"What about him?" Fennel asked, watching Wild Bill sputter and writhe from the gunshot wound to his chest. Fox must have reloaded with armor piercing rounds because every shot since had penetrated the killer's Kevlar.

"He tried to kill me," Axel said. "It seemed only fair."

THIRTY-SEVEN

Brad rubbed his face. "I hate paperwork."

"Are you almost finished?" I asked.

He pushed back from his chair. "With the important stuff. The rest will wait until tomorrow." He turned and peered down the hallway. "Who do you think they'll believe? Us or Axel Kincaid?"

"Kincaid won't lie," I said.

"That would be a first," Brad said. "Like the way he denied sleeping with Marilyn."

"Why do you think he's sleeping with Marilyn?" I asked, hating having to keep a secret from my partner. But maybe it made us even for the softball thing.

"C'mon, Liv, why would a wealthy woman like that change her will to leave everything to a lowlife like Axel Kincaid? She's gotta be banging him."

"If he's that good in the sack, maybe I should sleep with him too."

Brad looked up, all joking aside. "No."

"Why not?" I teased.

"It's bad enough Emma slept with a killer. You don't need to follow suit."

"Shit, Emma."

"Don't worry, Jake's with her."

"That does not make it better. It makes it worse. The last thing she needs is to date Voletek as a rebound, or worse yet, she might try to set me up with him."

"Well, Jake's a better choice than Kincaid. At least he's a cop, not a would-be killer."

"Do you think he'd invite me to your softball games?"

"No."

"Fine, then I guess I'll have to go with option C," I said.

"Become a nun?" Fennel asked.

"Yeah."

"Good choice." Fennel grinned, but his smile fell as Winston's door opened. "How do you think this mess is going to come down on us? Kincaid shot a cuffed man, and we didn't stop him."

"We had no way of knowing Axel would do that," I said. "According to the EMTs, Dreyfuss should pull through. He killed six people, shot two cops, and tried to blow us up. My gut says Axel will walk. He always walks. He'll probably tell his buddies in city council and the mayor's office to give us medals for helping him out."

Brad shook his head. "Great, we're practically accomplices."

"Chill. It's not worth it. You're mad because you didn't see it coming." I swallowed and signed the bottom of the form I filled out. "I didn't either. I never expected Axel to shoot him. But what really pisses me off is that I didn't realize the truth about Eric sooner. He went after Emma to get to me."

"It's a good thing you don't take work home with you," Fennel said.

"If I wasn't in the midst of moving, I would have."

Brad let out an exhausted grunt. "Shit, it's moving day."

"You haven't slept in two days. You deserve a break. I'll take care of it. You go home and get some rest."

"If I don't help you move, who will?"

"I got people. I'll find someone. Hey, do you still have the number for Speedy Delivery?"

"No," he pointed a finger at my face, "don't even joke. That's not funny." He reached for his jacket. "You don't have that much stuff at Emma's. It shouldn't take us too long to get it all loaded and unloaded. The rest of your crap is at your parents' place. Does your dad need help moving it?"

"No, he has it covered."

"Okay, I'll be at Emma's at three on one condition."

"What's that?"

"You break the news to her about Eric."

"Shit."

Brad laughed and headed for the door. "Have fun with that one, DeMarco. I'll see you at three. You still having the housewarming tonight after we move your stuff in?"

"Yep."

"Good, after all this, you definitely owe me a nice home-cooked meal and all the wine I can drink."

"You got it, partner."

Deadly Dealings

Note from the Author:

The events in this story occur concurrently with the events established in *Burning Embers*. If you haven't read that book yet and want to learn more about Detective Jake Voletek and the arson case he's investigating, please check it out. It features Alexis Parker, another tough female detective, but unlike Liv, Alex is a former federal agent now working in the private sector. I'm sure you'll love her and her pals as much as Liv and Brad.

To find out more about the Alexis Parker series check out my website:
www.alexisparkerseries.com

* * *

Thank you for taking the time to read this book. I hope you enjoyed it as much as I enjoyed writing it. If so, please consider leaving a review wherever you purchased this title. Reviews are always appreciated and help other readers decide to give my books a try.

* * *

Don't worry, another Liv DeMarco novel is on the way. Sign up to be notified about it and future releases by visiting:
http://www.alexisparkerseries.com/newsletter

Deadly Dealings

ABOUT THE AUTHOR

G.K. Parks is the author of the Alexis Parker series. The first novel, *Likely Suspects,* tells the story of Alexis' first foray into the private sector.

G.K. Parks received a Bachelor of Arts in Political Science and History. After spending some time in law school, G.K. changed paths and earned a Master of Arts in Criminology/Criminal Justice. Now all that education is being put to use creating a fictional world based upon years of study and research.

You can find additional information on G.K. Parks and the Alexis Parker series by visiting our website at
www.alexisparkerseries.com

Made in the USA
Middletown, DE
21 August 2025